BETH EHEMANN

Cement
Heart

Dedication

This book is dedicated to Michelle Finkle,
who not only gave me the idea for it when it came to her in a dream over a
year ago,
but has helped me raise this baby as if it were her own.
I love you to pieces, Michelle.
Thank you for being the most amazing friend.

Prologue

I FELT THEIR EYES ON me as I stared at the ground, taking my time. Some of them knew me, some of them didn't, but they were all focused on me, wondering what I was about to say. It was a lot of pressure to have a couple hundred people hanging on my every word, praying that I'd be the one to come up with the magical phrase, some fucking generic sentence that would make them feel better. Take away their pain. How could I take away theirs when mine was so real, so raw?

I deserved this pain, every second of it.

It was my fault we were there.

I'd caused this.

I'd killed him.

Chapter

1

MY COCK JERKED IN ANTICIPATION as she slowly sank to her knees, eyeing me like a lioness about to devour her prey. She licked her dark red lips and roughly pushed me back onto my bed seconds before her tongue gently flicked the head of my dick. I fought the urge to shove my hands into her blond hair and start thrusting like some teenage punk getting sucked off for the first time behind a middle school.

Patience, Viper.

I knew the reward that was coming and it would definitely be worth it, so long as I could keep from coating her throat too early. She wasted no time, moaning as she moved her warm mouth up and down my shaft. Her hand slid in between my legs, pushing them apart so she could cup my balls.

Seriously? The balls? Already? Amateur.

"You started without me?" Her brunette friend appeared in my bedroom doorway, pouting as she crossed her arms over her huge tits.

"Come on in." I linked my fingers and tucked my hands behind my head. "There's plenty to go around."

She ran her tongue between her teeth and top lip as her eyes trailed slowly from mine, down the length of my body, and back up again, settling on my dick. "I can see that." Her top lip curled at the corner as she stared.

The blonde, Claire—Corrine—Chloe, whatever her name was, sat up but continued stroking me with her hand. "Come join me, Heather," she suggested seductively to her friend, tilting her head to the side as she batted her eyelashes.

Heather strolled leisurely across my guest room, her curves emphasizing all the best parts of her body. Just the way she walked—her tits bouncing with each step, the light shining through the window and glistening off her skin—was hot.

I'm not saying I wasn't looking forward to being sandwiched in between the two of them, but let's just say if her little blond friend had decided it was a good time to go for a walk, I wouldn't have stopped her.

Heather lifted her knee onto the corner of my bed and crawled like a sexy, needy little cat over to what's-her-name. They raised up onto their knees and started kissing right over me. Eyes closed, tongues dueling . . . they devoured each other. Heather grabbed the back of her friend's head and pulled on her hair, exposing her neck. She slowly kissed her way down to blond girl's tits, where she eagerly pulled her nipple into her mouth, moaning as she sucked. Watching them go at it was almost as gratifying as if they were doing it to me.

Almost.

"Ahem." I cleared my throat playfully.

Heather's lips made a slapping sound as she pulled them from her friend's nipple. She grinned at me. "Sorry. Guess we got a little carried away."

"No, no . . . I'm good with carried away," I responded. "Just carry me with you."

She looked up at her partner. "I think he wants some too, Crystal. What do you think?"

Crystal! That's her name!

"I think that can be arranged," Crystal cooed as she sat back down next to me.

"What should we do first?" Heather asked, licking her lips as she stared right into my eyes.

Crystal slowly ran her finger up my leg and swirled it around on my stomach. "Hmmm, what do *you* wanna do?" She was looking straight at Heather.

"Well, let's not let this thing go to waste, huh?" Heather's gaze moved from Crystal's to mine as she bent down and wrapped her mouth around my cock.

"Wait for me." Crystal giggled as she dipped her head down toward Heather, who immediately backed off to allow her friend access.

And then . . . it was on.

They were hungry. They were fierce. They attacked my dick like it was the only popsicle in the middle of a scorching desert. One on the right, one on the left, their lips touching at the top and the bottom, they ran their mouths in unison the whole length of my shaft. I wasn't sure there was anything hotter than hearing not one but two women moan as their heads bobbed up and down on my lap. The faster they moved, the closer I was to coming, but blowing my load all over my stomach wasn't something I was into, so I slowly pushed myself up on my elbows and cleared my throat. Immediately, Heather came up for air and smiled at me. Before I could say anything, Crystal threw one leg over my hips and positioned herself over me.

"Whoa, whoa! Slow down," I blurted, trying to scoot out from under her as fast as I could. "My boy doesn't inspect any caves without protective gear."

Crystal's eyebrows pulled together. "Huh?"

"He means he wants to wear a condom." Heather rolled her eyes.

"Oh." Crystal covered her mouth and giggled. "I get it."

"You're cute and shit, but I have no desire to see what our DNA would look like mixed together." I winked at her.

I was no stranger to one-night stands, that was obvious, but

I did have rules about what I would and wouldn't do during sex. Rule number one—always wear a condom. Always. Too many women would kill for a chance at twenty percent of my paycheck.

Rule number two—never go down on one-night stands. Ever.

Two hours ago, I'd been having a late lunch at a bar down the street and this dynamic duo was just a couple of girls sitting next to me. I hadn't even noticed them until they got up and started grinding on each other on the dance floor. Next thing I knew, I was buying them drinks while they told me all about how much they loved hockey and how cute the little black ball, as Crystal called it, was on the ice.

Oh yeah, real big hockey fans.

Anyway, not a chance in hell was my tongue going anywhere near their pussies. My covered-up dick, fine, but not my mouth.

Rule number three—*if* I brought them back to my place, as opposed to my car, an alley, or the bar bathroom, we did not have sex in my bedroom. *Always* the guest room. I liked my guests to take off pretty quickly after we were done, and the last thing I needed was their tacky perfume smelling up my pillow. My room was my domain, my place to relax and unwind.

I grabbed a condom out of the nightstand and rolled it onto my dick before climbing up on my knees.

"You, lie down," I said to Crystal, pointing toward the bed.

She moved quickly, lying on her back and eagerly opening her legs for me. "Go ahead, take me."

"Nope." I grinned at her, slowly shaking my head. "I'm gonna take care of Heather while she takes care of you." A small smirk appeared on Crystal's lips as she looked from me to Heather. I followed her gaze, waiting to see if Heather was going to object or not.

Her bright blue eyes stared back at me as she bit her bottom lip and slowly raised one seductive eyebrow. "Wouldn't be the first time."

Holy shit.

Heather wasted no time, dropping to all fours and burying her face in between her friend's legs. The instant Heather's mouth made contact, Crystal's mouth dropped open and her eyes glazed over.

"Oh my God," she moaned.

Heather's round, perfect little ass was up in the air, her swollen pussy peeking out the bottom, inviting me in. And I RSVP'd in a big fucking way. I didn't even check to see if she was wet enough for me. I knew that she was.

She gasped as I roughly pushed myself inside her. I was barely five pumps in when I could tell that Crystal was about to come. Clearly Heather knew what the hell she was doing. Crystal's chest rose up and down quickly, panting as she shoved her hands into Heather's dark hair and squeezed.

"Heather! Yes!" she yelled out, squeezing her eyes tight. "Fuck! Yes!"

The squeals coming out of Crystal's pouty little mouth made my balls tighten as I fucked Heather faster, my fingers digging into her hips as I pulled her hard against me. Just as Crystal came down from her high, Heather laid her head on Crystal's thigh and started her own. She shoved her hand in between her legs and rubbed circles around her clit as I drove into her over and over and over again.

She started to cry out, teetering on the brink as Crystal encouraged both of us. "Fuck her, Viper. Harder. Faster. She's right there . . ."

So was I.

Heather's hand shot out and squeezed the sheets into a ball as she came hard, her groans filling the room as I squeezed her ass and filled the condom.

"It's not so much the release itself that's euphoric, but the build-up. Don't you agree?" Crystal said to Heather.

I rolled my eyes and clicked the remote again, trying to drown her out with sports. Any kind of sports. At that point, I'd have watched badminton.

"Don't you agree?"

"Oh, absolutely." Heather nodded. "I mean, sex is such an intimate encounter between two people, and when one of those people can heighten your senses like that and take you to that special place . . ." She threw her head back and exhaled loudly.

Jesus. My hand takes me to that special place all the fucking time. Relax.

"Exactly," Crystal agreed. "And I'm thinking"—she slowly crept across the couch and straddled me—"maybe I help you find that special place again right now. What do you say?" She leaned in and started kissing my neck, but all I could think was it'd been an hour since we fucked. How the hell was I gonna get them out of my house? My phone buzzed. She didn't stop kissing as I leaned over and started reading the text from Darla.

> D: Hey, shithead. I got off work early. Wanna buy me dinner?

Bingo!

> Absolutely. Meet you at Stumpy's in 45?

> D: Perfect! I'm bringing Kacie and Brody with me. Why don't you grab Mike and Michelle?

I shot Big Mike a quick text to see if he could grab a sitter and then it was time to start acting.

"Oh no!" I sat up straight, gently nudging her off of my lap. "It's my grandma; she's not feeling well. I gotta go!"

Crystal's hand flew up over her mouth and Heather's eyes grew huge as I hurried into my bedroom.

"Is she okay? Do you want me to go with you?" Heather called from the living room.

"No, that's okay," I hollered back. "I don't know how long

I'll be, and I'm sure you guys have to get home to . . . things."

"Okay." Heather sounded sad.

"Why don't you write your numbers down and leave them on the counter?"

"Okay, we will!" Crystal chimed excitedly. "Are you almost ready? We wanna say good-bye."

I laid my forehead against the back of the bedroom door and groaned. I hated this part, the promise-to-call-them-even-though-I-know-I-never-will part. It's not that I felt bad about the lying; that was part of life. It was faking that I was sad to see them go.

I walked into the kitchen and Crystal was leaning against the kitchen table with her arms folded across her chest, sticking her bottom lip out.

"Don't be sad." I tried not to sound annoyed. "Things happen. We'll do this again."

Lie.

"I know, we just had so much fun," she pouted. It only made me more anxious to get her out of my damn house.

Crystal reached up to kiss me and suddenly I remembered why I'd brought her home in the first place. That girl had a mouth capable of working magic, whether it was on my tongue or my cock.

"Wait, you don't have a car here!" I exclaimed, using that as an excuse to pull back from her.

She wiped her lips with the back of her hand and shook her head.

"Here." I walked over to the hockey puck-shaped cookie jar on my counter and pulled out two twenty-dollar bills. "Let me pay for a cab for you guys."

"You don't have to do that." Heather held her hands up as I walked toward them with the money.

"No, I want to. It's the least I can do for having to leave so suddenly. Please."

9

"Thank you so much, Viper. It's sweet of you to do that for us. You're so considerate." Crystal threw her arms around my neck, and as I hugged her back, I peeked at that cookie jar, which held stacks of twenty-dollar bills exactly for this occasion, and smiled to myself.

Once they closed the front door, I turned back to the counter and picked up the piece of paper they'd left. The bottom of the paper glistened with two lip prints from where they'd each kissed it.

Cute, but no thanks.

I opened a drawer and tossed the piece of paper inside with all the others. Some men had notches in their headboards. I had a drawer full of numbers that I'd never call.

A little bit later, I'd just finished getting ready when my phone buzzed. It was Big Mike telling me they were outside.

"That was fast," I said, climbing into the backseat of his Tahoe. "Hi, Michelle."

"Hey, Viper." She looked back and smiled at me.

"I know. We're never lucky enough to find a sitter on such short notice, but my sister's in town and staying with us, so she said to go," Mike answered as he pulled out into traffic.

"Taylor?"

"Yes, Taylor."

Big Mike had one younger sister and she had been the reason for me making a deposit at the spank bank more than once. She had long blond hair and even longer legs that I dreamed about having wrapped around my waist while I fucked her against a wall.

"Stop it," Mike snapped playfully.

"Stop what?" I shot back.

"Thinking about her. I can feel it." He glared at me in the rearview mirror. "She's my sister, which makes her absolutely, one-hundred and fifty percent off-limits."

Michelle smiled and shook her head as I let out a guilty laugh. "Ah, Mikey, my boy, you know me so well."

"Yeah, yeah." He rolled his eyes.

We drove for a little bit before pulling off the highway into the parking lot of the run-down, hole-in-the-wall bar that had quickly become our new favorite place. Brody had found Stumpy's on accident after taking a wrong turn one night.

Go figure.

Way back when he and Kacie were still dating and he'd been driving there to see her all the time, he'd been on his way home and had to piss. The first parking lot he'd found was Stumpy's. It just so happened to be almost exactly halfway between the city and Brody's new house, so it was the perfect meeting spot for all of us.

We walked into the dark, quiet bar and found Brody, Kacie, and Darla already there, seated at our usual table in the back corner. Kacie waved us over as Darla stood and skipped over to me, pulling me in for a hug.

"Hey there, stud."

"Hey." I squeezed her back, hard.

Being with Darla was easy. She used me just like I used her, and there were no expectations when we said good-bye. Not only was she one of the women who I'd break rules number two and three for, but I didn't cringe when I rolled over in the morning and she was still there. The fact that she loved sports just as much as I did was a huge bonus. Being with her was like having a best friend I could fuck anytime I wanted. I knew she saw other men, and she knew I saw other women, but that didn't matter. We were what we were with no promises.

We all sat down at the table as the waitress walked up and passed out menus that we probably wouldn't even need.

"Portland!" I jumped up when I realized just who our

waitress was and pulled her into a bear hug.

The force of my hug made her drop her pen and paper as I lifted her off of the ground.

"Hi, Viper. Put me down." She giggled, squirming out of my arms. She bent down and picked her stuff up. "What can I start you guys off with? A pitcher?"

"Make it two," Brody answered.

"Got it." She punched my arm and winked at me as she walked away.

"Your tongue is hanging out of your mouth," Darla teased, nudging me back to reality. I hadn't even realized I was staring at Portland as she walked away.

"Seriously, dude. Control yourself," Mike teased.

"I can't help it." I finally turned back to the table. "She has an ass that keeps me up at night. Shit, that ass gets me *up* whenever I think about it too long."

Kacie and Michelle groaned and rolled their eyes.

"I'm gonna get her. Mark my words, I'm gonna get her," I said confidently.

To everyone else, she was Anna, but to me, she'd always be Portland. She'd moved here a couple of months ago from Portland, against her parents' wishes, to live with her boyfriend. Before she'd even finished unpacking, she found out he was cheating on her and he moved out. Trying to save face with her parents, she'd decided to stick it out and keep the lease for a year. I met her shortly thereafter and was attracted instantly. Her long jet-black hair and tattooed arms were my ultimate weakness, and I'd vowed to spend that same year trying to get her into bed, but she resisted every advance I'd made. Little did she know I hadn't brought out the big guns yet.

"I don't get how you put up with this hornball," Kacie said to Darla as she nodded her head toward me.

Darla shrugged. "He's not mine."

"Whatever." Michelle grabbed a peanut out of the bowl and

tossed it at Darla. "You are the closest thing to a girlfriend he's ever had."

"Actually, that's not true," objected Brody. "Remember Kat? She lived with him for like what . . . five minutes?"

"Don't remind me about *that* crazy bitch." I groaned as I dropped my head onto the table.

"That's the same nutjob that called my phone, right?" Darla asked.

"Wait, she called you?" Kacie asked incredulously. "You never told me that!"

"Really? I thought I had," she answered. "Yeah, right after we started fooling around, she called me to warn me about his evil ways."

Michelle's mouth hung open in shock as she reached over and grabbed another peanut. "What did you say?"

"I told her that she better not call me again or I'd show her what evil really was." Darla laughed.

"Okay, here you guys go." Portland walked back up to the table carrying a pitcher of ice-cold beer in each hand. Between the beer and her perky tits in the same eyeshot, my dick was getting hard right there at the table.

She set the pitchers down and took our food order.

"Can I get a water too?" Kacie asked.

"Sure thing. I'll be right back with that and then put these in." She smiled and walked away, disappearing through the saloon doors into the kitchen.

"Okay, enough about Viper's deranged relationships with women. What else is new with everyone here?" Brody asked as he started pouring beer into glasses and sliding them around the table.

Portland returned with Kacie's water and set it down.

"Maura's sleeping through the night, finally!" Michelle said cheerfully.

Mike raised his glass in the air. "I'll drink to that."

We all raised our glasses and bumped them together in the middle.

"How old is she now?" Darla asked.

Big Mike sighed. "Six months. Took her forever."

"Wait,"—Michelle narrowed her eyes at Kacie—"why are you drinking water?"

Like someone turned the dial up on her face, Kacie's cheeks flushed instantly. She cleared her throat. "Uh . . . I'm driving."

"Bullshit," Darla called her out. "Brody drove here."

"And I'm driving home," Kacie shot back defensively.

Brody looked down at the table, playing with an empty peanut shell as he tried to hide his smile.

"No way." Darla looked from him to her. "You two did it again, didn't you?"

"Did what?" I was clueless.

"Are you?" Darla ignored me as she pushed Kacie to answer her. Kacie turned her head toward Brody, silently begging for backup.

"Don't look at me." He laughed, holding his hands up defensively. "I'm not the fertile one."

"Oh my God! You are!" Michelle squealed as she clapped her hands together.

"Are what? What the hell is going on?" I growled as I looked around the table, annoyed that I was obviously the only one who didn't know what was going on.

Brody peeked down at Kacie, who'd covered her face with her hands. "Kacie's pregnant."

Darla and Michelle hopped off of their stools and ran around to Kacie's side of the table, wrapping their arms around her.

"Pregnant?" I blurted out. "Isn't Emma like . . . a newborn still?"

Kacie giggled as Darla and Michelle released her. "She's

almost one and a half."

Brody grinned. "They'll be a little over two years apart." Kacie rested her cheek on Brody's shoulder, staring up at him. She closed her eyes as he gently kissed her forehead.

"I'm happy for you guys, truly." Mike had a tear in his eye as he raised his glass again. We all lifted our glasses one more time.

"You're such a fucking pansy ass," I teased as Mike wiped his eye.

"He's not a pansy." Michelle leaned over and kissed his cheek. "He's a sweet, sensitive man who appreciates family."

"If by sensitive you mean he has a vagina," I joked before turning my attention to Brody and Kacie. "Really though, I am happy for you guys. Is this one gonna have a penis, unlike Mike?"

"We don't know." Kacie laughed as Mike reached over and punched my arm. "Still too early. And because it's so early, we're asking you guys to keep this to yourselves. You all know how it can be when the media catches wind of something personal in our lives, and I'm not ready for that yet. Not until I'm further along."

"Oh, honey. That goes without saying," Michelle agreed, shaking her head. "Damn vultures."

"Man, look at this. You guys are all on your second, third, tenth kids, and here I am living by myself, with no one to come home to at night, no family to love, no one to talk to . . ." I said as seriously as I could. They all stared wide-eyed at me, not sure how to respond. "Suckers!" I bellowed, laughing as I ducked the hail of peanuts.

Chapter 2

"**M**ORNING, SUNSHINE."

My head throbbed as I cracked one eye open the very next morning. Darla was sitting on the edge of my bed, smiling at me as she tied her shoes.

Blinking away the sleep, I leaned up on one elbow. "Where you going?"

"You're off work for the summer, but the rest of us aren't," she teased as she disappeared into my walk-in closet. "What are your plans for the rest of the day anyway?"

I sat all the way up and stretched my arms out. "I think I'm gonna go visit my grandma."

"Oh yeah?" She reappeared from my closet wearing a Minnesota Wild sweatshirt.

"Hey, that's my favorite one," I whined playfully.

"I know." She smiled at me. "So . . . your grandma, huh? Do you visit her often?"

"Not as much as I should." I sighed, feeling guilty. "It's hard to get over there during the season, so I spend as much time with her as I can during the off-season. We're kindred spirits, actually."

She stopped moving and stared at me for a second,

processing what I'd just said. "Kindred spirits? You and your *grandmother?*"

"Yep." I laughed. "Believe it or not. Gam's not a typical grandma. She looks like it on the outside, but on the inside she's wild and crazy."

"Hmmm." She tilted her head to the side. "I'd like to meet her sometime."

I nodded. "I'm sure you will."

"All right, I gotta go." Grabbing her purse off my dresser, she walked over and bent down to kiss me good-bye.

"What about my hoodie?" I mumbled through the kiss.

Darla pulled away and narrowed her eyes at me. "I'll bring it back, you big baby."

I yawned and lay back down on the bed. "You coming back tonight?"

"Maybe." She blew me a kiss and turned down the hall.

"What do you mean maybe?" I called after her.

"Gotta see what other offers present themselves," she yelled back from my kitchen.

I couldn't help but smile as I heard the clink of the cookie jar on the counter.

She knows me so damn well.

Gam's little ranch house was modest but really well taken care of, considering her stubborn eighty-nine-year-old ass wouldn't let me hire a landscaper. Not a flower out of place or a bush overgrown. It was her pride and joy, other than me of course.

The hum of my motorcycle brought Gam out to her front porch.

She tipped her watering can toward some weird pink puffballs in a pot as I took my helmet off and secured it to the back of my bike.

"You're so goddamn loud. The whole neighborhood knows

when my grandson comes over." She smiled, shaking her head. I walked up the white wooden steps to her porch and she offered me her cheek.

"Gimmie a break." I kissed her. "These old bats living in your community can't hear shit."

"You win." She nodded. "Here, come sit."

We walked over to the two white wicker chairs on her porch, and I collapsed into one, still tired and a bit hungover from the night before.

She stared down at me, studying my face. "You look like hell."

"Thanks. I feel like hell."

"Let me get you something to drink." She patted my knee and disappeared into the house.

I rested my head against the back of the chair and closed my eyes, taking a deep breath. Her porch smelled sweet from all the flowers that surrounded it. A bird annoyingly chirped somewhere from one of the twenty bright-colored birdhouses I'd hung in her trees a few years ago. Birds were her passion, especially cardinals. They were her favorite. She would sit and watch them all day long and talked about them like they were her friends. She also talked about the squirrels. Scratch that, more like bitched about the squirrels. Holy shit did she hate them.

The door hinge creaked as she came back out carrying a tray with our drinks in mason jars, as usual.

"Here, drink this." She handed me a glass of sweet tea along with a couple aspirin. "And take those. You really do look like shit."

I smiled and shook my head as I washed the pills down with a swig of tea.

"So, what's new with you?" I leaned back in my chair.

"Well, I'm not dead yet, so that's something to celebrate." She raised her jar in the air before taking a drink.

I looked back and forth from my glass to hers. "Why does

your tea look different?"

"Because my tea is whiskey." She grinned proudly.

"Whiskey?" I stared at it incredulously before checking the time on my phone. "It's ten thirty in the morning."

"Lawrence, when you're my age, you learn to do things when you want to do them, not when it's socially acceptable. Hell, who knows if I'll still be around at dinner time? While we're on the subject, I had half a tub of mint chocolate chip ice cream for dinner last night. Cheers!" She raised her glass again and winked at me.

The silver curls on top of her head didn't budge unless the wind blew at hurricane levels, the skin on her face was covered in wrinkles and laugh lines, and her glasses were thicker than my . . . hockey stick, but all of that was very deceiving. Knitting wasn't her thing, she didn't bake, and she didn't complain about loud music or kids walking on her lawn. She was a foul-mouthed, whiskey-drinking badass who told it like it was and didn't take crap from anyone. Even though she often complained about getting old, other than a bum knee and a little glaucoma, her health was great, and I was beyond thankful for that.

"How's your knee feeling?" I asked. "The weather's been weird the last couple days, really damp."

"Oh, you know . . . the usual." She shrugged. "If I sit too long, it tightens up. If I stand too long, it tightens up. When I get up in the morning, it's tight. When I go to bed at night, it's tight."

"At least you're consistent," I joked.

"Enough about my old bones. Have you talked to your parents lately?"

The muscles in my arms tightened. "Nope," I answered sharply, looking her straight in the eye, a gentle warning not to ask any more questions about it.

She stared back at me, squinting slightly as she tried to decide whether or not to push it.

"Have you talked to Ben? He was here last week."

"I know. He told me," I said, thankful she'd decided against talking about my parents. "He called last week. Said everything is still on track, so that's good."

Ben Goldberg was the best financial adviser in all of Minnesota. Not only did he stop me from pissing all my money away on beer and strip clubs, I paid him a little extra to help take care of my grandma. She'd received a small insurance claim from my grandpa's death, and while she lived simply, it was nowhere near enough to last her the rest of her life. Ben told her he'd invested it wisely and not only was it still there, but she was making a little on it every month. Little did she know she'd run out of money two years ago. A couple times a year, Ben went over finances with her in . . . layman's terms. She didn't understand percentages and IRAs and all that confusing shit, so she had no idea I paid Ben to pad her account. All she needed was him to reassure her that she was still set. I was supporting her one hundred percent, paying for anything and everything she needed, and that was strictly between Ben and me. If she knew the truth, she'd march her old, stubborn ass down to Starbucks or some shit like that and get a job. That was the last thing I wanted. She'd spent her whole life working hard as a cook, and I wanted her to worry about nothing more than her flowers and her birds.

"Damn it!" She jumped up from her chair and glared into the yard.

I followed her stare and turned around just as an ice cube whizzed past my head toward a squirrel that had stealthily climbed a tree and dropped down onto one of her birdhouses.

"Whoa, whoa! What the hell are you doing?" I held my arm up, shielding my face from another ice cube.

"That little bastard is looking for seed in the houses!" she yelled, raising her right arm and throwing another cube, barely missing the squirrel.

I looked down at the tray, finally noticing the cup with

nothing but ice in it. "You were prepared for this?"

"Yeah, he does this all the time!" She launched another cube, this time making contact with the poor little guy's belly. He jumped from the swinging house back up to the tree and disappeared.

"He'll be back . . . and I'll be ready." She sat back down in the chair, keeping a careful eye on the tree.

"Is this what you do with yourself all day?"

"Pretty much."

"So what else is on your agenda this week, other than squirrel hunting?" I teased, nodding toward the tree.

She shrugged. "The ladies gave me a hard time for missing cards last week, so I suppose I'll have to do that on Monday. It's supposed to rain Tuesday, so I'll most likely lie around in my underwear and watch TV."

Like I said, kindred spirits.

She continued, "Probably *The Price is Right.* Drew Carey is a cutie. He can leave his shoes under my bed anytime."

"Ugh." I cringed. "Gross. Why do you talk like that?"

"Hey, I'm old, not dead. Some of those young men on TV really get my motor running." She wiggled her eyebrows up and down.

"Come on! Knock it off. I don't want to hear about this." I laughed and covered my ears with my hands.

"You know, Lawrence, in my day, I was pretty hot to trot," she bragged proudly.

"I don't think I want to know what that means." I sighed.

"It means the boys thought your old granny was pretty cute, and granny loved the boys right back." She stared off into space, thinking about her past. She smirked and raised one eyebrow. "Especially the ones in uniform. Boy, was I a sucker for a man in a uniform."

"Can we be done with this conversation now?" I pleaded, rubbing my eyes with the heels of my hands. "I'm trying to keep my breakfast down."

Gam laughed loudly, clearly enjoying my discomfort. "Why did you want to know what I was doing anyway?"

"I was going to come by again. Maybe Wednesday?"

"Let me check my schedule." Her dark brown eyes looked up toward the ceiling of her covered porch and then back down at me. "Yep, I'm free."

"Good. I'm gonna come take you to breakfast."

"You are?"

"I am."

"Hmmm . . ." Thinking about it, she chuckled to herself. "Make it brunch. I like to sleep in."

Chapter
3

"**H**EY! COME ON IN." BIG Mike's smiling face greeted me as the wooden door opened. He was holding Maura in his right arm, facing out, as I stepped inside. As soon as I stepped through the door, she grinned up at me, her arms flapping wildly as drool hung off her chin.

I caught the spit with my finger and wiped it on Mike's face as I walked by. "Kind of like having a puppy, huh?"

He laughed, wiping his cheek with his sleeve. "Asshole."

I walked toward the back of his large, comfortable house and into the kitchen. Matthew was sitting at the counter eating a bowl of macaroni and cheese.

"Hi!" He waved at me, grinning just as big as his sister had.

"Hey, buddy!" I walked over and high-fived him. "How's it shaking?"

He scrunched his little eyebrows together and looked up at me. "How's *what* shaking?"

"Never mind, bud." I laughed and he went back to his noodles.

"Matthew, never take anything Uncle Viper says literally. It's a very important lesson we all need to learn at one point or another," Mike teased as he set Maura down in some weird-looking baby contraption.

"You two aren't going to corrupt my son, are you?" Michelle breezed into the kitchen.

"That's the plan," I answered.

Mike tilted his head to the side, smiling slightly as he watched her frantically open drawer after drawer. "What are you looking for?"

"My credit card. I can't find—Here it is!" She grinned, holding her gold card up in the air.

"Where are you going anyway?" I asked.

She shoved the card into her purse. "Book club."

I frowned at her. "Why do you need a credit card for book club?"

Mike looked at me and rolled his eyes. "Why do they have book club at a pub?"

"Correction,"—she held her finger up in the air—"it's at a martini bar. Way classier than a pub."

"Mmhmm, if you say so." She walked over and stood up high on her tippy toes to give Mike a kiss. He smacked her ass as she walked away. Her perfume tickled my nose and I realized I'd never really seen her dress up before. Not like this. She actually looked . . . hot.

"Okay, baby . . ." She threw her purse over her shoulder and walked over to Matthew, then knelt down next to him and kissed his cheek. "I love you. Have fun tonight."

"Love you too, Momma."

She wiped her lipstick off his cheek with her hand and whispered something in his ear, making him giggle. Then she left. Again with the damn perfume.

Perfume on a woman is like a secret weapon against men. It flies up our noses and heads straight for our brains, making us completely pussy drunk. We suddenly turn into bees that need to stick our little bee dicks into a woman's flower for a taste of that sweet, sweet nectar. Intoxicating.

"What did Mom say to you?" Big Mike asked Matthew.

"She said you and Uncle Viper are crazy, so I'm in charge tonight." He giggled again and shoved a huge bite of noodles into his mouth.

"Oh, really? Then what are we doing tonight, boss?" Mike walked over and picked up Maura, who had started fussing in her swing. She was six months old already but still so tiny in Mike's huge paw.

"We're gonna . . ." His little face twisted and contorted as he thought about what he wanted to do. "Let's eat lots of cookies and watch *Teenage Mutant Ninja Turtles!*"

I shrugged. "Sounds good to me."

An hour later, Maura had eaten, puked weird white shit all over Mike's shirt, and passed out in another baby apparatus in the corner of the family room while Big Mike, Matthew, and I each lay on a different part of the sectional, watching the Minnesota Twins beat the crap out of the White Sox.

"So this is what you do with your Friday nights, huh?" I asked Mike as I glanced around the room, fascinated by the simplicity of the evening.

"Pretty much." He smiled proudly. "Awesome, huh?"

"Sure." I shrugged. "If you don't like women with tits."

"Really?" Mike glared at me before looking over at Matthew, who was too busy watching TV to pay attention to us. "Come on, Finkle, you know one day you'll be an old married man like me with a wife and house full of little kids." He picked up the remote and changed the channel from the baseball game to some obnoxious cartoon with a singing yellow sponge.

I stared in disgust as the porous little bastard danced around the screen and poked his big pink friend in the gut. "Not if it means having to watch this shit."

Matthew gasped, his mouth hanging open as his head twisted quickly toward me and then over to his dad.

Big Mike tried to hold in his laugh. "Try not to swear, okay?"

Jesus, it would be easier not to eat for a week than it would be not to swear.

"Sorry. But no, you and Brody live in a different universe than me."

He frowned. "What do you mean?"

"He's like you now. Busy with the family all the time and preoccupied."

"He's not preoccupied, he just has different priorities now. Unfortunately, being your wingman at the bar has taken a backseat to his wife and kids."

"I know, and trust me, the last thing I need is a wingman. It's just weird. I hardly see him anymore."

"It hasn't been so bad, though. You and I have been hanging out a lot more." He smiled a big, goofy grin at me.

"Easy there, big guy. Reel your vagina back in." I glanced over at him and shot him a small, playful smile. "It has been nice, though, hanging out I mean. I've been over here so often lately your couch is starting to take on the imprint of my a—" I cleared my throat. "—butt."

We sat in awkward silence for a minute, trying to figure out how to make our conversation manly again.

"It's not so bad, you know? Wife, kids, the whole thing. It's actually pretty awesome." He nodded toward Matthew. "That one looks at me like I'm a superhero for something simple like throwing frozen waffles in the toaster, and that sleepy little girl smiles all the time, even in the middle of the night."

"Sorry, you lost me at 'middle of the night.'"

"Oh, bull. Half the time you don't crawl home until the middle of the night. Stop acting like you couldn't handle a 2 a.m. feeding."

"I need my beauty sleep."

"That I'll agree with, ugly."

I picked a bottle cap up off of the coffee table and launched it across the couch at him, fist-pumping when it bounced off the top of his head. "And why the fu—" I caught myself and looked at Matthew, who was staring right at me, listening to every word we were saying. "—heck are you feeding her at two in the morning anyway? Isn't that the woman's job?"

Big Mike's eyes grew wide and a heavy laugh escaped him. "Viper, my boy, you have a lot to learn. First, never say anything is her *job* or you'll be parking it on the couch for a long time with a serious 'dry spell,' if you know what I mean," he said, making air quotes with his fingers.

"I wasn't being a pig. I was being serious," I defended. "I thought they had the . . . *equipment* to take care of that."

"They do, but sometimes that equipment gets clogged or doesn't produce enough milk or she's just plain tired and you have to step it up."

Clogged?

I held my hand up to stop him from going any further. "Okay, okay. I get it. No more."

Mike smirked at me without saying a word.

"What? Stop it." I was uncomfortable with him staring at me like he was.

"I can see it."

"See what?"

"You." He grinned. "With a kid."

"No fu—" I caught myself again—barely. "No way."

"I'm not kidding. You're all rough and tough, but I can totally picture you schlepping some mini-Viper around with you to games and practices, showing him off."

"Absolutely not." I shook my head firmly. "The last thing this world needs is another Viper."

"Well, I agree with that too, but I think it would soften that cement heart of yours."

"I like my cement heart." I sighed.

Before he continued his quest to talk me into becoming a father, we heard the front door close. Mike sat up and peeked over the edge of the couch toward the kitchen.

"Hi," Michelle sighed as she tossed her purse onto the island.

"Hey." Mike sat up further. "What are you doing back so soon?"

"A couple of the girls couldn't make it because their kids were sick, so we had a small group tonight. We pretty much just had dinner and called it a night." She walked over and checked on Maura briefly before kissing Matthew on the forehead and sitting down on the couch next to Mike with another heavy sigh.

"I'm sorry. You sound bummed." Big Mike lifted his arm and tucked it behind her head, pulling her in tight.

"I am a little, but now I get to hang with my favorite people instead." She lifted her head and smiled at him.

"Mom?" Matthew asked.

"Yes, baby?"

He twisted his little face, thinking hard about whatever it was he was going to say next. "You're kind of a woman, right?"

Michelle giggled and tilted her head to the side. "Yes, honey, I am. Why?"

"I was just wondering . . ." He paused and wiped his nose with the back of his hand. "What are tits?"

Michelle sat up straight and gasped as Big Mike cringed, shutting his eyes tight.

"That's my cue!" I hopped up and slapped Mike on the shoulder on my way out of the room. "See ya tomorrow, buddy. Nice seeing you again, Michelle!"

Chapter

4

"WHAT'S UP, LADIES?" I exclaimed as I crashed loudly through the wooden doors of the Minnesota Wild locker room.

Everyone turned in my direction briefly and then went back to whatever they were doing, except for Brody and Big Mike, who rolled their eyes in unison.

I hung my bag on my hook and turned toward them. Brody's arms were crossed over his chest as he eyed me suspiciously. "Why are you so chipper?"

"Because I'm young and alive and drop-dead gorgeous," I bragged.

"You're not that young, and you're definitely not drop-dead gorgeous, but you are alive, so one out of three ain't so bad." Brody laughed.

Big Mike glared at me. "Barely alive."

"Oh, shit." I stared back at him, suddenly remembering the tit incident from the night before. "How bad was it after I left?"

Brody scrunched his eyebrows and looked back and forth between the two of us. "What did I miss?"

"This moron"—Big Mike smacked my chest hard with the back of his hand—"doesn't know how to watch his mouth

31

around kids. Matthew asked Michelle what a tit was last night."

The edges of Brody's lips turned white from him pushing them together so hard as he tried not to laugh.

"It's not funny!" Mike grumbled.

Brody nodded in agreement but didn't keep his composure for long. His hand slapped over his mouth as he let out a big laugh. "I'm sorry, but it's fucking hysterical."

Brody laughing made me laugh, and eventually even Mike cracked a smile.

"Okay, seriously. How bad was it?" I asked, feeling almost guilty, but not really.

"It was"—Mike let out a heavy sigh—"not great. She explained to him what a tit was and why we don't use that word. Then she marched around the kitchen mumbling something about you being grounded from the house until the kids go to college."

"Grounded?" I busted out laughing again. "I haven't been grounded since . . . ever."

"Bullshit," Brody disagreed. "There's no way *you* were never grounded as a teenager."

"It's true. I was a fucking angel. Still am," I teased as I pulled my shirt over my head and tossed it in my bag.

"Holy shit, everyone back up." Brody held his arms straight out to his sides and took a giant step back. "Lightning is going to strike the locker room any second."

"So wait,"—I ignored him and looked at Mike—"since we're grounded, does this mean you're not coming over tonight?"

Mike's eyes darted to Brody's and back to mine. "What's tonight?"

"You have the memory of a fucking goldfish," I said as I picked a towel up off the bench and whipped it at his head. "Poker night, remember?"

Brody ran his hands through his hair. "Oh, shit. I forgot."

"Tough," I barked at him. "You have to be there, both of

you."

Brody held his hands up in front of him defensively. "Relax, I'm going. I just forgot."

Mike nodded. "I'll be there too. Who else will be there?"

"I texted Andy, Viktor, and Louie, but I've only heard back from Louie so far."

Mike glanced around the room to make sure everyone was out of earshot. "Oh I'm sure Louie responded the second he got your text." He laughed as he sat down on the bench to lace up his skates. "He's so far up your ass that when you open your mouth to talk, I see his eyes staring at me from the back of your throat."

The sentence was barely out of Big Mike's mouth when Louie popped his head around the corner. "Viper, are you going on the ice or working out first?"

Brody let out a loud roar as he dropped to the bench and high-fived Mike, who was laughing just as hard.

"Uh, not sure. Probably the weight room," I answered.

"Okay." He nodded and disappeared back around the corner.

I turned around to Brody and Mike, who were still laughing so hard they could hardly breathe. "Fuck you both. Be at my place at eight o'clock." I grabbed my iPod and headed out toward the weight room.

"You sure we can't come earlier?" Big Mike teased in between breaths. "I can think of at least one person who'd like to get there earlier."

I flipped him off and kept walking.

"I'm a little early. Hope that's okay." Louie smiled as he stood on my front porch.

You've got to be fucking kidding me.

"It's fine," I lied. "Come on in."

Louie was the young and all too eager backup goalie for our

team. He was a cocky little pain in the ass who seemed to always be two steps behind me, but for the most part, he was harmless. His arrogance turned most of the guys on the team off, and they gave him a lot of shit for it. Personally, I liked his attitude, so I kinda took him under my wing.

"Nice place!" His eyes darted around my kitchen as he set a case of beer on the kitchen table.

"Thanks. I wanted to buy a condo, but my grandma insisted I needed a yard." I sighed.

He shoved his hands into his jeans pockets and walked over to look out the back window. "Nice yard!"

"Thanks. Again."

"Wait . . ." He turned back around with a puzzled look on his face. "Is that a trampoline out there?"

"Yep."

"You don't have kids, right?"

"Nope."

"Then why do you have a trampoline?"

Chuckling to myself, I shook my head as I loaded the beer into the fridge. "What's a trampoline for, Louie?"

"Uh . . . for people to . . . jump?"

"Right. And what's the best part when you're fucking a girl and she's on top?"

I could practically smell the thick black smoke his brain was producing as he thought hard about what I'd just asked.

Three . . . two . . . one . . .

"Oooh! I get it!" His excitement turned into confusion almost instantly. "Wait . . . really? Chicks come over here to jump on your trampoline?"

"No, they come over to hang out with me, and I sweetly coax them into the backyard where I sit on a recliner and drink a beer while they jump up and down on the trampoline, preferably in a bikini."

"You have a recliner out there too?" he exclaimed, turning back to the window.

I tilted my head to the side and scratched it, completely baffled at his response. "*That* is what you got out of what I just said?"

Before he could answer, the doorbell rang.

Thank God.

As I was heading toward the front door, it swung open. Brody, Mike, and Andy poured into the house, arguing over the baseball game.

"Bullshit! That was a bad call at the plate. He was safe at home, and if you couldn't see that, then I think we need a new goalie," Mike ranted.

"He was out," Brody argued back. "The ball beat him by at least four steps."

Andy nodded as they walked by, leaving my front door wide open.

"What were you guys raised in a barn?" I called after them as I walked over to shut the door.

Holy shit. I sound like Gam.

"Wait for us!" Michelle giggled, pushing the door back open.

Kacie reached up and kissed my cheek. "Hey, Uncle V."

My eyes practically bulged out of my head as they shuffled past me. "Hold up," I commanded. "What are *you guys* doing here?"

"We love poker night!" Michelle cheered, throwing her arms in the air.

"We called Darla too. She'll be here once she's off work," Kacie added. Noticing my lack of enthusiasm to see them, she added, "Awww, don't worry. We aren't here to ruin your boys' night. I brought guacamole and wine." They turned and walked toward the kitchen.

"Wine doesn't belong at *poker night*," I yelled after them as I shut the door—again.

At least they called Darla and invited her too. The odds of getting laid by something other than my hand just increased about a thousand percent.

Two hours had passed and we hadn't even touched one card, but I was cool with it. We were still having a good time shooting the shit around the kitchen table. Darla had just gotten to my house and immediately parked herself on my lap. I was zoning out as she told Kacie and Michelle about the new doctor that had just started at the hospital. Apparently he had dreamy eyes and a killer ass.

"So did you guys exchange numbers?" Kacie leaned in close to Darla, almost whispering.

If it was for my benefit, I didn't need her to be quiet. Darla was a beautiful, single girl who was free to date—and fuck—whoever she wanted. So was I. I liked our freedom with each other.

"No, but we work together two more times this week. I totally checked his schedule." She giggled.

Darla *never* giggled.

"You should ask him out for coffee or something," Kacie urged her. "Make a move before another nurse on your floor snags him. A couple of those girls are major whores."

"Can I meet the whores?" Louie interrupted.

Kacie rolled her eyes. "You get enough whores."

"Speaking of whores, I was down in your basement last week, Viper . . ." Brody leaned back in his chair and crossed his arms over his chest.

"You have whores in your basement?" Louie's eyes were wide, and I swear I saw drool drip from the corner of his mouth.

I reached out and smacked him in the back of the head. "No, you idiot."

"You're a candy whore. I knew you had a stockpile, but my God. There must be twenty cases of Lemonheads along the wall." Brody shook his head slowly in amazement.

Turning in my lap slightly, Darla rested her arm around my shoulder. "Candy? In your basement? Why?"

"You don't know?" Louie looked incredulously at her.

Darla shook her head.

"Before every game," he continued, "Viper gives Big Mike a box of Lemonheads."

"You do?" she squeaked at me, clearly surprised.

"Yep. Every single game. Home or away." I reached my hand across the table and fist-bumped Mike.

"They've been doing it for a while now," Michelle added with a smile as she eye-fucked Mike. "I'm constantly throwing away empty boxes I find tucked in all corners of his car and office."

"I didn't know that," Darla said softly as she rubbed my temple with the back of her fingers.

"Oh, stop." I rolled my eyes as I grabbed her hand and kissed it. "It's not because I was worried he wanted a snack; it's purely superstition. I don't know why, but I gave him a box one game and we all played really well that night. Won a game we probably shouldn't have won. Ever since then, it's just been our thing." I shrugged.

"Awww," Kacie, Darla, and Michelle cooed together.

"Aren't they sweet?" Andy mocked as he clapped his hands together near his face and batted his eyelashes dramatically.

"We *are* fucking sweet," I bellowed arrogantly. "Our bromance is amazing. We're like a modern-day Romeo and Romeo."

"Whoa, whoa!" Big Mike held his hands up defensively and laughed. "I wouldn't go *that* far, Finkle."

"This is nothing new, though, this superstition thing with Viper," Brody said as he stood up and walked over to the fridge. "He's always been over-the-top . . . about more than just candy."

"What else?" Kacie asked.

"When he gets dressed before every game, he puts all his left pads on before his right ones." Louie laughed.

"Not only that," Mike jumped in at the end of Louie's sentence. "As long as I've played with him, he listens to the same song about a hundred times before every game. In the car on the way to the arena, while he's getting dressed, on his way out to the bench."

Darla crinkled her nose. "The same song? Over and over?"

"Fuck yeah." I nodded. "'Thunderstruck' by AC/DC. That song makes me want to run through a brick wall."

"I'll give him that. It *is* a badass song." Brody sat back at the table and set a bottle of Gatorade in front of him. "He also buys his own tape for his stick and will only use bright yellow."

"Maybe you should stop paying so much attention to my stick, Murphy," I teased, gently nudging Darla off my lap. I got up from the table and walked over to the fridge to grab another beer. "Anyone else want one?"

"Dude, you keep drinking beer like that in the off-season and you're not gonna be much use on the ice when it counts." Mike stood up and stretched his arms above his head.

"Psh." I waved him off. "Regardless of what, or how much, I drink, I could still skate circles around you."

"Oh, really?" He looked straight at me with his eyebrows raised. Suddenly I had his attention. "Wanna make it interesting?" he challenged with a smirk.

"Uh-oh." Andy sighed and dropped his head into his hands. "I hate when you idiots say things like that. It usually means I'm going to have a long day in the near future."

Ignoring Andy, I stared straight at Mike. "Yeah, let's make it interesting. Practice, Friday. You and me. One on one against Brody. Loser has to wear a pink tutu to workouts for an entire week."

Big Mike's eyes lit up as he walked across the kitchen holding his hand out for me to shake. "You're on."

Chapter
5

"WELL AREN'T YOU A FINE-looking piece of ass!" I hollered as I got out of my car and walked around it.

"Flattery will get you everywhere." Gam winked at me as she carefully walked down the front steps of her house.

I hurried over and took her hand, leading her to my car. "How are you feeling today?"

"Better than you look." She laughed as she climbed into my car.

"You tell me I look like shit every time you see me. It's starting to give me a complex," I joked as I closed the door and jogged around to my side.

"Oh, bull," she scoffed. "You know you're hot shit, and you don't need my confirmation for that."

"I was taught never to argue with my elders, so I'll agree with you." I wiggled my eyebrows up and down at her as she reached over and smacked my arm. "So, where we headed?"

She shrugged. "This was your idea. You choose."

"Well, are you in the mood for breakfast or lunch?"

"I don't care where we go or what we eat. Just make sure the place serves alcohol already." She winked again as I pulled out of her driveway.

We'd only been driving a couple of minutes when I pulled into a nice restaurant just outside of downtown called The Raspberry Cafe.

"*Here?*" she exclaimed.

I parked my car and turned toward her, confused by her response. "Yeah, why?"

She glanced down at her turquoise sweat suit and back up at me with her brows pulled in tight. "I'm a little underdressed for this place. Come to think of it, so are you."

"Who cares?" I waved her off. "Live a little. Besides, I've been here before—in sweats. They don't care. They know me here."

She sighed and picked her purse up off the floor of the car. "Fine, but you're paying."

I laughed and went around to her side of the car. She hooked her arm through mine as we slowly made our way into the restaurant. The smell of cinnamon smacked me in the face as I opened the big wooden doors and stepped back to let her go in ahead of me. The Raspberry Cafe was a contemporary yet rustic restaurant with real wooden beams on the ceiling and walls and stone accents on either side. What I liked best about the place were the tall wooden booths. They offered privacy, which is something I didn't always get when I was out in public. It wasn't like I couldn't walk through the grocery store without being attacked, but I had enough fans to keep things interesting.

"Hi. Welcome to The Raspberry Cafe," a busty, young olive-skinned girl greeted us as we walked in. "Two today?"

"That's right." I stared at her, trying to figure out if she was legal or not. Jailbait was a big fat no for me. Frankly, if she couldn't legally take a drink of alcohol, I had no desire to fuck her. Another rule of mine.

She grabbed two menus off the hostess stand and led us to a table in the back corner. I was thankful for the added privacy even though the restaurant wasn't busy.

"Thanks, dear." Gam smiled at her as she slid into the booth.

Once the hostess set the menus down and walked away, I slid in across from Gam.

"She was cute." She nodded in the direction the hostess had just walked.

"Sure." I shrugged.

"Think you'd date her?"

"I don't date anyone."

"Why not?"

I sighed, uncomfortable with the thought of discussing my love life with my grandmother. "I don't know. I don't really have time."

She pursed her lips and rolled her eyes. "Oh, that's crap, Lawrence, and you know it. You have more free time than you let on. You're off today. You could be taking a beautiful woman to brunch."

"I *am* having lunch with a beautiful woman." I reached over and kissed the top of her hand.

"Oh . . ." She grinned shyly. "You little shit. You're good. Got that charm from your papa."

"From what I hear he was quite the man. I'll take that as a compliment."

I'd never met my grandfather. He was the love of Gam's life, but he'd died before I was born. I could tell he was a great man just based on the way her eyes lit up when she talked about him. As a kid, instead of reading to me, she would tell me stories about their life before he died. From what I knew, he was a talented artist, a badass pilot, and a practical joker.

"He was quite the man," she responded, her eyes red-rimmed, "and your father was too."

Check, please.

"Don't roll your eyes at me," she scolded.

Oops.

"Sorry," I apologized coldly.

"Lawrence, your parents love you very much."

"That's great." I picked up my menu. "What are you getting?"

Her hand came over the top of my menu and smacked it down hard onto the table. "Right now? The brush-off from my grandson."

I sat back against the booth and sighed as I crossed my arms over my chest. "You're not getting the brush-off, but my memories of them are very different from yours. Can we just leave it at that, please?"

"No."

"You're a stubborn old lady, you know that?"

"Yes." She smiled proudly.

"Hi there. Sorry about the wait." A young waiter set down two glasses of water, spilling drops all over the table as his hands shook.

"You okay, boss?" I asked.

"Yeah. I just . . . I'm new and you're . . . you, and I'm a little nervous." He grabbed a napkin off of the table next to ours and wiped up the water as fast as he could.

"No problem." I laughed. "You a hockey fan?"

"Uh, yes. Yes, sir," he stammered.

"Well, I'm a fan of anyone who's going to bring me food, so let's take a picture together, I'll sign whatever you want me to, and we'll call it even, okay?"

His goofy, crooked smile let me know he liked my idea. After a few minutes of selfie taking and autograph signing, he finally seemed to calm down enough to take our drink and food order.

"That was sweet of you," Gam whispered once he was out of earshot. She took a sip of her water, trying to hide her proud smile behind her glass.

"Stop it," I grumbled.

"Stop what?"

"Smiling."

"I will not," she said stubbornly, lifting her chin in the air. "I'm having a nice brunch with my grandson, who happens to be a very sweet man."

"I'm not sweet, Gam. I'm barely sour. In fact, most days I'm downright inedible altogether."

"You may not think you're sweet, but I do." She nodded toward the door leading to the kitchen. "And so does that young man. He's probably back there calling all of his friends to tell them how cool you are. You made his day."

I stared at her with a deadpan expression on my face. "I just want pancakes."

Later that night, I was sitting at home playing Madden on my XBOX when my text alarm went off. It was from Darla.

> D: Hey, you busy? Can I come over?

> Hell yes. Bring a pizza.

"Hey!" Her huge smile was the first thing I saw when I opened the door a little while later.

"What's up, baby?" I reached out and pulled her in for a hug.

"Careful." She giggled, keeping the hand that held the pizza out straight. "You don't want tomato sauce and cheese all over the floor of your foyer."

I pulled back and took the pizza from her. "I'm so hungry I'd probably still lick it off the floor. Come on." I took her hand and led her back to the kitchen.

We sat at the breakfast bar and stuffed our faces with pizza, barely even talking to each other, for the next half hour.

"Okay," I sighed, wiping my hand on a napkin. "What's going on?"

She froze, staring back at me with a bite of pizza still in her mouth. Covering her mouth with her napkin, she shook her head slightly. "What?"

"You."

"Me?"

"Yeah, you're different. Something's up."

"I'm not different."

I read Darla like I read opponents on the ice. What came out of their mouths never mattered; that was just chatter. It was their body language that gave everything away. They would fake right and go left, but I was already on the left waiting for them. I knew what moves they were going to make before they did. It was the same with Darla. She was preoccupied, distant.

"You've been in my house for over half an hour, and not only have you been avoiding eye contact the whole time, you have yet to give me shit about . . . anything. Normally, you would've picked me apart for ten different things by now."

She balled her napkin up and tossed it down on her plate, shrugging. "I don't know what you're talking about."

I turned my stool to face her and pulled her legs so that she was facing me. "Bullshit. Don't lie to me. We don't do that."

She looked sad.

I cupped her face and rubbed her cheek with the pad of my thumb.

"Don't do that. Don't be nice to me." She took my hand off her face, kissing my palm before resting it in her lap. Not making eye contact, she continued, "I did come over here for a reason, but it wasn't to torment you like normal."

"The doctor, right?"

Her face swept up to mine, her shoulders finally relaxing for the first time since she'd walked through the door. "How did you know?"

I laughed. "I knew it the other night when you started talking about him."

"I'm so sorry." She looked down at her lap again.

"Hey,"—I tucked my finger under her chin and lifted her face—"why are you apologizing?"

"I don't know. It's just—We—"

"Don't," I interrupted. "Don't say you're sorry. You have nothing to be sorry for. Darla, we've never put labels on whatever this has been between us, and that's one of the reasons it's worked so well for us. We live our lives and whatever happens, happens. Something is happening for you. Don't you dare apologize for that."

A pathetic, depressing smile spread across her lips. "You've just always been so good to me."

"And that's not going to change if you start seeing someone. You'll always be one of my best friends."

"It's probably nothing anyway. We just went for coffee after work yesterday, but it was . . . different. Weird. Good weird." She shook her head. "I'm probably overreacting. He's going to decide he doesn't like me, and here I am making an ass out of myself over nothing."

"It's not nothing, D. You're making an ass out of yourself for a chance at everything, and it's adorable. You need to go for it. You need to see what this is." I squeezed her hand. "But just know, if he hurts you, I'll break both his fucking legs."

Chapter
6

FRIDAY MORNING CAME, AND IN spite of my talk the night before with Darla, I was pumped. Beyond pumped. I took a picture of my breakfast—oatmeal, a banana, and a Red Bull—and sent it to Big Mike to taunt him, along with a text that said:

Ready to get your ass kicked?

A few minutes later, he responded.

M: Ready to wear a tutu?

I laughed as I tucked my phone into my backpack, strapped it to my motorcycle, and took off.

Arriving at the arena after a nice therapeutic ride on my bike with my iPod blaring AC/DC in my ears, I was more pumped than when I'd left the house.

I pulled into the parking lot and parked in my usual spot in the far corner of the fenced-in lot.

"Uh-oh." Brody chuckled and slammed the door to his pickup truck as I walked toward the building. "He rode his motorcycle, Mike. That means he's feeling extra cocky."

Mike got out of the passenger side of Brody's truck and lifted his bag out of the bed. "That's okay. I had Wheaties this morning, so I am too."

I ignored his Wheaties comment. "Awww, you two drove together today. Aren't you cute?"

"My car is in the shop, but don't worry—" He walked over to me and wrapped his giant gorilla arms around my shoulders, squeezing me so hard I thought my head was gonna pop off. "—you're still my favorite."

"Weirdos." Brody shook his head as he walked past us.

"I told you our bromance was real," I shouted after him. "Next up: *Brokeback Mountain,* the hockey edition."

Once inside, it was time to get to work. We all knew that Coach Collins would kick our asses for dicking around on the ice if we didn't do what we needed to do in the weight room first, so we all went in there to knock that out together.

"I fucking hate leg day," I growled as I lifted 400 pounds off the squat rack and puffed my cheeks out, watching my form carefully in the mirror.

Down, up.

Down, up.

Down, up.

"I gotta go see the trainer about a weird pain I'm having in my calf," Big Mike said as he bent over and rubbed the back of his leg. "I'll be back in a bit."

I put the squat bar back on the rack and glared at him in the mirror. "Go get that shit taken care of. No backing out."

"Ha!" he bellowed loudly. "Back out? No way. I'll see ya in a bit."

I nodded in response and looked around for Brody, but he was off doing incline presses on his own, so I threw my earbuds in, turned on Korn, and focused on my reps for the next two hours.

"Holy shit. I can't move." I was lying on the floor in the corner of the weight room stretching when Brody appeared above me. He slowly sat down next to me, grunting and groaning the whole way down.

"I can move . . . my arms." I sighed, suddenly regretting doing all those extra sets of calf raises. My entire lower half was tight and achy. What a long fucking afternoon it was going to be. "Big Mike back yet?"

"Hell yeah." Brody laughed. "He's been out on the ice for half an hour already. He's pumped."

"Sweet." Knowing that Mike was out on the ice already, clearly trying to get a head start on what would surely be the ass-kicking of a lifetime had adrenaline flooding my body and speeding through my veins. "Let's go." I ignored my sore legs and jumped up, heading for the locker room to change.

Brody hustled down the tunnel trying to keep up with me as I practically jogged to the ice. Mike was out there shooting against Louie, who was manning the goal for him.

"You ready, pretty boy?" I called out as I skated over to them.

Big Mike smiled confidently and nodded. "Hell yeah. Louie is sticking around to watch. You wanna have one goalie and play with half the rink, or you wanna use both guys and play full?"

"We're old and my legs are killing me. Let's play half."

"Sounds good." Mike whistled to Louie and skated over to let him know we wouldn't need him.

In my initial hurry out to the ice, I'd dropped my bag on the bench. I skated over to it and pulled a hot pink tutu out, hanging it on a hook on the inside of the boards. "See this?" I yelled, pointing at the tutu. "This is what we're playing for, or playing against."

Mike skated over, stopping just a few feet from me. "It'll look great on you." He winked arrogantly.

"Hey!" Brody called out from the goalie box. "Let's get this show on the road. We're having dinner at Sophia's tonight, and Kacie'll kill me if I'm late."

"I'm ready." I skated out to the center, right behind Mike. "Any specific rules?"

He shrugged and shook his head. "Nothing I can think of. First guy to score three goals on Murphy wins. Play your ass off. Think that about covers it, yeah?"

"Sounds good." I held my fist up in the air and Mike punched it.

Game on.

Since we no longer needed Louie to play goalie for us, we gave him the job of dropping the puck. He skated over to center ice and Big Mike and I took our positions. Louie held the puck up in the air for two seconds and dropped it between us. Our sticks crashed together as we each tried to smack the puck out of the middle and off to the side, where we could gain control of it. I pushed the puck between Mike's legs and out the other side.

"Shit!" he yelled as I skated around him quickly and took control of the puck. I handled the puck out and around the goal, putting some distance in between Big Mike and myself. I looped around the other side, and before Mike could get in between me and the goal, I flicked my wrist and sent a snapshot toward the goal.

Blocked.

Fuck you, Murphy!

He passed the puck to Louie, who carried it back to the middle where we started all over again.

"You got lucky. It won't happen again," Mike grumbled around his mouth guard as his eyes shimmered with determination.

"Watch me." I tried to sound just as confident, but I wasn't a dummy. I was the enforcer. My main job during every game was to beat the crap out of any guy that hurt one of our guys and then sit in the penalty box. Scoring was not expected from me, and my puck handling wasn't near as strong as Mike's, so my cocky attitude had to make up for what I lacked in skills.

Louie dropped the puck, but Mike was right. He was faster off the draw than I was that time as he pulled the puck back toward himself and skated toward Brody. I did my best to catch up and get in between them, but Mike was quick. He weaved his stick left and right and when he had an open shot, he took it. The puck flashed like lightning over the ice. I followed it with my eyes and watched as Brody dropped to his knees to block it, but it bounced off the left post and crossed over the red line.

Son of a bitch!

I hung my head as Big Mike's hands flew up in the air in celebration.

"Nice shot," I congratulated as we met in the middle again.

"Thank you. Wanna just concede now and save yourself any more humiliation?" He laughed.

"Fuck that. Let's go." I crouched down again, impatiently waiting for Louie to drop his arm.

The black flash of the puck was barely in front me for a millisecond before I was swinging at it, trying to gain control, but once again, Big Mike was too fast. He swatted the puck off toward Brody this time, and we were in a full-on sprint to see who would get to it first. Mike beat me to it by no more than two seconds, and rather than swipe at it and steal it from him, I did what I know how to do. Lowering my shoulder, I crashed into Mike as hard as I could, sending him flying backward and landing on his ass. As his brain registered that this wasn't just some cordial hockey game, but a game of pride, he glared at me and scrambled to his feet. I hooked the puck and skated backward just a little bit to put space between us again. My handling wasn't good enough to get close to Brody and try and

51

fake him out. I needed to shoot from as far away as I could and hope that Brody would make a mistake. I wound up and shot it as hard as I could.

Blocked.

"Damn it!" I yelled out loud this time as my head hung low again, and I slowly made my way back to the center of the rink.

"Wow, Finkle." Big Mike was already there as I skated up. "Didn't know we were going all out like that. Thought this was just a friendly little one on one."

"I go hard every game, no matter who I'm playing. Wanna quit?" I was pissed, embarrassed. This match was my idea, and I was losing miserably.

He scoffed, "Hell no I'm not quitting."

We got into position again, and just like the three times before, my body shook as I stared at the ice, waiting to jump on the puck. My heart was racing, but not like it raced in a normal game. There was way more at stake here than just the humiliation of parading around in a pink tutu for a week. I didn't want to look like a loser in front of Louie *or* Brody, and I didn't want Big Mike to see me as weak.

I was so lost in my head thinking about what could go wrong if I lost that I nearly missed the puck drop. Big Mike easily gained control of it that time, but it gave me a chance to skate a little ahead of him and try to block his attempt at a close shot. Mike's eyes bore into mine as he moved the puck back and forth, weaving closer and closer to the goal. His top half went left, but I knew that was a ploy, so I went right. Sure enough, he ended up taking a shot from his right hip. It flew over my stick and, thankfully, bounced off Brody's glove. Before Brody could pick it up and slide it back to Louie, I caught it with my stick and moved back toward the middle of the ice. Out of nowhere, Mike came barreling at me. As he snuck an arm around me to try and steal the puck, his elbow collided hard with my bottom lip, jolting my head backward. Bright white stars dotted my vision as Mike skated away with the puck, going head-to-head with Brody once again.

Score.

I looked down at my practice jersey, which had a long line of dark red blood down the front of it. Slipping my glove off, I lifted my hand to my mouth and wiped my lip as the taste of blood coated my tongue.

"Shit. I'm sorry, Finkle," Big Mike said sincerely, a concerned look on his face. "I didn't mean to do that."

"No problem, baby!" I whooped. "It's all part of the game. Let's go."

Mike was up two to nothing, but no fucking way was I going to let him shut me out completely. The next goal was mine. Period. It felt like it took the puck ten whole minutes to fall from Louie's hand to the ice, but once it did, Mike and I were a mess of sticks and limbs. I got control this time, and I would fight like hell to keep it.

I skated around in full control of the puck as Mike camped out in front of Brody, waiting for me to make my move. It was hard enough to get through Mike, but getting through Brody at the same time would be tough. I kept skating close to Mike and then pulling back, hoping to draw him out farther onto the ice where I could skate around behind him and battle it out with Brody alone. After three circles in, Mike finally took the bait and skated out toward me, but my plan backfired. Instead of skating around him, he was able to reach in and poke the puck away from me, out the other side. I skated past it and he cut in behind and took control once again. That was it.

He was gonna score again.

He was gonna win.

I used every drop of adrenaline in my body and skated toward him like a freight train, determined to get that puck back before he got to Brody. He glided effortlessly along the ice, his eyes set on Brody and the goal, not even paying attention to me. Coming in from behind, I pulled my shoulder in tight and rammed into Big Mike as hard as I could. His body went flying toward the boards, abandoning the puck completely. I took control of it and in one swift motion, smacked it as hard as I could toward Brody, who barely had time to make a move for it.

Score.

I threw my hands up in the air and cheered in celebration as loud as I could.

"Finally!" I roared, my voice echoing through the empty arena. I turned immediately to heckle Brody, but he was frozen, staring past me. I turned around, following his eyes, and there was Mike, lying in a heap on the ice.

Lifeless.

Chapter
7

I FELT LIKE I WAS in a movie. Brody, Louie, and I all skated over to Mike as fast as we could.

"Mike, you okay?" I heard my own voice, but I didn't feel like I was talking. "Get up, man." He didn't move. He didn't respond. Pulling his shoulder gently, I tried to roll him over.

"Stop!" Brody grabbed my arm roughly. "You can't move him. Louie, go get Pete! And call 911."

Louie stood up and tried to skate away so fast his feet kept flying out from under him. Eventually he gained control and skated across the rink to go get Pete, the team trainer.

I'd heard people talk about a "stomach-sinking" feeling before, but until that moment, I'd never actually experienced it. But they were absolutely right. Inside I felt like I was falling, but in reality I wasn't moving at all.

"What happened?" My voice cracked, exposing the sheer panic coursing through my system. "I hit him and then went for the puck. I didn't even see what happened."

"I'm not really sure." Brody put his fingers on Mike's neck, checking for a pulse.

Holy fuck. A Pulse. How can he not have a pulse?

"I saw you hit him," he continued, "and then I watched the

puck for about half a second before his body sliding across the ice caught my attention. He crashed into the boards pretty hard, Viper. I think he might have been out at that point already."

I didn't think it was possible for my stomach to sink any lower, but it did.

Just then, Louie and Pete came racing across the ice.

"What happened?" Pete yelled, sliding to a stop next to Mike. Just like Brody, he checked for a pulse on Mike's wrist.

I swallowed hard and took a shaky breath. "I hit him."

Brody's eyes flew up to look at me, but I couldn't look back at him, so I just stared at Mike, silently begging my friend to wake up, to talk, to move an arm . . . anything.

Pete moved around to the other side of him and shined a light in his eyes as we heard the faint sound of a siren getting louder and louder. It felt like an hour later but was probably only seconds before a small team of paramedics slid across the ice as carefully as they could.

"What happened here?" asked the first guy who got to us.

"I—"

"He fell," Brody interrupted me. "We were playing a game of one on one and he got checked. I think it knocked him out, because when he slid into the boards, he was already pretty limp."

"Okay. Move back, please," he ordered.

The three of us backed up enough to allow them to circle around Mike and do what they needed to do. He still hadn't moved. Why the fuck wasn't he moving? I covered my face with my hands as my head spun.

Wake up, Mike. Please, wake the fuck up.

Brody put a hand on my shoulder and leaned in close. "Relax. He'll be okay."

The loud clank of the wheels of a stretcher hitting the ice echoed through the arena and pulled me out of my own head and back to reality. One paramedic was pushing it while another carried a neck brace and a backboard.

A neck brace.

A backboard.

Please, God, don't let him be paralyzed. Holy fuck. Please.

They worked quickly but carefully, placing the brace around Mike's neck and rolling him onto the backboard, where they secured him tightly.

"On three . . . one, two, three." The paramedics worked together to lift him onto the stretcher and made their way across the ice, toward the tunnel.

Pete turned to the three of us and sighed, running his hands through his hair. "I'm gonna follow the ambulance to the hospital. Does anyone know how to get ahold of his wife?"

"I'll call Michelle," Brody announced before turning to me. "Are you going to the hospital?"

I bit down hard, clenching my jaw.

Do. Not. Cry.

"That's the stupidest fucking thing you've ever asked me," I snapped and skated ahead of them toward the exit.

My vision was blurry, everything just slightly out of focus. My mind was racing with the worst scenarios possible, and a permanent lump that I couldn't swallow was lodged in my throat as I made my way across the ice toward the tunnel. Only one thing was bright and in focus.

That fucking pink tutu.

Chapter
8

BRODY AND I DROVE THE whole way to the hospital in silence. I stared out the window at nothing in particular, but my peripheral vision kept catching Brody look over at me.

Finally, as we pulled into the hospital parking lot, he sighed. "Listen, obviously this whole situation sucks, but let's not freak out until we know there's something to freak out about, okay?"

Too late.

"Yep," I answered coldly.

We walked into the emergency room, and Pete was already there.

"Hey," Brody said to him stiffly as we walked up. It was clear none of us wanted to be there. "Any news?"

Pete grabbed a tissue from a box on the desk and wiped his eyes. My heart sank again.

Why is he crying? What the fuck is going on?

"Not really." He shook his head. "They're prepping him for surgery right now. Did you call his wife?"

"Surgery?" Brody panicked. "What kind of surgery?"

Pete cleared his throat and took a deep breath, looking back and forth between Brody and me. "Apparently he had a seizure and started puking uncontrollably in the ambulance, so they did a CT scan immediately, and he has bleeding around his brain."

"Holy shit." Brody barely got the words out, sounding like he'd just had the wind knocked out of him. My head spun again. I felt like I might pass out, so I hurried over to the nearest chair, where I plopped down and rested my head in my hands. What the fuck happened? Two hours ago, we were heckling each other in the weight room about whose ass was going to look better in the tutu, and now they were rushing him into surgery with bleeding in his brain. I desperately wanted to switch places with him. I had no kids, no family other than Gam, no life. I should have been the one with a bleeding brain on my way into surgery. I looked around for the nearest trash can as my stomach rolled.

"Where is he?" A panicked voice grabbed my attention. I looked up just as the sliding glass doors were closing behind Michelle. Pete was filling her in on what the doctor had told him as I walked over to them.

"What the hell happened?" Her eyes filled with tears as she bit her bottom lip to keep it from trembling.

"We were on the ice, doing what we do, and he slid into the boards," Brody answered as he stared at the ground, deliberately not looking at me.

She wiped her eyes with the tissue Pete gave her and shook her head incredulously. "That doesn't make sense. He's fallen a million times before. Was he wearing his helmet?"

Brody nodded and I couldn't keep quiet anymore.

I cleared my throat. "It's my fault. We were playing one on one. The game got intense and I checked him."

Her eyes went from sad to angry faster than I'd ever seen. "*You* did this?" she hissed through clenched teeth.

I wanted to tell her it was an accident, that I didn't mean to hit him that hard, but nothing I could say at that moment would have taken away her anger. To be honest, I wanted her mad. I wanted her to take her fury and hate out on me, so I just nodded.

"Michelle, it was an accident—"

The words weren't even out of Brody's mouth before the side of my face stung with heat. I never saw her hand coming. She reeled back to hit me again, but Brody wrapped his arms around her waist, pulling her back. "Michelle! Stop! It was an accident!"

"You motherfucker!" she screamed at me, flailing like a wild animal in Brody's arms as tears rolled down her face. "How dare you? How dare you hit him like that? He's your friend!"

Brody struggled to hold her back. "He didn't mean to. We were just playing a game."

"Some fucking game it turned out to be, huh?" she continued yelling through her sobs. "You're standing here just fine, and my husband is in surgery! I hate you. Even when he's better, I'll still hate you! You don't deserve him!" **Ouch.**

I couldn't defend myself against anything she said. She was right, and if Brody had let her loose, I would've let her hit me. Over and over. I deserved it.

A security guard walked up to us. "Is everything okay over here, folks?"

"Clearly not," Pete said, "but we'll keep it down. Sorry."

Michelle had finally stopped kicking, but Brody was still holding her. "I'm gonna put you down, okay?" he said softly. "Don't do that again or they're gonna kick you out, and you won't be here when Mike wakes up."

She covered her face with her hands and started sobbing. Her shoulders bounced up and down and her legs started to give out as she turned toward Brody and wailed into his chest. Once again, he wrapped his arms around her, only this time it was to hold her up.

I walked quietly to the other side of the waiting room, knowing space for Michelle was the most important thing right now. After a couple hours, Kacie showed up and immediately went over to Michelle. They hugged and cried for a solid three minutes while Brody came over and sat by me.

The back of my head rested against the wall behind me as I stared straight ahead, refusing to look at him. "Where's Pete?"

"He left a while ago. He asked us to please keep him posted," he said quietly. "Viper, listen, about before—"

"Don't. I deserved it."

"No, you didn't. I understand she's upset, but this isn't your fault."

"Oh, really?" I finally glared at him out of the corner of my eye. "Then whose is it? Because from where I'm sitting, it's no one's fault *but* mine."

"Accidents happen. You can't take this on."

"Whatever," I snapped, staring straight ahead again.

Do. Not. Cry.

The double doors opened and a nurse appeared. Brody and I collectively held our breath as she looked around the room. "Michelle Asher?"

Michelle quickly lifted her head off of Kacie's shoulder and stood when she saw the nurse. "Yes?" she responded in a shaky voice. Kacie stood beside her and held her hand. The nurse smiled at them and walked over; Brody stood up and followed. I stayed behind. The four of them talked intimately for a good ten minutes before Michelle hugged Kacie and followed the nurse back through the doors. Kacie turned to Brody with tears in her eyes and wrapped her arms around his waist, squeezing tight. She closed her eyes as he hugged her back and rested his chin on the top of her head.

Fuck. What's happening?

Kacie's eyes opened and looked right at me. The second we made eye contact, I looked down at the ugly gray tile and shifted uncomfortably in my chair. A few seconds later, I felt her sit down next to me, but I refused to look up.

"Hey," she said softly.

"Hey."

"Are you okay?"

I didn't answer. Dumb question.

"Sorry, that was a dumb question." She laughed nervously.

"Yep."

"Oh, Viper." She hooked her tiny arm around my back and laid her head on my shoulder, not saying another word. I waited for her to ask something else or give me some bland speech about how it wasn't my fault, but she didn't, and I was grateful. Brody disappeared around the corner toward the bathroom sign and I finally decided to ask.

"Is he dead?"

She shot up straight. "What? No. Why would you think that?"

"I don't know." I shrugged. "The nurse came out, Michelle left, you and Brody hugged . . ."

"Oh, no. Sorry. I just wanted to hug him." She took a deep breath and exhaled slowly. "No, he's in the ICU. They did a craniectomy and now they're watching him closely."

"A craniectomy?" I finally looked over at her. "What the fuck is that?"

"His brain is swollen, so they removed a piece of his skull to allow for the swelling."

As if someone had punched it out of a sleepy haze, my heart started beating fast. "They removed part of his fucking skull?" my voice thundered. "Seriously?"

"Shhh." She frowned and held a finger up to her mouth, glancing around the waiting room. "Sit down," she ordered in a loud whisper.

I sat while she continued, "Yes, it's a pretty common procedure for someone whose brain is swelling."

Like a giant tsunami washing over a tiny island, my mind was instantly flooded with questions. "What do they do with the piece they took out?"

"I'm not positive in Mike's case, the nurse didn't say, but typically if they can save it, they tuck it into the patient's abdomen so it's preserved by his own body."

Holy shit.

"So he's gonna be okay?" I asked slowly.

Kacie's eyes looked up to the ceiling and for a quick second, I thought maybe she was praying. "Not sure. He's definitely not out of the woods. It's going to be a long recovery."

I looked back down at the floor and closed my eyes.

"Listen, Viper—"

"Don't," I stopped her.

"*You* don't," she scolded. I glared at her to scare her off, but she lifted her chin higher and kept going. "I'm not going to tell you how to feel right now because I have no idea how you feel. I've never hurt one of my friends like this. What I'm going to tell you is that regardless of what happens, it was an accident. You didn't set out to hurt him; it was an accident. Beating yourself up over it will only hurt both of you, and right now, we need all the positivity we can get. So feel sorry for yourself later. Fall apart and be pissed later, at home, but we need you to be strong for Big Mike now, and for the rest of us."

Do not cry.

"You're right." I nodded.

"Damn right I'm right." She looped her arm through mine and rested her head on my shoulder again, staring straight ahead with me. "I love you, Viper."

Fuck . . . Do. Not. Cry.

Thankfully, Brody rounded the corner again at the perfect time. "Hey." He walked over to us, looking exhausted with dark circles under his eyes. "We can go back to the private ICU waiting area, but we can't actually see him yet. You guys wanna?"

"Absolutely." Kacie hopped up and walked past Brody.

He laughed as he watched her walk by, full of independence and attitude. Shaking his head, he turned back to me. "You coming?"

I wanted to say no. I wanted to sit there and pout. I wanted to sit there and feel sorry for myself. I wanted to disappear.

But Kacie was right, so I stood up and nodded. "Lead the way."

Brody's hand clapped my shoulder hard and he offered a tight smile as he turned around.

"By the way," I added, "that woman you have there . . . hold on tight to her. She's pretty amazing."

Brody and I walked side by side toward the ICU waiting room. I'd never been in an Intensive Care Unit before. It was different. Instead of a hallway with rooms on each side, it was more like a pod—one central hub in the middle with all the patient rooms circled around it. Before we reached that central station, there was a waiting room on the right side. It was smaller than the waiting room in the ER, but it was also more private. When Brody and I walked in, it was empty except for Kacie and Michelle.

We rounded the corner and my eyes met Michelle's on accident. I didn't look away; neither did she. She didn't seem to be angry anymore, but I couldn't figure out exactly what she was.

"Hey." She sighed and puffed her cheeks out. "Can I talk to you?"

I shoved my hands into my pockets and nodded. "Sure."

"Ummm," Kacie stammered as she stood up, "Brody, I'm gonna go grab some coffee and water. Wanna come with and help me carry?"

"Sure,"—he looked back and forth between me and Michelle—"assuming I'm not needed here for security?"

Michelle sniffed and shook her head, looking down as she played with her wedding band. "No, we don't need security."

"All right, we'll be right back." Kacie pushed Brody's chest gently and they left the room. I sat down in a chair across from Michelle and waited. I had no idea what she wanted to say. A million different things ran through my head, and I was prepared to take whatever she needed to give out.

Finally, after a long awkward silence, she looked up at me with puffy, red-rimmed eyes and sighed heavily. "Viper, I'm so sorry."

What?

"Huh?"

"I'm sorry about the way I acted before, and I'm even sorrier about the things I said." She grabbed the wadded-up tissue off of the coffee table and started picking at it.

"You don't have to apologize, Michelle—"

Her eyes swept up to mine and she cut me off. "Yes. I do. No matter what happened, he really is your best friend, and you didn't deserve that from me. I know you love him, and I know he loves you. I was just . . ." Her voice trailed off as she shook her head back and forth.

My throat felt tight. I was getting choked up because she was choked up.

Do not cry.

I got up and went around the table to her couch and sat down. Not knowing how she would react, I hesitantly put my arm around her shoulders. Me hugging her may have been the last thing in the world she wanted at that very moment, but I couldn't help it. I had to hug her. Thankfully, not only did she not punch me in the face, but she leaned into me just a little and rested her head on my chest. "Don't say any more, okay? Let's just sit here and . . . I don't know," I sighed.

She sniffed. "Pray?"

"Nah," I said confidently. "Mike is as strong as they come. I'll be surprised if he's not trying to sign himself out of here this time tomorrow."

Chapter
9

"**M**ICHELLE?"
I was sound asleep and nearly jumped out of my skin when a nurse came into the waiting room and called Michelle's name. We'd dimmed the lights a few hours before to try and get some shut-eye, but the catnaps were few and far between until this last one, when I finally crashed. I blinked quickly to try and force the room into focus just as Michelle hopped up and walked toward the nurse. They disappeared around the corner as I sat up. Brody heard me and cracked his eyes open too.

"What's going on?" he whispered loudly, trying not to wake Kacie, who was still sleeping against his shoulder.

"I don't know." I rubbed my eyes with the heels of my hands. "The nurse just came in and called Michelle out. Hopefully Mike woke up and asked for her or something."

The words were barely out of my mouth when Michelle reappeared in the doorway, teary eyed. "What's going on?" Brody asked, no longer worried about whispering. Kacie jolted awake, blinked once or twice, and was instantly alert.

"I just talked to Dr. Reese." She sniffed. "Apparently Mike's had a stroke." Her voice gave out and she trailed off.

Kacie gasped and rushed over, pulling her in for a hug as

Brody and I sat, stunned.

"What does this mean?" Brody asked.

"They're doing an EEG in a little bit to check his brain function and then they'll know more," she mumbled through sobs into Kacie's shoulder.

My stomach dropped for the hundredth time in the last twenty hours.

Brain function? Holy shit.

Brody went over and sat on the other side of Michelle, gently resting his hand on her leg. "Has he woken up at all?" he asked.

Michelle never lifted her head to answer him, but Kacie looked at him with sad eyes, pressed her lips together, and shook her head slightly. "No, he's been out since yesterday at the rink."

Brody leaned forward and rested his elbows on his knees as he stared down at the ground. With each passing second, the room got smaller and smaller around me, and I suddenly needed to get out. I'd never been claustrophobic, but at that moment, I felt like I couldn't breathe in there.

"I'll . . . be back," I stammered as I wobbled to the doorway. Once in the hallway, I started jogging, desperately looking for an exit. Any exit.

I took two lefts, one right, and an elevator down to the main floor and I was finally outside. I thought for sure once I was out of that room and outside I would feel better, but I was wrong. No amount of sunshine and fresh air could take away the dread that had permanently planted itself in the pit of my stomach. I walked up and down the sidewalk with my fingers linked on the top of my head, trying to make sense of what was going on, but I couldn't.

"Viper!"

I turned when I heard my name to see Taylor, Big Mike's little sister, hurrying toward me with tears streaming down her face. She threw herself into my chest and started sobbing. I wrapped my arms around her and let her cry for several minutes. Once her shoulders stopped shaking and she was done, she pulled back and wiped her eyes with the sleeve of her shirt.

"Sorry, I don't know what came over me." She looked up at me and tried to smile. "I just saw you and all of a sudden, I lost it."

"It's okay. I've almost lost it myself a bunch of times."

"How is he? Is he awake yet?" Her eyes begged me for good news, any little sliver of hope to hold on to.

I couldn't bring myself to tell her what Dr. Reese had told Michelle, so I just shook my head. "Not yet."

"Can you take me up there? I have no idea where I'm going."

"Sure, follow me." I turned and headed back into the last building in the world I wanted to be in, not because I didn't want to be there for Mike and Michelle, but because I wanted to go back in time and undo what had been done . . . by me.

We took the elevator up to the third floor, made one left, two rights, and we were back to the waiting room. Michelle and Kacie were still sitting close together on the couch holding hands, and Brody was pacing on the phone. Once Michelle and Taylor saw each other, they both started hugging and crying again.

"I can't believe you came." Michelle sniffled as she pulled back and cupped Taylor's face in her hands. "You must've driven all night."

"Are you kidding? Of course I would be here." Taylor's breath hitched. "He's my only brother." When those words left her mouth, Michelle's face twisted and she bit her lip to keep from breaking down all over again. "Is he awake yet?" Taylor asked.

Michelle shook her head. "No, and unfortunately, he had a stroke this morning."

Taylor's hand flew up over her mouth as she gasped.

"But," Michelle added quickly, "the nurse came in right after Viper went downstairs and said that while he's nowhere near out of the woods, they've stabilized him for now, so we can go in one at a time to talk to him."

Michelle turned away from Taylor and looked at the rest of us. "Is it okay if I go in first?"

"Of course," Kacie answered immediately. "We wouldn't have it any other way."

"Thanks," she muttered quietly. "I'll be back soon."

As soon as Michelle was out of the room, Taylor let out a huge sigh and plopped down onto the couch next to Kacie. "This is unreal." She shook her head, staring incredulously at the coffee table.

Kacie nodded. "It is."

"Wait," Taylor looked around the room quickly, "Where are the kids?"

"Michelle said they're with her neighbor Jodi." Kacie responded.

"Oh, okay. So . . ." Taylor asked slowly, "what exactly happened? Michelle called, but we didn't really get into it over the phone. She just said there'd been an accident at practice."

I knew right then that I would hear that question over and over for the very near future, and every time someone asked what'd happened, I felt worse than the time before.

"Um . . ." Brody paused. He was choosing his words carefully. "We'd just finished our workout and he was playing a game one on one. He got checked and slid into the wall really hard."

She scrunched her eyebrows together and curled her top lip, clearly not liking what she'd just heard. "Who checked him?" she asked.

"Me," I spoke before Brody had a chance to. "It was me, Taylor."

Her eyes flashed over to mine for a quick second before she threw her hands up in the air. "Oh, thank God. I was worried it was done on purpose, like someone was out to hurt him." She turned back to me. "I'm sorry, Viper. This must be really hard on you too."

"Huh?" I was confused.

"This whole thing"—she waved her arm around the room—"must be hard for you too. I mean, clearly you didn't mean to do it, so this must suck for you especially. I'm so sorry."

She sounded as genuine as I'd ever heard another person sound, offering up *her* apology to *me,* the person who'd put us all in this situation. I was stunned. I didn't know how to answer that. I quickly glanced up at Kacie, who appeared to be reading my mind and was giving me a sympathetic I-told-you-so smile.

"I should be the one apologizing, Taylor," I finally said.

She shrugged. "I mean, if that makes you feel better, fine, but I don't think anyone here blames you." She looked at Brody and Kacie and then back at me. "I certainly don't."

"I appreciate it, but I still feel like a giant dick." I took a deep breath. "I wish I could go back in time and do it all over again."

"Well of course you do," she said matter-of-factly. "That's life. When something bad happens, we always wish we had a do over, but that's not how life works unfortunately. Shit happens and we have to react to it. Good shit, bad shit . . . it all happens, but I doubt anyone that has ever been around the two of you together thinks for one-half a second that you did this on purpose. You love him like a brother; we all know that."

Do. Not. Cry.

Clearing my throat, I looked down at the tile beneath my feet and nodded slowly. I was searching my brain for what to say next when Michelle somberly walked back into the room. We all stared, waiting for her to say something, anything.

Her eyes were red and swollen as she hugged herself tightly and sat on the couch next to Taylor.

"Honey," Taylor asked slowly, "are you okay?"

Michelle didn't say anything; she simply shrugged. "He looks awful. He has a bandage around his head, and he's hooked up to all these machines that are breathing for him. He doesn't look like my Mike anymore."

Without saying anything this time, I got up and left the room quietly. I needed the break I didn't get last time when I'd run into Taylor.

Two lefts, one right, and the elevator.

I found a bench right outside the door at the very moment my legs decided to give out. Who knew a hard-ass concrete bench could be so comforting? I ran my hands through my hair and rested my elbows on my knees, staring at the concrete slab below me. An ant slowly walked up to my foot and stopped. I wondered what it was like to be an ant. Did they have friends and families? Did they accidentally hurt each other? Did they feel guilt? I'd fought like hell my whole life to keep my feelings in check and never let people see them, but the last two days were testing that more than any other time in my life. I didn't know how much longer I could keep it together.

Praying was something we never did in my house growing up, but at that moment I felt the overwhelming urge to talk out loud to . . . someone.

Looking around to make sure I was alone, I took a deep breath and puffed my cheeks out, exhaling slowly.

I glanced up at the sky for just a second, quickly deciding I probably looked like a moron and that whoever I was going to talk to would probably hear me no matter where I was looking.

"Hey, whoever's up there. My name is Lawrence Finkle, but you probably know me as Viper. Anyway—" I cleared my throat, suddenly feeling very stupid that I was talking to myself, but so desperate I was willing to do anything. "—we've never had what I would call an active relationship, but right now I'm feeling pretty alone down here. I've fucked up a lot in my life, as you probably know, but I've always been able to talk myself out of any trouble I got into. Well, I've finally done something I can't fix. It was an accident, but I still can't fix it, and I could really use it at the moment. I don't really know how this works, but I'm willing to bargain. I'll do anything—go to church, donate time and money, stop fucking strangers. I mean it, anything. Just *please* . . . save my best friend. He's a good man with a wife and kids who need him. If you need to take someone, take me. No one gives a shit whether I'm here or not." My eyes started to feel hot and sting as I took another shaky breath.

"Mr. Finkle?"

Startled at the sound of my name, I stood and turned as a camera flashed in my eyes. Squinting and holding my hand up, I tried to block out another flash. "What the fuck?" I growled.

"Hi, Mr. Finkle. I'm Warren Sanders with the *Star Tribune* here in Minneapolis." He held his hand out for me to shake. I glared down at it and then back up at him without saying a word. He quickly pulled his hand back and continued, "We heard about what happened yesterday with Mike Asher, and we were just wondering if we could ask you a few questions. Like, maybe what exactly happened? What's his current condition? Anything you're willing to give us." He held a microphone in my face as the cameraman lifted a different camera onto his shoulder to film me.

Rage shot through me like a bullet shoots out of a gun.

"You want anything I'm willing to give you?" I asked coldly. "Well, I'm going to give you ten seconds to get that motherfucking camera out of my face before I shove that mic up your ass."

"Uh . . ." he stammered. "We won't keep you for long. We just want a quick statement."

Without hesitation, I took three steps and grabbed the camera from the guy behind him, lifted it above my head, and smashed it on the concrete. They both jumped back, their mouths hanging open as they stared at the ground.

"There!" I pointed to the shattered camera as I walked away. "There's your fucking statement."

Chapter
_10_

MY HANDS ENCASED THE HOT cup of disgusting coffee as I sat in the back corner of the cafeteria by the window. It had only been fifteen minutes since I smashed that dickhead's camera outside, and I already had three text messages sitting on my phone from Andy, unopened.

Brody rushed around the corner and peeked his head into the cafeteria, quickly scanning the room. He did a double take when he saw me and closed his eyes in relief before walking over.

"There you are." He sighed as he dropped down into the seat across from me.

"Where else would I be?"

"Oh, gee, I don't know . . . out front smashing cameras?" he said sarcastically.

I frowned at him. "How did you know about that already?"

He took his phone out of his pocket and set it on the table. "Andy texted me to hurry up and find you. Apparently some reporter from the _Star Tribune_ tweeted that you knocked his camera out of his hand or something. There was a picture of it shattered on the ground."

"Yeah, I knocked it out of his hand. Whoops," I said dryly, taking a sip of the tar-like coffee. "Why did I buy this?" I stared down at the cup. "I don't even like coffee."

"Finkle,"—Brody leaned forward on the table and folded his hands in front of him—"are you okay? I mean, I know this whole thing has moved faster than lightning, and it's not exactly a pleasant experience, but . . . how are you holding up?"

I couldn't believe he was asking me how *I* was. Our friend was lying upstairs with a hole in his head and tubes going into God knows where in his body, and Brody was worried about me.

"I'm fine."

"No you're not."

"You're right, I'm not, but I will be."

He narrowed his eyes and studied me for a minute, trying to decide if he should push me further. Thankfully, he decided against it. "All right," he finally said, "let's head back upstairs. Would you text Andy and let him know you're under control, please?" Grabbing my coffee cup, he stood and took it over to the garbage can.

I picked up my phone and, without reading any of Andy's messages, wrote back.

> I'll pay for whatever it cost, but I won't apologize.
> That asshole deserved it.

We weaved through the crowded hallway and made our way back to the elevator. "Did you go in yet?" I asked once we were alone.

"For a minute." He swallowed and stared at the drop ceiling tiles in the elevator, clearly avoiding my eyes. "I'm not gonna lie, it was tough to see. He's pretty jacked up."

I closed my eyes and nodded, not saying another word.

The elevator came to a stop on the third floor, and we were barely two steps from it when we heard loud crying. Brody's eyes flashed to mine quickly. "Oh shit!"

We started walking faster toward the waiting room, but just before we were about to round the last corner, Kacie ran right into Brody.

"Kacie!" Brody gently grabbed her shoulders and leaned back, looking straight into her eyes. "What's going on?"

"I was just coming to find you guys." She was out of breath and trying desperately not to cry. "You need to come back. It's bad."

"What's bad? What happened?" Brody asked.

"Mike. They did the EEG and a bunch of other tests." She swallowed and shook her head, unable to say any more.

"Kacie, baby, talk to me. *Please.*"

"There's nothing," she choked out. "He's brain-dead. Gone." Her hands covered her face and she started to sob as Brody cupped the back of her head, pulling her into his chest.

Gone. He's gone. How the fuck can he be gone?

Kacie had to have misunderstood something. There was no way Mike was gone. I rushed past them to the waiting room where Michelle was hysterical, kneeling on the ground and hugging herself, rocking back and forth. Taylor was kneeling next to her, staring into space with a dazed look on her face. Two nurses were rubbing Michelle's back, trying to get her to calm down enough to take a pill. The room started to spin. Then the world started to spin. Someone kept asking me if I was okay, but I couldn't tell exactly where it was coming from. Nurses were hustling in and out of the room, talking to each other, but all I could hear was the blood rushing through my ears.

"Sir, I said, 'Are you okay?'" was the last thing I heard.

My head was pounding. The back of it felt like someone had hit me over and over with a hammer. Peeking my eyes open just a tad, I was relieved to be waking up in my bed, beyond thankful that it had all been a really shitty nightmare. I cringed as I craned my neck to look at the clock on my nightstand.

No nightstand. No clock.

I lifted the blue blanket I didn't remember buying and looked down at my outfit.

Practice clothes.

I sat up suddenly and tried to look around but was overcome by the pressure in my head as I cupped it in my hands and winced in pain.

"Hey, there you are," an unfamiliar woman's voice said softly.

I opened one eye to peek at her, trying to move my head as little as possible. A nurse in blue scrubs stood at the end of my bed with her hands on her hips, smiling at me. "You gave us quite the scare." She walked over to the side of my bed and gently touched the back of my head. "How's this feel?"

The second her hand made contact with my head, I flinched. The pain was off the fucking charts.

"Shitty," I answered, leaning my head away from her hand. "What happened?"

She sighed. "You walked into the waiting room and passed out. Hit your head pretty hard too. You have a big ole bump back here."

Waiting room.

Fuck. It's not a dream.

"When did this happen? Where am I?" I was so confused, but the harder I tried to remember, the more my head hurt.

"Just about half an hour ago." She gently put her hand on my arm in an effort to calm me down. "Relax. We put you in an empty bed in the ICU so we could monitor you, make sure you were okay instead of sending you off to the ER."

It hurt like hell but I turned my head to the side to look at her. "I'm still in the ICU?"

"Yeah, we want you to rest for a bit."

"Fuck that." I stood up too quickly and the room started spinning again. Closing my eyes, I grabbed the side of the bed to steady myself.

"Please lie back down," she pleaded. "The last thing we need is for you to pass out again."

"I'll be fine," I snapped stubbornly. I knew she was just doing her job, but I didn't respond well to people telling me what to do. Never had, never would.

Finally regaining some control over my body, I slowly made my way to the door, holding on to anything I could for stability. The bright lights of the hallway hurt my eyes, but I narrowed them as much as I could and kept going. I rounded the corner of the waiting room, shocked to see it full of people now. Brody and Kacie were still there and Taylor, of course, but now Louie, Viktor, and a few other guys from the team were there too, huddled together and talking quietly. Big Mike's agent, Ross, was there as well, talking to Andy in the corner. The second I stepped into the room I felt like everyone turned and stared at me, silently judging the evil monster and what he'd done.

"Hey!" Brody stood and hurried over to me. "How are you?"

"I'm fine," I lied through gritted teeth. Trying not to move my head too much, I looked around the room again and noticed one person was missing. "Where's Michelle?"

"She's in with Mike," Brody said somberly.

My head snapped back toward Brody quickly, sending a shooting pain across the whole backside of my head from ear to ear, but I didn't care. "Did he wake up?"

"No." He shook his head, biting down hard as the corners of his jaw popped. Leaning in close, he put his hand on my shoulder. "He isn't gonna wake up, buddy. That's why Michelle is in there. She's with him and the chaplain."

The chaplain?

My heart starting pounding so hard I was worried it was going to explode right there in the waiting room. "The chaplain? What the fuck for?"

"He has no brain function . . . at all. Michelle's decided to donate his organs while they're still viable."

No brain function.

Donate his organs.

My brain repeated what Brody said over and over but refused

to comprehend it. How could this be happening? It was just hockey. You're not supposed to die from playing hockey. You're also not supposed to kill your best friend. My hands started to tingle as I wiped away a thin layer of sweat that had formed above my lip.

Louie turned away from the group and around to face me. His eyes grew huge and his jaw dropped when he looked at me. "Viper, are you okay? You look like shit."

Ignoring his comment, I moved over to a chair in the corner, as far away from him and everyone else as possible.

I couldn't wrap my head around what was happening. I didn't understand it. How could a young, healthy man be alert and smiling one minute and the next his brain was gone? How was I ever going to look at Michelle or his kids again? It was hard enough when I was worried that I'd broken his arm or something stupid. I would give anything for a broken arm instead of this.

Throughout the day, people filtered in and out of the room, each going in and taking their turn saying good-bye to Mike. I pretended to be asleep most of the time so people would leave me alone. I didn't want to talk. I didn't want to hug. I just wanted to be left alone.

With my eyes shut and my head leaning against the wall, I felt someone sit down next to me. "You can pretend all you want, but I know you're not sleeping," Brody said.

"Yes, I am. Go away," I insisted.

"Almost everyone is gone, you know. You can sit up now."

I opened my left eye just enough to see that the only people left in the room were Taylor, Brody, Michelle, Louie, and Ross. "Where's Kacie?" I asked.

Brody's elbows were resting on his knees, his hands folded out in front of him. "She's in with Mike," he answered quietly, wiping the corner of his eye.

I took a deep breath. "Did you already go in?"

He nodded and then looked at me. "You're the only one left, other than Michelle, who's going in last."

Fuck.

I hadn't seen Mike at all since they'd wheeled him off the ice on a stretcher, and this was the last place I wanted to have a reunion.

"I don't think I'm going in," I said flatly, closing my eyes again so I didn't have to see Brody's disapproving glare.

"What the fuck do you mean you're not going in?" His voice was low and stern. Turns out I didn't need to see his glare when his voice was that thick with judgment.

"Just what I said. I'm not going in," I repeated.

"Why?"

I finally lifted my head off of the wall and grimaced as I turned toward him slowly. "Why do you think, Murphy? What am I supposed to say? Sorry for putting you here?"

Brody stared down at the floor and sighed. "No, of course that's not what you're supposed to say, but I think you're going to regret not going in. I really do." He lifted his head toward me. "He was your best friend, Viper. Don't you want to say good-bye? Tell him you love him? Anything?"

I sighed.

Do not cry.

Even before I walked through the sliding glass doors, I could hear the rhythmic beeping coming from inside Big Mike's room. I knew that what I was about to see would be permanently burned into my memory. It wasn't something I wanted to see once, let alone forever. But Brody was right—I would always regret it if I didn't go in.

I took a deep breath.

Do not cry.

The beeping got louder as I pulled back the privacy curtain. Mike was lying still in the hospital bed. I stopped and stared at him, surprised by what I saw. He had a big bandage wrapped around his head, and other than a small white tube going up his nose and a blue hose taped near his mouth, he looked like he was sleeping, not brain-dead. The machine next to him hissed as it went up and down. I watched it for what felt like an hour.

Up and down.

Up and down.

Up and down.

Up until that point, I was mad at myself for what had happened, but being in that room with him, I started to get pissed at everything else too. We were in a hospital, a good fucking hospital. There had to be *something* they could do for him. Hockey doesn't kill people. The longer I stood there staring, the longer that machine would move up and down, which meant the longer he would be alive, which meant the better chance he had of waking up. He just needed time. Mike was one of the strongest guys I knew, and he could absolutely come out of this; he just needed time.

"Oh, I'm so sorry," a voice from behind me said.

I turned to see a nurse in blue scrubs frozen in the doorway, but I didn't say anything back.

"I just need to check his vitals real quick, then you can have all the time you need, okay?" She smiled cheerfully as she passed me and walked over to him.

All the time I need? I need forever. Okay? Can you make that happen?

"Is he in pain?" I asked.

She pressed her lips together and looked sadly down at Mike. "No, he's very comfortable."

He's not comfortable.

I watched her as she moved around him in a practiced way, like she'd done this a thousand times before. I had no clue what she was doing, and honestly, I didn't care. Unless she was going to wave a magic wand and wake my best friend up, I just wanted her to leave.

While she was doing whatever she was doing, I walked over to the small blue chair they had in the corner of the room and sat down.

Why was everything in hospitals always blue? Blue scrubs on the nurses, blue furniture in the rooms, blue curtains hanging on the windows, blue blankets on the beds. No wonder blue has always been such a depressing fucking color.

I pulled back the curtain and looked out the window next to me. It was sunny as hell outside and that pissed me off all over again. What pissed me off more were the people I saw going about their days, acting completely normal.

Two women sat on a blanket eating and laughing.

Bitches.

A man sitting on a bench pushed his glasses up the bridge of his nose and turned the page in his book.

Wonder if he's a doctor. Maybe he can save Mike.

"Okay, I'm done here. Take your time." She squeezed my arm as she walked by my chair.

I never even looked up at her. I'd never despised a woman's touch more than that very second. Closing the curtain and knowing I couldn't avoid it for much longer, I lowered my head into my hands and sighed. I was supposed to be saying good-bye to my best friend, but all I wanted to do was run out of the room and down the hall and forget the last three days had ever happened.

Do not cry.

"I've never said good-bye like this to anyone before," I said in a shaky voice, still staring down at the ground. "I don't know how to begin or what to say."

I paused, half expecting him to sit up and answer me.

"How did we get here?" I finally sat back in the chair and looked up at him. "A few days ago we were sitting at my house, *not* playing poker, and now we're here. One stupid bet led to this. One stupid bet plus my stupid pride."

Another long pause while I stared up at the ceiling. Every muscle in my body ached from the tension I felt sitting there in that room with my dying best friend.

My brother.

"I'm sorry, Mike. I'm so, so fucking sorry." My eyes stung as they started to water, but I didn't care anymore. "I wish I could go back. I wish I could take that hit back. I'd wear that fucking tutu every day for the rest of my life." Tears ran down my cheeks, and they felt good. So fucking good.

"This is just so fucking unfair. *I* did this. *I* should be the one lying in that bed, and you should be going home tonight with Michelle and the kids. I hope you know I would give anything to make that happen."

My mind raced a mile a minute.

"I have to make that happen. I have to find a way to make this right. One of the last conversations we ever had, you teased me about having a cement heart. I have to prove that's not true, and the only way I can do that is to take care of Michelle and the kids for you." I hurried over to the bed, my blood rushing through my body as I took his hand. Practically begging, I continued, "I mean it, Mike. Whatever they need until Maura is eighteen. I'll be the stand-in. I won't be near as good as you would've been, but I'll do it." I let out a sob, something I hadn't done in years. "I'll do anything for you. I love you."

Mike died at 7:21 p.m.

Chapter
11

MY DOORBELL RANG FOR THE third time, but I didn't move off of my couch. I knew who it was, and I didn't care. Within a minute, Brody appeared at the sliding glass door in my kitchen, cupping his face with his hands as he peeked through the door. He saw me staring back at him.

"Hey!" he yelled as he banged on the glass. "Open the damn door!"

My arms and legs felt like they weighed a hundred pounds each, and it took all my strength to peel myself off of the couch and go unlock the door.

"What the fuck?" He frowned, closing the door behind him. "Did you hear me ringing the bell?"

I walked over and lay back on my couch again. "Yep."

"Why aren't you dressed? We have to leave."

I lifted my head and looked back at him, finally noticing the sharp black suit he was wearing, before rolling away.

"Viper!" he called again, sounding annoyed. "Get dressed! I just dropped Kacie, Andy, and Darla at the church. Come on!"

Funerals suck. No one wants to get dressed up and sit in a stuffy church and listen to people say the same bland crap about someone they loved. To top it all off, Michelle asked *me* to say something at the service. I'd tried to sit down and write out a speech several times over the last couple days, but that just wasn't me. I wasn't a planner. I figured I'd just get up there and say the first thing that came to mind.

"Hey! Asshole!" Brody shouted from the kitchen. "Stop ignoring me. Get up!"

I groaned as I got off the couch and headed toward my bedroom to get dressed.

"Don't forget to bring your jersey!" he called out as I walked down the hall.

"Wait . . ." I stopped and turned back toward the kitchen. "What? Why?"

Brody grabbed a water bottle from the fridge and leaned against the island as he cracked it open. "Some of the guys thought it would be meaningful to wear our jerseys instead of our jackets during the service."

"Great," I mumbled and closed my bedroom door.

The street leading up to the Cathedral of St. Paul was crowded with people, some making their way to the church to pay their respects, others gawking at the people coming and going. Bloodthirsty reporters and cameramen tried to get as close to the church as they could, all trying to snap pictures of crying teammates or get the money shot of the grieving widow.

"Try not to break any cameras today, okay?" Brody said smugly, as if he were reading my mind.

Ignoring his comment, I put my sunglasses on and squeezed my jersey tight in my hand.

Just get through today.

Brody pulled into a parking space a block from the church, put his truck in park, and sat back in his seat without turning the engine off. Looking straight ahead, he took a deep breath and let it out slowly. "You ready for this?"

"Not even kinda." I stared straight ahead and zoned out too.

The sun was shining bright and the sky was crystal blue, not a cloud to be seen. A perfect Minnesota day, except for the absolute horror of burying my best friend.

Brody turned his truck off and grabbed his jersey out of the backseat. "Let's get this over with." We hopped out and started making our way down the street. The closer we got to the church, the thicker the crowd grew. We both kept our heads down and tried to make it through the hordes of people without being recognized. Once we finally got to the steps leading up to the cathedral, the whispers were too loud to ignore and the cameras were clicking as fast as they could.

"Move please," I barked at a couple people in jogging clothes on the steps, clearly there being nosy pains in the ass.

"Geez," the girl snapped as I brushed past her.

I stopped and started to turn back around, but Brody was behind me and pushed me to keep moving up the steps. His nostrils flared and I knew he was annoyed too, but he shook his head. "Don't. Not worth it."

We walked through the big wooden doors of the cathedral into the lobby. People dressed in all black stood around talking and laughing as if it were just a normal day.

Fucking assholes.

Brody craned his neck, looking into the actual church. "It looks like most of the guys are here and they have their jerseys on. You gonna change?"

I nodded.

"All right, me too. Let's do that fast."

We hustled off to the restroom and changed into our Wild jerseys, heading back toward the church as soon as we were done. Brody was taking his time walking through the lobby, shaking a few hands and chatting with people, but I was in no mood, so I passed him quickly and headed up the aisle, looking for a familiar face. As I scanned the pews already filled with people, Darla stood up and waved at me. I waved back and walked toward her, Kacie, and the rest of the group.

As I got closer, Darla stepped out from the pew and stared at me with the saddest eyes I'd ever seen. Her chin started to tremble and a tear fell down her cheek as she pulled me in for a giant hug, which I gladly accepted.

"Hey," she said softly into my shoulder.

I cleared my throat. "Hey."

We hadn't seen each other since the accident. She'd been swamped at work while Mike was in the hospital, and when the whole gang had a little get-together the other night at Mike and Michelle's house, I ignored the thirty or so texts from various people begging me to come over.

"How are you?" She sounded sincere, like she actually gave a shit how I was doing. I wanted so badly to tell her how I really was, but lying was always easier.

"I'm fine."

She pulled back and looked at me with puffy, red eyes, shaking her head. "No you're not."

I smiled, kissed her cheek, and scooted past her into the pew next to Kacie, Michelle, Andy, and a few other friends. They all chatted quietly while I stared straight ahead at the big wooden casket.

Do not cry.

Next to the casket were more flowers than I'd ever seen in my whole life, and pictures of Mike were everywhere. Some hockey pictures, but mostly pictures of him with his parents when he was little, him with Taylor, and of course him with Michelle and their kids. His jersey was draped across the end of the closed casket with his stick leaning against it. The sight of it was almost too much for me.

Brody slid past me in the pew and sat down between Kacie and me just as the organ started playing.

Once the priest started his service, I zoned out. I wasn't religious so most of it went over my head, plus I'd started panicking about what I was going to say when it was my turn. There were way more people there than I'd been anticipating.

Not surprising, though. Mike is a great man. Was.

I didn't think I'd ever get used to talking about him in the past tense.

"Lawrence Finkle."

The sound of my name jolted me back to reality.

Game time.

I took a deep breath and stood up as Darla grabbed my hand. She gave me a tight smile and squeezed gently, trying to comfort me. I appreciated her gesture, but it was pointless.

A week ago, my life had been normal. My biggest worry had been who I'd be spending the night with or did my bike need to be washed, but now, I was sitting in a church with my best friend dead in a box, dreading walking up the steps in front of me. The priest cleared his throat, pulling me out of my own head once more. I was still standing in the pew aisle, staring down at Darla, though I wasn't really looking at her. More like through her. She pulled her brows together and leaned in close.

"You okay? Can you do this?"

I swallowed a lump the size of a golf ball. "No, I'm not okay, but I *have* to do this."

She offered up another sympathetic smile as I let go of her hand and scooted out into the center aisle. My shoes echoed loudly with each step I took toward the front.

I made my way up a couple of stairs toward Father O'Malley. He pursed his lips together and nodded toward the podium as he took a step back. The last thing in the world I wanted to do was turn to face all those people, but it was too late to back out now. I spun on my heel and wrapped my hands around the edges of the wooden podium without looking up.

I felt their eyes on me as I stared at the ground, taking my time. Some of them knew me, some of them didn't, but they were all focused on me, wondering what I was about to say. It was a lot of pressure to have a couple hundred people hanging on my every word, praying that I'd be the one to come up with the magical phrase, some fucking generic sentence that would make them feel better. Take away their pain. How could I take away theirs when mine was so real, so raw?

I deserved this pain, every second of it.

It was my fault we were there.

I'd caused this.

I'd killed him.

Father O'Malley cleared his throat again, and I turned my head to the left slightly, looking at him out of the corner of my eye. He stepped forward and held his hand over the microphone. "Can you do this, son? If you're not ready—"

"No, I'm ready," I protested, harsher than I'd meant to. I looked at him and attempted a smile. "I just needed a minute. Sorry."

"Take your time." He moved his hand away from the microphone and stepped back again, folding his hands in front of him.

Obviously I can't. You keep clearing your fucking throat.

I took another deep breath and looked out into the crowd. "Hi."

Really? Hi? Nice start, asshole.

"Some of you know me, some don't. My name is Vip— Lawrence Finkle—and I want to be here as much as you all do."

A small gasp came from somewhere in the back of the church, and a couple people frowned in confusion.

"Please bear with me. I'm not a plan ahead kind of guy, so I'm winging this today. What I meant by that was I'd rather be anywhere on the planet other than here, saying good-bye to our friend." I took a shaky breath, determined not to lose it, certainly not up there in front of all those people.

"Calling him a friend is an understatement. He wasn't my

friend; he was my brother. Not biologically of course, but we were as close as brothers, maybe closer. I was there when his kids were born, and he was there . . . for me. All the time. That's the kind of guy he was. He'd give you the shirt off his back if you asked."

I sighed and ran my hands through my hair. "I don't know why I'm telling you guys this. If you're sitting in this room, you already knew that about him. I'm guessing every single person in here can think of some way he helped them, or better yet, some goofy story about how he made them laugh."

The low rumble of laughter vibrated through the room.

"What happened is . . . terrible, but that's not how I want to remember him. I want to think about all the times he made me laugh in the locker room. I want to remember him grinning like an idiot when he sent me a picture of him holding his new baby girl. I want to remember the man who had my back no matter what, no questions asked, and trust me, sometimes he should've asked questions."

Another small wave of laughter and I wondered if I'd said enough. I just wanted to be done. I looked down at Michelle, who was sitting in the pew with tears in her eyes, gently rocking a sleeping Maura back and forth while Matthew rested his head on her arm. Maura would never know her father. Matthew would never *remember* his father, and it was all my fault. Michelle leaned down and gently kissed the top of Maura's head, and the lump in my throat came back, bigger than the last time. I blinked hard and shook my head slightly, trying to regain my composure. I needed to stop; it was too much. Way too fucking much.

"Anyway . . . Big Mike was amazing, but you all know that or you wouldn't be here. Thanks for coming," I finished abruptly and stepped down the steps as the crowd started chattering quietly, probably about my sudden departure, but I didn't give a shit. Once again, their eyes were glued to me, the weird guy who could barely form a complete sentence up there. As I walked down the aisle, I paused briefly at the row I'd come from. Darla scooted in so I could sit down, but I shook my head. "No. I'm leaving, but do me a favor, please?" I handed her a small box of Lemonheads. "Set these on the casket at the end, okay?"

She blinked and frowned up at me, completely confused. "Wait. Aren't you—"

"No, I need to go," I interrupted and rushed toward the exit.

I needed air.

I needed to escape.

I headed straight out the doors.

Straight out into a shitty world that would never be the same again.

Chapter
12

Michelle

ONE MONTH, NINE DAYS, AND twenty-two hours. That's how long it'd been since my husband, the love of my life, took his last breath in this world. The last five and a half weeks had been the absolute worst of my life. I'd been trying hard to establish a new normal, but how do you go on when the person you were supposed to spend the rest of your life with kisses you good-bye, goes to work, and never comes home again? It was beyond unexpected. A complete shock. He'd been ripped away from me so suddenly that I was still reeling, as if it'd just happened.

We had dreams. We had goals. We weren't done yet. We had wanted to buy a house on the ocean in North Carolina and spend our summers there. We wanted to travel the country and see one baseball game in every stadium. We wanted to go to Paris. We wanted another baby. Damn it, we weren't done.

I sat in the kitchen, lost so deep in my thoughts that the ring of the doorbell made me gasp out loud. Hurrying up to the front of the house, I was pleasantly surprised to see Kacie's face smiling at me through the glass.

"Hey!" I said cheerfully as I opened the door.

"Hey yourself!" She held Emma in one arm but wrapped the other one around me and squeezed hard. "We were in the neighborhood, so I thought I'd drop by. Is this a bad time?"

I laughed as she pulled back. "I feel like lately it's always a bad time, but no, please come in. Hi, girls," I said to Lucy and Piper. They chirped hello in unison and waved as they followed Kacie into the house. "Matthew is going to be *so* happy to see you guys. He's bored out of his mind in the playroom."

I tried to smile as big as I could as they ran past me and down the hall to the playroom, a room they'd become very familiar with over the past couple of weeks. Kacie had stopped by numerous times just to see how I was doing, and I couldn't have been more appreciative. She had three daughters of her own and was pregnant with baby number four, yet she drove an hour just to check on me. I was so lucky to have her.

"How ya doing?" Kacie set her bag on the kitchen table and turned back to me.

My eyes stung and I shrugged. Why was it that when anyone asked how I was doing, I instantly lost it?

"Hold that thought." She disappeared into the playroom and set Emma down. "Watch her for me for a couple minutes, okay?" I heard her say to Lucy and Piper before she came back to the kitchen.

"Oh my God, look at you!" I squealed, staring at her belly.

She looked down at her stomach and back up at me. "I know. What the hell? Last week I was still small, and all of a sudden, I've popped."

"You totally popped." I wrapped my hands around her stomach. "Feeling any kicks yet?"

"Not really. A flutter here and there, but nothing substantial. I tried to make Brody feel one last night, but he told me I just had gas and he refused to feel gas." She rolled her eyes and sat at the table.

"Want some coffee?"

She nodded eagerly. "Yes, please. I would love some."

I took a sage green mug out of the cabinet and poured her a fresh hot cup of coffee—no sugar, extra cream, just the way she liked it.

"Here ya go."

"Thanks." She smiled, dumping extra cream in it like she always did. "So, how's your week been?"

I sighed. "Aside from Matthew asking me every three minutes when his daddy is coming home? Great."

Kacie's face fell. "I'm so sorry."

"It is what it is." I waved her off, not wanting to be a Debbie Downer—again. "I know I have to get used to it; it's just so damn hard."

"I can't even imagine." She shook her head slowly, her green eyes starting to water. "Did you decide what you're going to do about the house?"

I looked around my dream kitchen and sighed again. "Yeah, I think I'm gonna keep it for now. Thankfully, Mike was a smart money man and he invested wisely. If I'm careful, I can continue to stay home with the kids."

Her eyes grew wide and she reached out and touched my hand. "That's great. What a relief, huh?"

I nodded. It *was* a relief. I didn't want to sell the house we'd built together, the house I loved so much. Mike's parents had both passed, my mom had died when I was in high school, and my dad was remarried and living on the West Coast. For a while, I'd thought about selling the house and moving closer to him, but we didn't have a great relationship as it was, so I didn't see the point in uprooting the kids.

"I think Taylor's gonna move here," I told her.

"That would be amazing!"

"I know. I'm excited for the kids to have their aunt here. I think it'll be good for them and an extra hand for me if I need it." I walked back to the cabinet and grabbed the bag of goldfish crackers. "Sorry,"—I lifted them in the air—"I haven't been to the store, so my snack selection is limited."

"Oh, please." Kacie laughed and snatched some crackers out of the bag. "These are practically a food group at our house."

"So how is everyone else? Have you talked to Darla lately? Andy? Viper?" I poured some fish into a bowl and set it between us.

"Andy's good. Busy. Very busy. Darla is good. Things appear to be progressing nicely with the doctor." She wiggled her eyebrows up and down.

"Oh, really?"

"Yep. He's taking her to his hometown this weekend to meet the folks."

"Whoa." I took a sip of coffee. "That's kinda soon, no?"

Kacie shrugged. "They've been seeing each other for like a month and a half, so not really."

"Wow," I exclaimed in disbelief. "Has it really been that long already? It's so strange, sometimes it feels like the accident was months ago, and then the next minute it seems like no time has passed at all."

"I know, honey. It'll get easier." Kacie reached over and rubbed my hand again.

"Speaking of the accident, have you talked to Viper at all?"

Kacie shook her head slowly and sighed. "No, actually. Brody is worried about him. He's kinda gone off the rails."

"What do you mean?" I tossed a couple more crackers into my mouth.

"I don't know. It's weird." Her foot bounced up and down nervously. "They haven't talked much at all, as far as I know. He's almost always late for workouts, if he even shows up in the first place. Brody calls and texts . . . he doesn't answer."

"Momma!" Matthew whined as he ran down the hall from the playroom. "Lucy and Piper are playing house and they want me to be the daddy. I don't wanna be the daddy. I wanna be the monster who lives in the sewer."

I let out a hearty laugh while Kacie hollered down the hall. "Girls! Stop teasing him, please. Let him be whatever he wants."

"Sorry!" they both yelled back in monotone.

Kacie looked at me and bit her bottom lip, trying not to laugh. "The monster in the sewer?"

Still laughing, I rolled my eyes. "Clearly he's been watching too much *Teenage Mutant Ninja Turtles* lately. Actually, he's been watching too much of everything lately. When I don't feel like getting out of bed, it's just become so easy to put the TV on for him."

"Oh, please." Kacie waved me off. "Welcome to parenting. You don't want to know how much TV the girls watch. You do what you gotta do to get through the day, right?"

"Ain't that the truth." I smiled at her just as Maura started fussing in the monitor. "Oh,"—I set my coffee cup down—"I better grab her. I'll be right back."

"We'll let you get back to your day. I don't want to take up your whole morning."

I stopped in the kitchen doorway and turned back to her, probably looking more pathetic than I'd meant to. "Do you have to go?"

"Not at all. I just didn't want to bug you."

"You're not bugging me at all," I replied, happy that she was staying. "You're saving me."

Kacie smiled at me and sat back in the chair. "In that case, I'm all yours."

"Great!" I started up the stairs to the nursery. "I'll get Maura, we'll chat for a bit, and I'll order a pizza in a while."

"You had me at pizza!" She giggled from the kitchen.

Chapter
13

"**H**EY!" PORTLAND SMILED AND HURRIED over to me the minute I walked into Stumpy's. Damn, she looked fucking hot. A little red T-shirt that dipped low in the front showed off her beautiful, full tits and tight black shorts made it hard for me to keep my hands—amongst other appendages—to myself.

"How are you, baby girl?" I picked her up and spun her around.

When I set her down, she looked past me. "Where's everyone else?"

"Just me tonight." I held my hands up. "I came for the best burger in the state, and to see you, of course."

"Awww." She grinned and batted her eyelashes at me. "Well, sit wherever you want. I'll be out in a minute to take your order."

She turned and walked back to the kitchen while I made my way to the table we all normally sat at together. I knew it seemed silly to have one person at an eight-person table, but I didn't care. It was ours and I was sitting there.

The Twins game was playing on the TV above my head, but I was too busy watching Portland strut that hot little ass of hers around the restaurant to care. The way she walked was more entertaining than any baseball game I'd ever seen.

She sighed as she walked up to my table and gave me a big grin. "Okay. What can I get you tonight, Viper?"

"I'm gonna have an order of potato skins and a burger, medium."

She chewed on her juicy bottom lip as she wrote down my order. "Got it. What to drink?"

"Just a root beer, please."

"You and your root beer." Tilting her head to the side, she narrowed her eyes at me. "You get that almost every time you come here. Not a lot of people order that."

"I'm full of surprises." I wiggled my eyebrows up and down at her. She rolled her eyes and started to walk away, but I called her back. "Hey!"

She turned back and rested her elbows on the table.

"Let me ask you something, Portland." I leaned in close. "I get asked at least once a day for my phone number from random women. You've had my number for a few months now. Why haven't you ever used it?"

Her cheeks flushed as she shrugged and looked down at the table, nervously picking off an old sticker. "I don't know," she said in a low, shy voice. "I'm not sure how long I'm staying here, and getting involved with someone makes things messier, ya know?"

"I *don't* know. My life is hockey. Nothing more. Nothing less. If you ever change your mind, just remember it doesn't have to be messy." I smirked at her. "At least not outside of the bedroom."

"Oh my God!" she squealed, her face growing as red as her T-shirt as she laughed and walked away.

For the next hour, every time Portland was at my table or near my table, I tried to convince her to come home with me. After being turned down for the tenth time, the group of women playing pool in the corner started looking better and better. The tallest of the group, a leggy brunette, kept staring at me, then looking away every time I stared back.

She thought I was smiling at her, when in reality, I was laughing. Did girls really think that worked? The play-shy-to-try-to-get-you-to-come-over thing? Fuck that. If you want to come over and say hi, say hi.

To my surprise, she did just that a few minutes later.

"This is going to sound really weird,"—she giggled as she came over to my table—"but my friend and I have a bet going about you . . ."

Weak. I've heard that one already.

"She thinks you're a famous hockey player, but I told her no way." She giggled again and shook her head, her bangs swishing back and forth. "Who's right?"

"Not you."

She gasped as her mouth fell open.

Looks big enough.

"You *are* a famous hockey player!" She clapped her hands together and jumped up and down. "That's so exciting. I've never met anyone famous before. What's your name?"

"Viper," I answered as she dragged the chair back from the table and sat down across from me.

"Oooh, sexy." She licked her lips and lifted her eyebrows once at me. "I'm Jade."

And just like that, was a done deal.

Three hours later, we crashed through the front door of my house, barely inside before we started ripping our clothes off. We were both naked from the waist up, bumping into this wall and that wall like bulls in a china shop, when we finally made our way to the hall. She pulled away from me and started toward my bedroom when I gently yanked her hand back.

"No, not that one. In here." I led her to the guest room.

"This is *your* room?" She turned her nose up slightly as she looked around the room. "I figured it'd be . . . I don't know . . . decorated better?"

"Did you come here to bash my paint colors or fuck me?" I growled as I crashed into her, claiming her mouth and shoving my hands into her hair.

She let out a pleasant moan as our tongues slid around each other's mouths, sucking and teasing. Her hand slid down my stomach and into my jeans, wrapping around my hard dick. That was the kind of girl I liked—no need to romance, no need for an hour of foreplay, just straight down to business. I unbuttoned her jeans and stepped back as she wiggled out of them and hopped onto the bed. Shoving my own jeans down as fast as I could, I grabbed a condom out of the nightstand and rolled it on. I jumped into bed in one swift movement, grabbed her legs, and hooked them around my waist as I pushed my cock into her roughly. She let out a loud gasp, and part of me hoped it wasn't too hard for her, but mostly I didn't care. I needed a pussy to get lost in, and she was the willing recipient.

My hands were wrapped tightly around her thighs, lifting her ass off of the bed just a little so I had better control of how hard I fucked. Her fingers grabbed my wrists and her nails dug in as she opened her mouth and closed her eyes, thoroughly enjoying it.

I didn't hold back.

I couldn't hold back.

I closed my eyes and crashed into her over and over and over.

"Lock your legs around me," I said gruffly. Still not getting the leverage I wanted, I leaned forward and grabbed the top of the headboard with both arms, giving me the extra boost I needed.

"Oh, yes!" she called out as I drove into her as hard as I could. "Oh, fuck! Yes!"

Ten seconds later, my balls tightened and I came hard with four long grunts. I opened my eyes and looked down at Jade.

Her eyes were wild and she was biting her lip, trying not to smile.

"What?" I slid out of her and tossed the condom in the garbage before heading into the connected bathroom.

"Nothing." She giggled, rolling over to face the bathroom doorway. "That. It was hot. Intense."

Please. On a scale of one to ten, it was a six at best.

I stood in the bathroom doorway, wiping my dick off with a towel, and stared at her. She wasn't the most beautiful girl I'd ever been with, but she was definitely cute and she seemed pretty cool, not as ditzy as most of the others. Typically, I would have already been in my kitchen getting money out of the cookie jar, but that night I was willing to break my own rule and let her stay, assuming she wanted to.

"You gonna stay or do you wanna go?" I asked as I pulled my pants on.

She shrugged. "What do you want me to do?"

I glanced down at her lying innocently on my guest bed, oblivious to the fact that I'd just used her to try and forget the last two months of my life, and something in me ached. I surprised myself when I responded, "Stay. Please."

My phone buzzed for the fifth time before I even considered rolling over and looking at it. I was lying in bed on my stomach with my hands under the pillow as I cracked one eye open to see my blue voice mail light blinking.

"Who was it?" Jade yawned as I rolled my eyes.

"I don't know. I obviously didn't answer it," I said sarcastically.

She moved in close and hooked her arm over my shoulder, annoyingly hugging me from behind. The cuddling had been a nice change last night, but in the daylight she was just another girl who'd been had in my guest bedroom. Before she could get comfortable, I lifted her hand and slid out from under it, grabbing my phone off of the nightstand on the way out to the living room. Three new voice mails. Two from Brody and one from Gam.

Gam! Shit!

I cringed and hit the button to listen to her voice mail.

"Hi, Lawrence, it's me, your old, delicate grandmother, who's just suffered the unfortunate humiliation of being blown off by her grandson. Do you find it as ironic as I do that *I* am the one calling to check on *you?* Anyway, I'm going to go make myself some lunch now, seeing as how you're not here and I'm starving. Maybe we can try again next week and you'll actually show, assuming I'm still alive and kicking. Give me a call and let me know you're okay, please. Love you."

Might as well check out the voice mail from Brody too.

"Finkle, it's me. Where are you? You missed workouts— again. Call me."

Deciding I didn't give a shit about his other message, I turned my phone off and tossed it onto the coffee table. I closed my eyes and let my head fall back against the couch.

"Penny for your thoughts . . ." She sat on the other side of the couch, wrapped in a bedsheet.

First, why the hell didn't you get dressed? Second, how the fuck am I gonna get you out of my house?

"Nothing," I sighed, closing my eyes again.

"Well, here's the deal . . ." I felt her move in closer. "I have to run because I have some errands and stuff to do today, but how about later I come back and we have a repeat of last night?"

I stood up and walked to my cookie jar, suddenly wanting her as far away from me as possible. "That sounds great, but I have plans." I walked over and handed her cab money. "Thanks, though. It was fun."

She stared down at the money and frowned. "What's this for?"

"Cab fare."

Narrowing her eyes, she looked at me sideways. "I followed

you here. My car is out front, remember?"

"Oh." I tried to think back to last night but couldn't. "My bad. Well, you can keep it anyway."

I could feel her anger from five feet away as she jumped off of the couch, wadded up the money in her hand, and threw it at me. "You dick! I'm not some hooker!" She stomped off to the guest room, reappeared a few seconds later in her clothes, and glared at me on her way to the front door.

"Thanks again!" I called after her.

She slammed the door, and that was the last of Jade.

Chapter
14

LIKE AN EMBARRASSED DOG THAT just got caught pissing all over the carpet, I tucked my proverbial tail between my legs and climbed the front steps of Gam's house, holding a bouquet of flowers.

It took her a minute to get to the front door, and when she did, she crossed her arms over her chest and glared at me. She glanced down at the flowers I was carrying and back up at me. "There better be a flask in that bouquet." She opened the door and let me in.

"I really am sorry," I said a few minutes later, propping my feet up on her coffee table.

"Mmhmm." She glared at me playfully out of the corner of her eye as she carried a blue vase with her new flowers in it over to her dining room table and set it in the middle. Sighing as she sat down in the chair across from me, she crossed her arms again. "You know this is the third time you've blown me off recently, right?"

"Third? No way," I defended.

She nodded sternly. "Oh yes it is, my friend. I wrote each date down on my calendar."

I frowned. "Why would you do that?"

"Just in case I needed to prove it. Do I?"

Sighing, I threw my hands up in defeat. "Nope. I give up."
She really did have a calendar in her kitchen and she kept
meticulous records. I had no doubt scribbled on three different
squares was something about her asshole grandson not showing
up when he was supposed to.

"What's going on with you?" Concern filled her voice.

"Nothing. I'm fine. Why?"

"Oh please." She rolled her eyes. "I know you better than
almost anyone. You're not fine. Is it the accident?"

Just the mention of the accident made my chest tight. I'd tried
very hard over the last couple of months *not* to talk about it with
anyone, but Gam wasn't just anyone. She did know me better
than anyone, so I had to give her just enough to keep her happy
without really getting into it.

"Of course it still bothers me." My head fell back against the
couch and I stared up at the ceiling. "He was my best friend. I
talked to him every single day, and now he's just . . . gone."

"Have you talked to him since the accident?"

I lifted my head off of the couch quickly and looked at her
like she was nuts. "How much whiskey have you had this
morning?"

"Shut up, you brat. I'm serious. Have you been to his grave?
Have you talked to him? It might help."

"No. I can't go there." I shook my head. "I'm not ready."

I stood to grab my buzzing phone out of my pocket. Brody
was calling.

"Who is it?" Gam asked.

"Brody." I set my phone on the coffee table. "I'll call him
back. He's probably calling to yell at me anyway. I'm not in the
mood."

"Why would he yell at you?"

My text message alert sounded, and I sighed as I picked my
phone up again. "I missed another workout."

Sure enough, a text from Brody.

B: Coach Collins wants to talk to you. Call me
ASAP.

Shit.

"Hang on a minute, Gam. I need to call him back real quick."
I dialed Brody's number and stepped into Gam's kitchen for a
little privacy.

"Where the hell are you?" Brody answered.

"Wow. Good morning to you too." I laughed.

"Where. Are. You?" he repeated.

"At my grandma's. Why?"

"Collins wants you to come in. Today. He's going to call you,
but I figured I'd give you a heads-up first." Brody sighed into the
phone. "He's pissed, Viper. He had a closed-door meeting with
Fletcher *and* Leipold today."

*Shit again. A meeting with the general manager and the owner does not
sound good.*

"Okay, I'll head over there now."

I thanked Brody for looking out for me and we hung up.

"Uh-oh, that doesn't sound good," Gam said as I walked back
into her living room.

"No, it doesn't." I shoved my phone into my back pocket and
crossed my arms as I leaned against the door frame. "Apparently
Collins has his panties in a wad that I missed an optional
workout, and now he's looking for me."

"You better take care of that." She stood up and walked
toward me with her arms out.

I wrapped my arms around her and hugged her tight, holding
that hug for as long as I could. Sometimes being comforted by
someone who loves you unconditionally was the most basic
necessity in the world.

I took a deep breath and knocked on the door to Coach Collins's
office.

"Come in," he yelled from behind the doorway.

I opened the door just enough to slip inside and closed it quietly behind me.

Collins looked up from his computer over his glasses. "Well,"—he leaned back in his chair and linked his fingers behind his head—"look what the cat dragged in."

"Actually, it's more like look what Brody dragged in. He told me you wanted to talk to me," I joked, slowly making my way across his big office to the chair in front of his desk.

I sat and waited for him to talk, but he didn't. He just stared at me for a long time. First, he studied my face; then he looked off into space and pulled his eyebrows in tight, deep in thought about something.

Finally, he cleared his throat. "I have four daughters, Finkle."

What?

"Yes, sir. I know that."

"We had our first daughter and my wife and I were elated. We were over the moon for my second daughter too, though at that point I was already itching for a son. Then we had my third daughter, and I was convinced I could only make girls." He leaned forward in his chair and took his glasses off, placing them down and folding his hands on his desk. "My wife was done. Three was enough. I begged her for one more. I knew I would finally get my son. After three long years, she agreed to try one more time. We got another girl."

I laughed, nervously chewing at the skin on my fingers.

"Of course we love all of them, don't think we could love them more if we tried, but at the time . . . I wanted a son. When I was hired to coach this team, I was thrilled, but not just because I got to combine my two loves, hockey and coaching. I was most excited about inheriting twenty-three sons." He sniffed and cleared his throat again. "Two months ago, I didn't just lose one of those sons to a tragic accident, I lost two."

Do not cry.

"Finkle, you're never here. And when you are here, you're not *here*."

I looked down, focusing on a dark spot on the front of his desk, and nodded.

"The big wigs have noticed, and they were here today. They're concerned about your ability to play this upcoming season. They say you're not dependable anymore."

My eyes shot up to his. "I *am* dependable, Coach. You know that."

"Do I, Finkle?" he snapped. "How would I know that? I know that we have workouts and practices and you're always missing. I know that members of your team have called you and you've ignored them. I know that you've blown off not one, not two but three small charity functions this summer that you were scheduled to appear at."

I bounced anxiously in my seat.

Am I getting fired?

"I know what happened with Big Mike has been hard on you, son. I get that. But the team has to move forward—" He paused and let out a heavy sigh. "—and if we can't count on you, we're going to move on without you."

"Coach, you know how much this team means to me," I pleaded. "I'll do better."

"It's not me you need to convince, Finkle. It's them. And right now they don't have a lot of faith. They've decided in order for you to continue wearing a Wild jersey this upcoming season, you need to see the team psychologist, Dr. Shawn Roberts."

My shoulders slumped and I rolled my eyes. "Come on! Are you serious?"

"Yes, Finkle. I am."

"Well, I'm not seeing a goddamn shrink." I stood up and ran my hands through my hair as I paced his office.

"If you won't do this, then I can't guarantee I can protect you." His warning was stern.

I turned back toward his desk and threw my hands up in the air. "Can I have a few days to think about it?"

"You have twenty-four hours. If you don't have an appointment set up with Dr. Roberts within that time frame, I'm not sure what will happen."

The last thing in the world I wanted to do was lay on some shrink's couch and have him judge me while I went on and on about my fucking feelings. How was that going to fix me anyway? I made a mistake; I just needed time to move past it on my own.

"I really don't think this is necessary—"

"Lawrence," he interrupted. "It's not up for discussion."

My hands balled into fists and I clamped my jaw down hard before I said something I was going to regret. I turned around and marched toward the door, grabbing the doorknob so violently I'm surprised I didn't rip it right off the door.

"Remember, you have twenty-four hours, son," he called out as the door shut behind me.

Really? Son? Fuck you.

I got into the elevator and punched the button for the lobby. I was so angry I could barely see straight. Who did those assholes think they were that they could make decisions for me? Why couldn't they just let me live my life and do my fucking job? The elevator doors opened and I stomped out, barely missing a group of men standing right outside the doors, and headed straight for the parking lot. I just wanted to get on my bike and drive away. Far away, for hours, and not think about hockey or Mike or Coach Collins or therapists.

Once I got to my bike, I sat down but didn't start it. I didn't drive away. Where was I going to go? Even if I drove for two days straight, not only would my problems still be there when I got back, they would be worse.

I felt defeated, but I took my phone out of my pocket.

"This is Mia," Coach Collins's secretary answered.

"Hey, Mia. It's Viper."

"Hey," she said, sounding sad. I was so sick of sympathy.

"Would you do me a favor, please?"

"Sure."

"Would you call that Dr. Roberts and set up an appointment for me?"

"Of course. Any specific day or time?"

"I don't give a shit. Just set it up and text me with the details when you're done, okay?"

"You got it, Viper."

"Then go into Coach Collins's office and tell him I have twenty-three hours and fifty minutes to spare."

Chapter 15

TWO DAYS AGO, MIA HAD texted me with the time and address of my meeting with Dr. Shawn Roberts. My meeting was in an hour and I was still lying in bed, dreading the thought of going to meet this asshole. I'm sure he was some cocky fuck who was going to tell me to take a deep breath and relax. I hadn't even met him yet and I already hated him.

Finally, I forced myself out of bed and into the shower. The drive to his office only took me about ten minutes, and I was thankful for that. Small victories, right? I parked my bike outside a boring-looking brown brick building with boring pink flowers in a boring planter out front and checked my phone one more time for the message from Mia.

Suite 301.

The elevator opened on the third floor, and I found suite 301 at the end of the hallway.

Here goes nothing.

I took a deep breath and hesitantly pushed the door open. I'd never been in a psychologist's office before, so while I wasn't sure what to expect, I kinda figured it would look like a regular old doctor's office. I was wrong. There was one small couch and no receptionist. Frankly, the walk-in closet at my house was bigger than that office. There was another door on the far side of the room. A light switch next to it had a sign above it that read: Please flip switch up at your scheduled appointment time. Thank you, Dr. Roberts."

"This is weird," I said out loud as I looked around the room.

The clock on the wall caught my attention. It read 11:10. I was ten minutes late. Oops. I flipped the switch up and turned to sit down on the couch. My ass hadn't even hit the seat when the door sprang open.

"Lawrence?" A short, smoking hot woman with slick, shoulder-length black hair was standing in the doorway.

The receptionist is in there? Weird.

"Yeah, that's me." I held my hand out. "I'm here to see Dr. Roberts."

"I know." She laughed as she shook my hand. "I *am* Dr. Roberts. Come on in."

Reeling from the shock, I followed her into her office. "Wait. *You're* Dr. Roberts?" I asked incredulously.

"Yep." She nodded as she reached behind me and shut the door.

"You're Dr. *Shawn* Roberts?"

"Yes." She laughed again.

"But Shawn is a man's name."

She raised her eyebrows and shrugged. "My mother didn't think so. Please, have a seat." Motioning toward the couch, she sat in the chair across from me and smiled.

Are you fucking kidding me?

The Gods must have been smiling down on me after all. *She* was my therapist? How fucking lucky could a guy get? This was going to be a breeze. I'd turn on the old Viper charm and be in and out of here in one session, tops. And if I was *really* lucky, I'd escape with a blow job and a new phone number to add to my drawer.

"So." Still smiling, she tucked a piece of hair behind her ear and crossed her legs. "Your appointment was a last-minute addition to my schedule, so I know almost nothing about you, other than your name and that you play for the Wild. Why don't you tell me why you're here?"

To fuck you senseless.

"Honestly? I'm here because my coach made me come."

"Ah . . ." She nodded. "So this wasn't your idea?"

"Not even fucking close."

"I see." She stood and walked behind her desk, which was off to the side of the room. "Do you want anything to drink? Water? Coke? Orange Juice?"

"Nope."

"Suit yourself." She shrugged. The leather in the couch crackled as I leaned over and craned my neck, trying to get a better look at her ass as she bent over to grab a bottle of water out of the fridge tucked in the corner. She stood up quickly and caught me staring. A shy smile crept across her face and I knew it wouldn't be long. Thank God I had a condom in these jeans from last week. Doctor or not, rule number one still applied.

"I know what you're thinking." Sitting back down across from me, she cracked the top off her water bottle and lifted it to her lips, not taking her eyes off of me for a second.

I leaned back against the couch and stretched my arms across the top of it, smiling at her. "You do, huh?"

"Yep." She set her water bottle down on the coffee table and leaned in close. "And you can stop thinking it right now."

"Huh?"

"You're not the first male athlete who's sat on that couch, you know? Most of them come in here expecting to find a man, and then they see me and think I'm gonna be some easy conquest for them."

Holy shit.

"If I were a bettin' gal, I would say that's exactly what you were thinking too. Am I right?" She sat back and crossed her arms, silently challenging me with the lift of one eyebrow.

"No," I denied sternly.

"Okay, Pinocchio." Her condescending laugh filled the room. "Why don't we talk about why you're here now?"

I stared straight at her without saying a fucking word.

"Okay, why don't you tell me a little about yourself instead?"

Nothing. I wasn't about to give that arrogant bitch any information. She wanted it? She'd have to work for it.

"Alrighty then." She sighed, obviously frustrated at my stubbornness. "Let's do this. I'll tell you a little about myself and if you want to jump in and contribute, you can."

She paused for me to respond; instead, I yawned.

"As you already know, my name is Shawn Roberts. I grew up on the north side of Chicago and lived there until I was ten, when we moved to Texas so I could train for the Olympics full-time. In 2000, I went to Sydney with the women's gymnastics team and was the favorite to win gold on the balance beam, but in a horrific practice the day after we got there, I fell off the beam and landed wrong. I shattered my ankle, and that was the end of my career. So I came home, regrouped, went to college, and here I am." She held her hands up as she smiled proudly at me. "Your turn."

"My name is Viper, and I don't talk about my personal life with strangers," I said dryly.

She nodded and flicked her tongue in between her teeth and top lip as she looked around the room. "Okay. Well, this is definitely going to be an interesting ride, isn't it?"

I was annoyed, pissed the fuck off. I didn't want to be there in the first place, and the last thing I needed was this little tart giving me a hard time and riding my ass. She was fine as hell but a total bitch.

"You're a condescending pain in the ass, you know that?" I growled. "And what the fuck do you mean 'interesting ride'? I came to this appointment because I was forced to. Now I'm leaving." I stood up, grabbed my keys off the coffee table, and

headed toward the door.

"That's fine. You can go,"—she stood up and walked over to her desk nonchalantly—"but that's the wrong door."

My hand was inches from the doorknob when I froze.

What?

Spinning around, I took two steps toward her desk. "What?"

"See that door?" She smugly pointed to another door on the other side of her office. "That's the one you leave through."

I sighed in frustration and marched to the other side of the room.

"When do you want to come back?" she asked just as I got to the door.

At that point, all I could do was laugh. "You've got to be shitting me." I rolled my eyes as I turned back to her one more time.

Her eyes lifted to mine just a little and she shrugged. "No, I'm not *shitting* you. I have the power to decide when it is you're ready to be done with treatment, and seeing as how I don't even know why you're here in the first place . . . nope, not ready." She picked a pen up off her desk and chewed on the end as she flipped the pages of a calendar in front of her. "Soooo . . . you wanna come back or no?"

Unfuckingbelievable.

In that moment, I wasn't sure if I wanted to stab her in the eye with that pen or throw everything off her desk and fuck her on it. "Fine," I agreed stubbornly as I walked over and sat back down on the couch. "Can we just get this over with right now, then?"

She looked down at the chunky white watch that sat on her tiny, tan wrist and then back up at me, smiling. "Nope. I have another client coming in fifteen minutes and I'm *definitely* gonna need longer than that with you."

"Fine!" I yelled, jumping to my feet. "Then when?"

"I have an opening tomorrow . . ."—she tapped the pen

against her desk as she studied her calendar again—"at seven o'clock. Want it?"

"Sure," I sighed in defeat as I started walking toward the door again. "I didn't know therapists worked that late. See you tomorrow."

"Uh, Viper . . ."

I opened the door and turned back to face her.

She stood behind her desk, grinning at me with her hands on her hips. "That's seven o'clock in the *morning*."

Chapter
16

ONE OF THE REASONS I loved my job was that I didn't have to set an alarm in the summer. I could be as fucking lazy as I wanted to be and sleep as late as I wanted. Workouts and practices were optional, though highly recommended, but there was no set time. Fucking time. The annoying beep, beep, beep of my alarm sounded from my phone and I swatted at it to make it stop.

I rolled onto my back and stared up at my ceiling. My meeting with Dr. Roberts yesterday had been mentally exhausting, and I was *not* looking forward to going back and doing it all over again. If she'd been telling the truth, she knew nothing other than my name, and it wasn't safe for her to be digging around in my head. Shit, even *I* tried not to get lost in there.

My alarm sounded again and I turned if off for good this time.

6:50. Fuck.

I jumped out of bed, swished some mouthwash while I took a quick piss, and was out the door.

Suite 301. Same weird little office. Same weird little light switch.

"Good morning!" she cheered as she opened the door, smiling at me.

"Morning," I grumbled.

I sat on the couch as she sat in the chair across from me and stared.

"What?" I snapped defensively.

She crossed her legs and leaned forward, resting her elbow on her knee. "Here's the thing . . . clearly, you're going through some . . . stuff. I'd like to just talk to you like we're friends, about whatever you want. Eventually, any issues we need to address will bubble to the surface and we'll get to where we need to go. Do you agree?"

I didn't say anything. I just shrugged.

"I'm going to tell you a little about myself again, from a more personal standpoint this time. My name is Shawn, and I never wanted to be a doctor. I wanted to do flips my whole life and win a gold medal." She stood and walked over to the fridge again, grabbing two bottles of water this time, and she set one of them down in front of me. "That obviously didn't pan out because of my bum ankle, and I was angry for many, many years. Without sports in my life, I became a bit of a wild child as a teenager and did some things I swear I'll never talk about again. After my mom forced me into some counseling of my own, it became apparent to me that I needed sports in my life in one form or another. So . . . I began running. First 5Ks, then half marathons, then full marathons. There was no denying that deep down I was an athlete before everything else."

I sat and listened closely, more interested in her story than I would ever admit to being.

"In college, I joined a running club, which kept me on the straight and narrow. After three semesters of forcing myself to pretend I wanted to be a kindergarten teacher, I couldn't fight it anymore and switched my major to sports psychology. I eventually got my master's degree and started at the bottom in a private practice. I was forced—well, obligated—to quit that job and decided to start my own practice. So here I am."

Curiosity killed the Viper.

"Why were you forced to quit?" I couldn't help it. I was

captivated by her and the story she was telling me.

"I started sleeping with my boss."

Whoa. Not what I was expecting.

"For real?"

"Yeah, but it's okay. We're engaged now." She laughed, holding up her left hand. I was surprised she could lift it with that huge fucking rock on her ring finger.

"Congratulations."

A big smile spread across her face. "Thanks. The point of me telling you all this is I wanted you to know that I'm not perfect. I'm not perfect, and I won't judge you. I'm not a typical therapist in that I don't follow a pattern with my clients. They're all different, and they all require different things from me. Also, and I want you to really hear me say this, anything—*every single thing*—you say to me in this room stays in this room. I don't talk about it with friends, my fiancé, no one. It's between you and me and Muhammad Ali." She nodded toward the large black and white picture of the legendary boxer on the wall. "I expect the same courtesy in return. Anything I say *to* you or tell you about myself doesn't go past you. Got it?"

I nodded like a stubborn toddler who'd just met his match.

"I demand respect and I will give it back, but what I won't do is let you bullshit me. I'm going to piss you off and push you out of your comfort zone. Often. But that's my job. That's how this works. That's how you move forward."

Grabbing the water bottle off of the coffee table, I cracked it open and gulped until the whole thing was gone.

"I'm assuming that means you agree?" She laughed again. "Now, tell me a little about you."

I took a huge breath and held it for a second, finally exhaling slowly. I'd never had anyone that I could completely open up to before. The thought of spilling my guts to this woman was both terrifying and tempting. More than anything, I wanted someone I could tell everything to and be myself around without fear of judgment or someone spilling *their* guts to the media.

Baby steps, Viper.

"Well, you already know my name. I'm not sure what else you want to know."

"Okay, how about I ask you questions and you answer them?"

"All right."

She stood and walked back to the fridge, grabbing another water bottle. "How long have you played hockey?"

"Professionally?"

"Sure." She shrugged as she set the bottle down in front of me.

"Eight years."

"And not professionally?"

"Uh . . . since I was about ten."

"Why hockey?"

I pressed my lips together and scratched my chin. "What do you mean?"

"Just what I said. Why hockey? Why not baseball or golf or something else?"

"First of all, golf isn't a sport. And B, I got into a lot of fights as a kid, so my parents figured if I was gonna fight regardless, might as well do it on the ice."

She narrowed her eyes and tilted her head to the side. "Why did you fight?"

"I had to."

"Why?"

"Next question."

Clearing her throat, she rested her chin on her hand and her elbow on the arm of the chair, not saying a word. "I'm gonna let that go—for now—but I can absolutely tell there's something there, so we *will* revisit it."

Good luck with that.

"Whatever." I rolled my eyes.

"Why don't you tell me about your relationships?"

"Elaborate, please."

"Your relationships, with people. Whoever you want to tell me about. Your family. A girlfriend. Maybe a boyfriend?"

If looks could kill, she would've been a corpse. "I don't have a boyfriend." I glared. "And I don't have a girlfriend either."

"Really?" Her body stiffened as her head jerked back slightly. "No girlfriend? With all that charm?"

"Ha ha, very funny."

"Okay, okay. Forget boyfriends and girlfriends. You have to love someone. Everyone does. Tell me about the most important person in your life."

I didn't hesitate with that answer; there was no need to think about it. "My grandma."

She squinted at me without saying a word.

I held my hands up defensively. "What?"

"Nothing." She continued staring at me with narrowed eyes. "I'm just trying to decide if you're being a smart-ass or if you're telling me the truth."

"Here's the thing. You want respect and I'll give that to you. I also will never lie to you. I hate liars. Loathe them, actually. I don't mean stupid little 'Sure, I'll call you in the morning' lies, but like real ones. If you ask me a question and I don't want to answer it, I'll tell you. If I want to answer it, I will."

"Fair enough." She nodded once. "Now tell me about this grandma of yours."

I couldn't help but smile when I thought about my grandma. "Well, I call her Gam, actually. When I was little, I couldn't say Grandma so I called her Gamma, and over time, the end just fell off, so now she's Gam. Anyway, she's my father's mother and my only real family. I love her more than anything."

"Wow." She bit the corner of her lip as she smiled at me, her dark brown eyes sparkling. "I'm pleasantly surprised. If you'd given me ten guesses, I don't know that I ever would have pegged you as a grandma's boy."

Nodding, I smiled back. "I'll wear that label proudly."

"Good, you should. Tell me more about her."

"Well, she's old . . . and sarcastic as hell. She drinks more whiskey than anyone I know and yells at squirrels all day long. She's a trip."

"Sounds like it." She laughed. "And you're closest to her? What did you mean your only 'real family'? Have the rest all passed on?"

I shook my head. "No, my parents are both still alive, but I'm an only child. Once you have perfection, why try to duplicate it, right?"

"Oh, naturally," she agreed sarcastically. "So wait . . . your parents are both alive, yet you said your grandmother was your only 'real family.' What does that mean?"

"Next," I barked.

"Fine. Let's talk about your relationships with females. Have you ever been married?"

"Fuck no!"

"Do you ever *want* to be married?"

"Yes. The minute Mila Kunis dumps that arrogant asshole, Ashton Kutcher, I'm going to propose to her. If that never happens, I guess I'm destined to be a bachelor forever." I stuck my bottom lip out and pouted at her dramatically.

"Okay, let's try that again, with less sarcasm this time."

"Okay . . . then the answer changes to no, I don't want to be married."

She tilted her head to the side and crossed her arms. "Why?"

"The thought of waking up with the same woman every day for the rest of my life makes my fucking skin crawl. I can't stand most women for more than twelve hours, let alone a significant amount of time."

"So you've *never* had a serious girlfriend?"

"I lived with a girl once, but I was never faithful to her, so I don't consider that serious. And I have one friend who I fucked regularly for over a year. Does that count as serious?"

"Maybe." She shrugged. "Did you love her?"

"As a friend. Not like *that*."

"Why not?" she pushed.

"It wasn't like that with me and Darla. She was like one of the guys, just with bigger tits and a hotter ass. She didn't want commitment and she didn't push me to give her more than I wanted to."

"Do you still see her?"

I bounced my head back and forth, left to right, as I thought about that question. "Kinda, when our whole group is together, but not on a one-on-one basis. She started seeing someone, so that's done."

"Okay, interesting. Tell me about this group."

"Why does this feel like an interview?"

"It kind of is." She grinned. "I'm just asking questions, trying to get a feel for who Lawrence Finkle really is."

I chuckled. "When you find out, let me know, okay?"

"Come on, we're getting there. Don't fizzle out on me now. Tell me about your friends, this group."

"There's just a group . . . of people . . . I hang out with. There's not much to tell. We haven't seen each other much lately."

"Why not?"

"I don't know." I shrugged.

"Hey, Pinocchio, you just lied to me again," she said sternly. "You promised never to do that."

Holy fuck.

"Things have just been different lately."

"I've let you blow me off twice now. This time I'm pushing. What's different and why?"

"One of the members of the group passed away." A huge lump formed in my throat. I did not want to talk about what had happened with a stranger, and as much as she was talking to me like we were, we weren't friends.

"I'm so sorry." Her tone was soothing and her face softened.

"So, anyway, it's just kinda changed the dynamic now. I don't know if they all hang out a lot or what, but I haven't gone if they do."

"Wait." She turned her head to the side and looked at me out of the corner of her eye. "Someone dying shouldn't make you want to leave the group. There's something you're not telling me."

Do it. Tell her. Rip the fucking bandage off.

"I killed him."

"You killed him?"

I stared down at the coffee table, not wanting to make eye contact with her, and nodded. "Yep."

She sat up straight in her chair, her eyes glued to me as she processed what I'd just said.

"What do you mean you *killed* him?"

"He was a teammate and we were playing a game, one on one. He was winning and I am too competitive. The game got more physical than it should have, and as he was about to score the winning goal, I checked him from behind. He slid into the boards really hard and all hell broke loose in his brain. He died a couple days later."

Her hand shot up and laid flat at the base of her neck as her mouth fell open. "Wow. I am *so* sorry, Viper."

"Needless to say," I continued, "I haven't hung out with that group much lately, because, you know . . . it's awkward."

"Okay, I get that, but you didn't *kill* him. It was an accident."

"We'll have to agree to disagree on that." I leaned forward

and snatched the extra water bottle off the table.

As I cracked the bottle open a light bulb near the door turned on, distracting both of us.

"Shit." She looked down at her watch. "That's my next client. And we were just getting into something."

"Oh no we weren't." I stood up and took my keys out of my pocket. "That's something we never have to talk about again."

"Fat chance," she argued. "I want you to come back tomorrow, okay?"

"Fine," I agreed, "but not before ten o'clock. This early shit is for the birds."

She walked back over to her desk and pulled her calendar out. "Damn." She tapped her finger on the page. "I'm booked up tomorrow. You know what"—she sighed, looking up at me—"I have a lunch break from one to two. Be here at one—not a minute later. There's a little deli one block north of here. Tell them you want a number four for Shawn. They know me there. They'll make it just the way I like it."

Chapter
17

THE NEXT MORNING, I WAS up and showered early, ready to go. I wouldn't say I was excited to get back to Shawn's office, but I wasn't dreading it as much as I'd been the last two times. I stopped and took a quick look at the phone number on my kitchen counter from the night before.

Madison

612-555-2369

I opened the drawer in my kitchen, tossed it in, and was on my way. A rainy, shitty day in Minnesota meant leaving the bike at home, so I parked my car in front of the Brown Bag Deli and hustled inside.

A bell rang as I stepped through the door, catching the attention of the middle-aged woman behind the counter.

"Hey, sweet cheeks!" she said cheerfully. "What can I get ya?"

"Uh . . ." I laughed. "I'm supposed to order a number four for Shawn. I have no idea what that is or what that means, but she said you'd make it just the way she likes it."

"Ah! I know exactly who you're talking about. Coming right up." She turned around and gave the order to the cook through the window as I took a seat at the counter near the front.

I couldn't believe the place was only ten minutes from my house, yet I'd never known it existed. The inside was decorated to look old-fashioned—black and white checkered tiles, tables and chairs with that silver rim around them, and a huge chalkboard with the menu written on it hung behind the counter. A huge glass case that held all sorts of cookies and desserts at the other end of the restaurant caught my attention, so I walked over to check it out.

"See anything you like?" the same woman asked as she walked up to the other side of the glass.

I glanced up at her name tag. Ruth.

"Hi, Ruth. Yeah, actually. I'll also take a cinnamon scone and a blueberry scone, please."

"Really?" The corner of her mouth lifted as she paused. "I took you for more of a . . . *meat guy* . . . but scones it is."

My mouth hung open as she turned around and grabbed a piece of tissue out of a box. She scooped the scones out of the glass case and put them in a little brown bag. "Anything else? A shake or float maybe?"

Wait. Floats?

"Oh, Ruth. You had me at float. Can I get a root beer float?"

"Damn. I'm off today. Once again, in my head you were an orange dreamsicle guy, but root beer it is." She giggled as she scooped vanilla ice cream into a big Styrofoam cup. "You're taking that sandwich down to Shawn now, right?"

Still laughing at the dirty bird cashier from the sandwich shop, I nodded as she handed me the cup over the counter.

"Hang on." She turned back to the counter and started dumping things into a blender while I continued looking through the cases.

"All right, cutie patootie, you already have your root beer float and here's your order. Blueberry scone, cinnamon scone, number four, no mayo, and a strawberry banana smoothie with ginseng." I frowned at her when she mentioned the smoothie, but she just winked at me. "They're the doc's favorite."

"Ruth,"—I grinned—"you're amazing. I might have to take you home with me."

"Don't say it unless you mean it, honey buns." She winked again.

I laughed out loud. It felt good. "How much do I owe ya?"

She punched a few buttons on her register. "Seventeen dollars and twenty cents, please."

"You'll definitely be seeing me again. Count on it." I winked back at her as I handed her a fifty-dollar bill and left.

As the elevator climbed to the third floor, I looked at the time on my phone.

12:53 p.m.

Made it with seven minutes to spare. Feeling proud of myself, I opened the door to the little waiting room and strutted over to the light switch, laughing as I flipped it up, then down, then up and down and up and down and up and down.

The door flew open and Shawn glared at me as she shook her head.

"My bad." I held my hands up in the air defensively as she closed it again.

A few minutes later, the door opened again. Thankfully, she wasn't glaring this time.

"Come in." She rolled her eyes, a slight smirk on her face.

"What's up, doc?" I grinned as I walked past her. "Sorry about that. I guess I got a little excited flicking the switch." I bit into my bottom lip, trying hard not to laugh. "Get it? Flicking the switch?" I set the food and drinks down on the coffee table.

She shut the door and sat down on the chair across from me.

"Yes, Lawrence. I got it. I may be a doctor, but I'm not a stiff idiot. My fiancé makes the same perverted hornball jokes as the rest of the male population."

I took her sandwich out of the bag and pushed her smoothie toward her. "I can't take credit for that. Ruth told me you'd like it."

Her shoulders slumped and she clapped her hands to her chest. "Isn't she the *best?* I was hoping you'd meet her."

"She's pretty awesome. I told her I'd be coming back."

She tapped my cup with her straw before pushing it into the smoothie. "What's that?"

"Root beer float."

Covering her mouth with her hand, she coughed loud, trying not to spit it everywhere.

"What?" I exclaimed.

"You, with a root beer float. It's like you instantly transformed into a five-year-old sitting on my couch."

"Wow," I said sarcastically as she laughed out loud. "I'm so glad I went and bought you lunch and came back here today."

"I'm sorry. I'm sorry. You're right." She took a quick bite of her sandwich and a swig of her smoothie. "Let's get down to it."

I wiggled my eyebrows up and down at her. "Now you're talking."

"Not that, testosterone head." She rolled her eyes. "Where did we leave off yesterday?"

"We were talking about Gam."

"No, we were done with that. And I'm pretty sure your nose is growing, *again*." She wiped her mouth on a napkin and sat back. "I believe we were talking about why you ditched your friends so suddenly after the accident."

Just like that the mood in the room shifted.

"I didn't ditch my friends," I snapped defensively as I took a bite of cinnamon scone.

"You said there was an accident. You said it was your fault. You said you stopped hanging out with them. Right?"

"Well, yeah, but—"

"Do you know if they've all hung out since the accident?" She took another bite of her sandwich and set it back down

"Yeah, they have."

"And?" She moved her hand in a small circle, motioning for me to keep going.

"And what?"

"Did they call or text you?"

"Next question."

"No way!" She jerked back, sat up straight in her chair, and pointed at me. "No way are you getting out of this one. They've invited you to hang with them, haven't they? And you've said no, haven't you? Why?"

"I don't know."

"*Why?*" she pushed.

"Because."

"Because *why?*"

"Because I don't want them looking at me, okay?" I yelled as I jumped up from the couch. "Because I know all they see when they look at me is the monster who killed his best friend. The monster who made his best friend's wife a widow. The monster who left his best friend's kids fatherless."

She licked her lips and crossed her arms over her chest as the smirk on her face grew bigger and bigger.

I plopped down on the couch, completely emotionally exhausted, and glared at her. "What the fuck are you smiling at?"

"You." She continued to smile proudly.

"Me what?"

"I told you I'd piss you off and push you. And I will again, but this is *great* news, Lawrence! Now we've identified an issue to work on." She clapped her hands in excitement.

"Shawn, I have way more issues than you could possibly ever fix. And please stop calling me Lawrence. Call me Viper."

"You don't need to be *fixed,* Viper. I know this is just the tip of the iceberg, but this really is a good thing. You're opening up, and we're on the way to getting you healed. And please, call me Dr. Roberts." She laughed as she packed up her garbage and threw it away. "Okay, come on." She glanced down at her watch. "My two o'clock will be here soon and he's never late. We only have a little more time. Tell me about your friend that passed."

I shrugged, picking at the skin on my fingers. "There's not much to tell. He's my best friend."

"Okay. You said he was married?"

Was. There was that past tense shit again. Still not used to it.

"Yes."

"And he had kids?"

"Two. A son and a daughter."

"Okay, and how is your relationship with them now? Have you kept in touch?"

The guilt of knowing that I hadn't said one word to Michelle since Mike's funeral was enough to make me lose my breath. My heart started racing, and I wiped the sweat from my palms on my pants.

"Viper?" Dr. Robert's leaned in. "Stay with me. What's happening right now?"

"Nothing. It's hot in here. Can we open a window?"

"Sure." Her brows pulled in tight and she watched me cautiously as she walked over to the window and cracked it. She sat back down across from me and didn't say anything for a few minutes as I concentrated on breathing slow and controlling my pulse.

"Are you okay?" she finally said quietly.

"Yeah, I'm fine."

"Can we talk about it?"

I sighed. "Can we not?"

She raised her hand, looking at her watch again quickly. "He's going to be here any minute, but I really don't want to end like this. What was that about?"

"Cement heart," I mumbled.

"Huh?"

"Mike told me once that I had a cement heart, and in the room—the hospital room—" I shook my head, not wanting to finish.

"Keep going," she ordered.

"In the room, when I went in to tell him good-bye, I also told him I'd take his place with his family. That I'd be there until the baby was eighteen, for anything they needed."

"Aaaaand now you haven't talked to them at all?"

I nodded.

"So first this horrific accident happens, which you feel responsible for, then he dies, and even though you've promised to be there for his family, you haven't been?"

I took a deep breath and nodded again. It was hard to hear it said back to me.

"Here's what I want you to do between now and our next appointment," she started. We both looked up at the lightbulb that flashed by the door. She stood and finished picking up the garbage off the table. "I want you to think seriously about what kind of man you are now and what kind of man you want to be."

"What do you mean?"

"Just what I said. Think about it. And come back Monday at three in the afternoon, okay?"

Chapter
18

Michelle

THE MONITOR LIT UP WITH the sounds of Maura babbling happily in her crib. I rolled onto my side and turned on the video monitor so I could watch her. I sat up in shock when the grainy black and white screen came into focus, clearly showing my independent little eight-month-old standing in her crib. She wobbled back and forth, hanging on to the side rail for dear life. My heart raced with excitement, and out of habit, I turned around to share the news . . . with an empty side of the bed.

Those were the saddest moments. The moments I knew he would have been just as excited as I was for a new milestone in the kids' lives. Even if he were out of town with the team, I would have called him on FaceTime and we would have been excited together. Now, I sat alone in my bedroom, staring at our baby girl, equal parts excited and heartbroken. A couple times when Matthew had said something funny at school or Maura cut a tooth, I'd called to tell Taylor. She'd done her best to fill the void of not having another parent to share it with, but it just wasn't the same.

My eyes started to water, and I knew before I even got out of bed it was going to be one of those days. I'd been doing better. Three months since his death and the crying was getting less and less. As long as my heart was beating and there was breath in my body, I'd never stop missing him, but I was trying hard to focus on the good memories instead of the unknown future.

My bedroom door creaked as it pushed open just a crack and a tiny head peeked in.

"Hey, buddy." I wiped my eyes and waved him over.

He walked slowly, staring at me with unsure eyes, and climbed in my bed. "Why are you sad, momma?"

"Oh." I cleared my throat. "I'm just missing daddy today."

His little head nodded up and down in agreement, though I wasn't sure he knew what he was agreeing to. I tucked the blankets up under his chin and laid my head on the pillow next to him, taking a deep breath and smelling his hair. He still smelled like soap from last night's bath. He scooted in close and I hugged him tight, looking outside at the rain streaming down the window.

"Momma?"

"Yes, baby?"

"I'm hungry."

I rolled over onto my side to face him, resting my head on my hand. "Me too. What should we have?"

He sat up in bed and thrust his little fists in the air. "Gummy bears!"

Laughing, I grabbed him and pulled him back down by me, tickling his sides. "We can't have gummy bears for breakfast." I poked and kissed his neck as he giggled wildly.

"Stop!" he panted in between giggles.

I quit tickling him and he sighed and looked up at me, not saying a word, just staring into my eyes. I brushed the fine brown hair from his forehead and rubbed his soft skin with the back of my fingers.

What the hell?

"You know what? Gummy bears it is."

His mouth fell open as he gasped, then he stood up quickly, cheering as he jumped up and down on my bed. "Woohoo!"

"Just this once, though, okay?" I added. "This isn't gonna be a new trend. *And* . . . you have to have an apple too. Deal?"

"Deal!" He held his hand out for me to shake.

"Come on!" Instead of shaking his hand, I turned around for him to jump on my back. "Let's go get your sister out of her crib."

"What do you think of a nice quiet day at home today?" I asked Matthew as milk dripped from his chin and dropped back into his bowl of Froot Loops. Thankfully, once we got downstairs he decided that he wanted something a little more filling than just gummy bears.

He shrugged and nodded.

"Maybe this afternoon we'll take a little trip to the library?"

"Yeah." He nodded more excitedly. "I wanna play at the train table."

"You got it!" I tried to sound upbeat.

Since Mike had died, little Matthew didn't smile as much anymore. He always seemed sad and lost, and maybe it was my imagination, but I felt like he stared at the front door a lot.

As I was cutting a pancake into teeny tiny pieces for Maura, the text alert sounded on my phone.

Hey. You around today?

I stared down at my phone, trying hard to remember whose number it was. Finally, I responded.

I'm so sorry. Who is this?

While I finished cutting Maura's pancakes, I kept one eye on my phone, waiting for it to buzz again. Finally, it did.

It's Viper. I was hoping I could stop by.

Viper? That's weird.

Oh, sure. I'm making a run to the library, but not till later. Come by whenever. :)

I'd barely put the phone down and it buzzed again.

Thanks. I'll be by in about twenty minutes.

That was weird. I'd barely talked to him at all since Mike died and not once since the funeral. I set the phone down on the counter and went back to cutting Maura's pancakes.

A little while later, the doorbell rang. I went up front and opened it as quick as I could, waving Viper in out of the rain.

"Hey." He smiled as he came through the door.

"Hey. This is unexpected." I closed the door behind him. "The kids are in the kitchen eating breakfast. Follow me."

"Viper!" Matthew yelled. The second he saw Mike's best friend walk into the kitchen, he jumped out of the kitchen chair and rushed over, leaping into Viper's arms.

Viper squatted down and scooped him up happily. "What's up, buddy?" Matthew wrapped his arms and legs around Viper like a monkey and squeezed.

"I haven't seen you in a long time." Matthew said.

"I know, buddy. I'm sorry about that," Viper responded. "Look at how big your sister got." He walked over and knelt down toward Maura, who grinned a huge grin up at him. "Whoa! She has teeth!"

"Yep." I laughed. "A few of them. She bites hard too."

"Momma,"—Matthew turned to me—"I'm done eating. Can I go play?"

"Sure, baby," I said as he squirmed out of Viper's arms and disappeared down the hall.

"Wow. He doesn't stop moving, does he?" Viper ran his hands through his wet hair.

"Or talking." I laughed. "Pull up a seat. If I stop feeding her for too long, it gets pretty loud in here." I barely had the spoon off the plate and she already had her mouth open like a little bird.

The wooden chair made a loud noise as it scraped across the kitchen floor. Viper sat down and sighed. I waited for him to fill me in on why he was there, but he didn't start talking. After a minute of awkward silence, I set the bowl down and turned to face him. He had a pained look on his face as he stared into the family room.

"Is it weird being here?" I finally asked.

He jumped a little, as though he'd forgotten I was even there.

"Kinda." He shrugged. "It's just tough."

I offered up a small smile. "Tell me about it."

"That's actually why I'm here, to talk to you about Mike." He cleared his throat. "First of all, I want to apologize . . . for what happened."

"Viper—"

"Don't, please. Just let me get it out." He scooted his chair a little closer. "Everyone keeps telling me that it was an accident and I, more than anyone, know that it was, but it still doesn't change the outcome. I just need you to know how truly sorry, from the bottom of my heart, I am. I would give anything to take his place."

My throat felt tight as my eyes welled up with tears. "I appreciate it, Viper, but the apology is completely unnecessary. It was an accident. I know how much you loved him, and I totally know how much he loved you. It's just an all-around shitty situation."

I walked over and grabbed a tissue from the box on my kitchen counter.

"That's not the only apology I owe you." He sighed.

I narrowed my eyes at him and sat back down. "What do you mean?"

"Something you don't know is that when I went into his room . . . to say good-bye . . . I made a promise to him to help you and the kids with whatever you could possibly need until Maura is eighteen years old, longer if you needed it."

My heart sank. I was completely blown away by his gesture to my husband. "You said that?"

He nodded. "And here he's been gone a few months already and I haven't even come by once. I feel like a dick." He looked down the hall toward the playroom and cringed. "Sorry."

I looked back at the hall and realized he was worried about Matthew hearing him swear. "Oh, don't worry about him. When the *Ninja Turtles* are on, he doesn't hear much else."

"I love those guys too," he said with a crooked smile. "Anyway, I feel like I've let him down all over again, and I let you down too, even though you didn't know about the promise. Still, I knew about it and I'm sorry."

"Viper, it's okay." I reached out and gently rubbed his hand. "What brought all this on? I mean, why today?"

He shrugged and stared down at his hands. "Someone asked me yesterday what kind of man I was and what kind of man I wanted to be. All I could think about was this promise that I'd broken. I thought about it all night. I couldn't sleep." He finally looked up at me. "I almost texted you at three in the morning, but then I realized that was a jackass thing to do."

"Oh, I was probably awake anyway. I don't sleep very well these days." I sighed.

"I'll have to remember that." He laughed nervously. "Anyway . . . is there anything I can help with? Anything at all I can do to make this easier on you?"

"That really is sweet of you, but we're getting by. One long-ass day at a time."

"All right." He stood up and shoved his hands into his jeans pockets like a nervous teenager. "Well, I'm not gonna take up any more of your day. Plus, I need a nap after my long night. You have my number now." He nodded toward my cell phone on the counter and looked me straight in the eye. "Please call me if you think of anything at all that you need, Michelle. And I'm going to check on you from time to time, if that's okay?"

"I would like that." I smiled sincerely at him. "Thanks for coming by, Viper. This was unexpected but very nice." He started to walk past me to the front door, and I don't know what came over me, but I reached out and wrapped my arms around him. I think I just needed to be close to someone else who'd been close to Mike. He took a shaky breath and hugged me back, tight. We stood like that for a couple seconds until Maura started yelling because she was out of pancakes.

Viper laughed and pulled back, bending down to kiss the top of her head. "I get pissed when I'm out of food too, little one." He stood up and called down the hall, "Hey, ninja turtle head, get out here and give me a hug good-bye!"

Matthew came flying around the corner, sprinting straight for Viper. They hugged each other for a long time too. "Are you gonna come back soon?" Matthew asked.

"You want me to come back?"

Matthew nodded furiously.

"You got it, buddy. I'll come back very soon." He leaned in and closed his eyes as he kissed Matthew's forehead. He set Matthew down, waved at me one more time, and slipped out the door.

Matthew smiled the whole rest of the day.

Chapter *19*

"**W**HOA! WHAT THE FUCK?" BRODY froze in the doorway of the weight room and stared at me. "Am I seeing things?"

"Shut up, asshole." I glared at him in the mirror while I continued my bicep curls.

"Not only are you here,"—he walked toward me—"but you're here *earlier* than me? I feel like I'm in *The Twilight Zone* right now."

I dropped the dumbbells onto the rack and grabbed my towel to wipe the sweat off my face, ignoring him completely.

He walked over and sat on the bench next to me, dropping his bag on the floor. "You know I'm just giving you shit, right? I'm happy to see you here."

"Thanks."

"Like, *really* happy."

"I heard you the first time." I laughed.

"I'm guessing the sit-down you had with Collins went well, then?"

I realized then just how much I'd shut Brody out over the last couple months. He had no idea about my meeting and what I was being required to do. A year ago, we wouldn't have gone a day without talking, let alone a week or more.

"Uh, it went okay." I looked around the room to make sure no one was within earshot. "The big wigs are making me see a therapist."

He lifted his eyebrows and his eyes grew huge. "For real?"

"Yep." I nodded.

"Yikes." Brody shook his head. "That's gonna be interesting."

"I've already seen her."

"*Her?*"

"Her."

"Holy shit. Poor girl. It's like feeding a baby antelope to a hungry lion."

I picked the dumbbells up off of the rack and started lifting again. "It's actually been okay. I kinda like her."

"You like her, or you *like* her?"

"Oh, she's hot as hell, and I would've fucked her senseless, but I can't for two reasons." I puffed my cheeks out as I finished my set. "First, she's engaged. Second, she read me like a fucking book and knew my game before I could even start playing it. This chick is a serious mind reader."

"Wow. Lawrence Finkle has met his match. Who would've thought?" He stood up, scooped his bag up off the floor, and flung it over his shoulder. "Hey!" His eyes flashed up to mine. "Speaking of chicks, guess what?"

"What?"

"We're having another girl!" He smiled proudly at me.

"Seriously?" I turned to face him. "Does your dick not know how to make boys or what?"

Brody picked the damp towel up off the rack and threw it at my face. "Just say congratulations, asshole."

"Congratulations, asshole," I joked.

He rolled his eyes and turned toward the door. "I'm gonna

grab a bite to eat after I'm done with my workout. Wanna join me?"

"Thanks, but I can't. I have . . . plans."

He turned to face me. "With the mind reader?"

I nodded.

He stood there and stared at me for another second before grinning. "Proud of you, brother."

"Proud of you too . . . big daddy."

After workouts, I showered quickly and hustled to Dr. Roberts's office, getting there with only one minute to spare. I flipped the light switch and took my phone out, shooting a quick text to Michelle.

> Hey. Just checking on you to see if you need anything.

The minute I hit send, the door opened and Dr. Roberts stood smiling at me in the doorway. "You've been on time twice in a row now. I'm impressed." She waved me in cheerfully.

"Don't get used to it. I can almost feel myself getting ready to oversleep," I teased as I walked past her, silencing my phone and shoving it into my back pocket.

"Ha ha." She sat in the chair across from me. "So, how was your weekend?"

"It was good."

"Did you do anything exciting?"

"Not really."

She turned her head to the side and looked at me out of the corner of her eye. "I feel like there might be something more to that 'not really.' Why don't you tell me about it?"

"There's really nothing to tell." I shrugged. "I talked to someone I haven't talked to in a long time, went to the grocery store, got laid, worked out—"

"Wait, wait, wait." She closed her eyes and shook her head, trying to process everything I'd just thrown out there. "You talked to an old friend—"

"Well," I interrupted, "more like a friend of a friend. It was Mike's wife."

"Mike. *The* Mike?"

I nodded.

"Wow. How did that come about?"

"I thought about what you said, all night long, actually. I couldn't stop thinking about it. About what kind of man I was and what kind of man I wanted to be." I paused.

"And . . ."

I cleared my throat. "And I don't want to be the kind of guy that makes promises and doesn't keep them. I know that guy. He sucks."

"Good! I'm proud of you for being proactive about this. How did it go?"

"Um . . . okay. It was hard at first, being in that house. Being with her. All of it. But it ended well. It ended really well."

Life was weird. If someone had told me a month ago that I'd be sitting in a therapist's office, spilling my guts, and actually enjoying it, I would have told that person they were off their fucking rocker. But I couldn't deny it. If any good was going to come out of this thing with Mike, then it was going to be a brand new Viper. A better Viper.

She was leaning forward in her chair with her elbows resting on her knee, listening closely. "Tell me more. What did you say? What did she say?"

"First, I apologized for what happened to Mike, then I told her about what I promised him in the hospital room. I told her I felt awful that I hadn't contacted her at all and then I asked if she needed anything."

The corners of her mouth turned downward and her eyebrows dipped low as she shook her head slowly. "You know, for someone who tries so hard to be a badass and keep people at arm's length, you really are a great guy."

"I'm not great," I denied, annoyed that she was praising someone like me. "Did you miss the part where I told you I had a one-night stand? I went to my favorite bar, for the second time in a week, in an attempt to talk the waitress into coming home with me. She turned me down—again—so I set my sights on another innocent woman. A woman who didn't know who I was or what I do for a living. She simply thought I was cute. I brought her home, fucked her brains out, gave her cab money, and sent her on her way. She left her number in hopes that I would call her again. Instead, I tossed it into my kitchen drawer on top of the other five hundred or so scraps of paper with phone numbers on them." I rolled my eyes. "Yeah, real great guy. I'll be back. I gotta piss." I got up and stomped out of Dr. Roberts's office, down the hall to a bathroom near the elevator.

I didn't have to piss.

I needed out of that room.

One minute I was okay with talking and working some things out, and the next I wanted to leave and never go back in there. I didn't deserve praise, certainly not from someone like her. I was a heartless bastard. I pulled my phone out of my pocket to check how much longer I had to sit in that room and noticed I had a text . . . from Michelle.

M: Hey. Thanks so much for asking, but nope . . . we're good. :)

That text calmed me more than any mindless fuck ever could. I'd done what I was supposed to do. I'd followed through, for once. Gripping the side of the counter, I stared at my reflection in the mirror. The reflection of a man who was desperately trying to change, trying to find himself but didn't know how.

This therapist is a gift, you fuckhead. Don't mess this up. Listen to her.

I slowly walked back to her office. She was waiting for me, sitting in the exact same spot she had been in when I'd had a tantrum and left. The leather crinkled as I sat back down and took a deep breath. "Sorry about that."

"Don't apologize," she said softly. "Don't ever apologize for how you're feeling. I'm never going to tell you how you're feeling is wrong or that you should feel a different way about something. Your feelings are yours and yours alone."

"You just said the word 'feelings' like twelve times in three sentences," I teased, trying to lighten the mood. "Here's the thing . . . I don't know what's going on with me. Six months ago, I was happy. I was playing amazing hockey, had the best friends in the world, fucking whoever I wanted . . . life was great. In one stupid moment, it all changed, and now I can't get that happiness back. I don't remember what happy feels like anymore. Everything is dark and dreary, and even when I'm balls-deep inside a woman I just met, I'm not happy. She's just a thing. Just something I'm using to fill a void and try and find a moment of happiness, but it doesn't work anymore."

"Wow." Dr. Roberts stared at me. "That was intense, Viper. You know yourself better than most people. Most people don't know that they aren't happy. Most people don't admit that they're using drugs or alcohol or sex to cope."

"Wait." My head was spinning so fast I couldn't catch it. "You lost me."

"You use sex the same way some people use drugs and alcohol. I'm not saying you're addicted because you're not out getting hookers or masturbating excessively, that I know of, but you definitely use it as a distraction from dealing with whatever it is you're going through."

"No way. That's bullshit. I've always had one-night stands and sex with strangers."

Okay, saying that out loud sounds a little strange.

"How many women would you say you've slept with in your lifetime?"

I raised one eyebrow at her without saying a word.

"Okay, scratch that. How many one-night stands would you

guess you averaged a week *before* the accident?"

Am I really sitting in a therapist's office trying to calculate the average number of women I fuck per week?

"One, maybe two typically."

"Okay, and since the accident?"

"Three to five."

Her eyes grew slightly bigger when she heard that number.

I shrugged. "I'm just being honest."

"No, I'm glad you are. Viper, don't you see? You're out there trying desperately to find your next fix so that you don't have to deal with what's really happening inside of you."

I stood up and started pacing the small room, rubbing my temples with my fingers. "Well how the fuck do I fix that?"

"Do you trust me?"

I stopped walking and spun to face her. "Fuck."

"Do. You. Trust. Me?" she repeated, emphasizing each word like it was its own sentence.

"Two weeks ago, I didn't know you existed." I strolled over and plopped back down on the couch.

She crossed her arms over her chest and raised an eyebrow at me, clearly waiting for my answer.

"Yes, I trust you." I sighed, nervous as fuck about what she was going to say next.

"Good. Then I need seven days from you."

"Huh?"

"Seven days. I need you to completely abstain from sex for seven days."

"You're out of your fucking mind."

"Maybe, and maybe not. Can you just try it? It's one week."

"Sure. I'll just call my friend Brody over to nail boards over my doors and windows so I can't leave." I covered my face with my hands and sighed again.

"Calm down, drama queen. I didn't say you couldn't eat for a week, I simply said no sex."

"Wait, can I—"

"And no sex acts. No oral—giving or receiving—no petting, no making out, nothing. And I want you to go to the bar where you said you normally pick up women, at least once."

Petting?

"Petting?"

She tilted her head back and forth. "You know . . . caressing, touching, all of that."

"You're trying to say I can't touch any tits?"

"Yes, that's what I'm saying."

The light by the door flipped on before I could protest and tell her she was crazy—again.

Her face lit up. "Perfect timing!" She sprang from her chair and went over to open the exit door for me. "Seven days. You can do it."

I'm glad one of us thinks so.

"Wait,"—I was almost through the door when I remembered to ask something—"can I rough up the suspect by myself?"

She frowned at me. "What suspect?"

"Ya know, can I charm the snake? Unclog the drain? Slap the sausage?"

I wished I had a video camera on her face as she realized what I was talking about. Her eyes bulged and she pressed her lips together tightly as she pushed me through the door. "Good-bye, Lawrence."

I swear I heard her laugh on the other side of the door as she closed it behind me and I walked away.

Chapter
20

THE FIRST FOUR DAYS HAD been easy. I hadn't thought about my dick except when I'd held it to piss. On day five, the Viking started talking to me. He was twitchy and ready to play. Ignoring it became harder and harder, literally. I was trying to settle into a new normal that concentrated on something other than where I was going to find a woman for the night. My "fix," as Dr. Roberts called it.

One of the positives of my new normal was my contact with Michelle. I'd remembered to text her every morning when I woke up and ask how her and the kids were and if she needed anything. Every day she responded the same way.

> M: Thanks, but so far, so good. :)

She didn't need me and that was okay. As long as she knew I was there, just in case, I could sleep at night. I'd visited Gam not once but twice, and I hadn't missed one workout. In fact, I'd been putting in extra time at the gym. All in all, it'd been a great week, but I still had the weekend to go before I could strut into Dr. Roberts's office Tuesday afternoon and prove to her that I could go a week without sex, standing on my head. And . . . one of Dr. Roberts's stipulations was that I had to leave the house and go out once, but she hadn't said anything in the rules about not bringing backup, so I called Brody and Kacie to have them

155

meet me at Stumpy's.

I got there before anyone else and grabbed our usual table in the corner. The saloon doors opened and Portland came striding over to the table with a big smile on her face.

"Hey, you!" She beamed.

"Hey."

I didn't know how to act. Typically, I would have jumped up and hugged her and said something inappropriate, but it was only day five, and I had to behave.

Portland tilted her head to the side and chewed on the end of her pen. "You okay?"

"Yeah." I tried to sound as casual as possible. "Why?"

"I don't know, you just seem different."

"Nah, I'm good. Just tired. It's been a long week."

"Okay." She smiled. "You want a root beer?"

"Sure."

"All right. I'll be right back."

She turned around and had just disappeared into the kitchen when suddenly, two little hands covered my eyes.

"Guess who?" a female asked, but it was clear she was trying to disguise her voice.

"Uh . . ." I was stumped. I'd picked up so many girls at this bar it literally could have been anyone. "Is it . . ."

"Your worst nightmare!" A man laughed. I knew that voice for certain. I pulled the hands down and Brody was already sitting across the table from me, cracking open a peanut. Still holding her hands, I looked to my left and saw Kacie.

"Did I get ya?" She grinned, wrapping her arms around me.

I nodded and laughed. "You totally did. I had no idea who the fuck it was."

As Kacie came around to sit at the table, I noticed she wasn't alone. Michelle followed behind her.

"Hey!" I was excited to see her.

"Hey yourself, stranger." She moved in for a quick hug too. "Long time no talk, huh?"

"Yeah, really. It's been what, almost eight hours?"

"You guys talked today?" Kacie stared back and forth between the two of us. "When?"

Michelle gave me a small smile before glancing over at Kacie. "Viper has been really sweet. He's been texting me every morning to see if the kids and I are okay or if we need anything."

Brody's and Kacie's faces mirrored each other. Complete shock.

"What the hell are you making those faces for?" I snapped at them.

"I'm just stunned to hear someone call you *sweet*. I don't think that's ever happened before," Brody joked. I picked up a peanut and threw it at him.

Kacie's face lit up as she looked past me and started waving. I turned in my seat, just enough to see Darla's smiling face walking toward us, dragging a man along behind her.

"Hey, everyone!" Darla said cheerfully as she walked up, looking at everyone except me. "Kacie, Brody, you guys remember Neil. Michelle and Viper, this is Neil, my boyfriend." She motioned toward the guy in a suit standing just behind her. He stepped forward and held his hand out for me to shake. I looked down at it and back up at Darla, who was biting her lip with her brows drawn in together, clearly anxious about my reaction.

Grasping Neil's hand tight in my own, I shook his hand and smiled. "Hi, Neil. Nice to meet you."

He smiled back, showing off a row of perfect white teeth that looked more like pieces of Chiclets gum than actual teeth. "Nice to meet you too, Viper. I'm a huge fan."

Wonderful.

He turned and shook Michelle's hand, offering her the same fake-ass smile. Darla took a step behind him and looked to me

157

for my approval. Instead, I rolled my eyes and pretended to gag.

"Why don't you guys have a seat?" Kacie asked, scooting her stool closer to Brody to make more room. Portland came back from the kitchen carrying my root beer and set it in front of me.

"Is that root beer?" Neil laughed, looking down at my bottle.

"Yeah," I said firmly, staring him in the eye as Darla rested her head on his shoulder and cringed.

"What can I get everyone else?" Portland asked as she took out her pen and pad of paper.

Brody held up his index finger. "Beer."

Michelle pointed at him. "Copy that."

"Make it three," Darla added.

"Do you have sparkling water?" Neil asked Portland.

"I have regular water," Portland answered innocently, "but I can put ice in it so it sparkles."

"Never mind. I'll take a beer also." Neil looked annoyed with her, and that annoyed me.

"Can I get a coffee, Anna?" Kacie asked.

"Sure. We don't have any made, but I'll get a fresh pot started for you." Portland smiled at her. "Be right back, guys."

"Coffee? Now?" Brody looked at the time on his phone. "You're gonna be up half the night."

"Yeah, well the girls had that birthday party at the jumpy house place after school, and if I don't get something to keep me up, I'm going to be sleeping on this table within five minutes." She stuck her tongue out at him playfully and squealed as Brody caught it between his lips. While Brody and Kacie slurped each other's faces off, I looked to my left to see Darla and Neil leaned in close, nose to nose as they laughed about something quietly. I sighed and stared straight ahead at the same time Michelle looked back at me and shrugged, a tight smile on her lips. We both felt it, the awkwardness of being the oddball out. I wasn't worried about being the oddball. I was used to being alone, and it didn't scare me. But she was new to this alone thing, and I was

concerned that everyone else so obviously coupling off would weird her out. I smiled back at her and gestured over toward the pool table area. She nodded eagerly and stood from the table.

"I didn't know you played pool." She looked up at me and grinned as we made our way across the bar.

"I don't,"—I shrugged, pointing straight ahead—"but I like music, and there's a kickass jukebox in the corner past the pool tables. I figured we could pick out a few songs while the lovebirds all calm down."

She turned and looked at the jukebox in the corner, with its pink and green neon lights shining bright. Her eyes lit up. "Good call! We can dance while they—"

"Whoa." I stopped walking, holding my hands up in front of me.

Once she realized I was no longer in step with her, she stopped too and spun on her heel to face me. "What?"

"Viper doesn't dance."

She put her hands on her hips and pursed her lips together. "But Viper talks about himself in the third person?"

"Sometimes Viper does . . . as long as he's not dancing."

Rolling her eyes, she grabbed my hand and continued dragging me over to the jukebox. "Dancing is easy. You just wiggle."

"Bullshit," I teased. "It's a lot of pressure. You have to wiggle to the beat of the music and hope you don't look like a complete fucking moron while you're doing it and people are staring at you."

"Since when does Viper not like people staring at him?" She nudged me with her elbow as she flipped through the songs on the jukebox.

I took a couple dollars out of my pocket and slid them into the machine. "Since Viper learned that he can't wiggle to the music very well."

Michelle punched a couple of buttons on the jukebox and

turned to face me, leaning her hip against the machine. "Come on. I don't believe that. You're always talking about your sexual conquests and how many women you've been with, but a little thing like dancing freaks you out?"

"Yeah, it freaks me out!" I defended playfully. "I fuck in the dark and most of the time, hopefully, she has her eyes closed. So if I make a stupid face or move my arm in an awkward way, no one else is watching."

"Speaking of sexual conquests . . ." She craned her neck to look over my shoulder, back toward our table. I glanced back, following her stare. Portland was at our table with a big round tray carrying all the drinks.

I turned back to Michelle. "What? Portland? I've never fucked her."

"But you've wanted to."

"Hell yes."

"Why?"

"She's hot. Scorching fucking hot."

"Really?" Lifting up onto her tippy toes to get a better look at Portland, she took a deep breath and puffed her cheeks out.

"Why are you asking? Where is this coming from?" I asked.

"I was married to Mike for seven years, together for nine. I haven't dated since I was practically her age, and I'm *not* ready now, but I loved being in love—" She paused, her eyes lowering sadly to the floor. "—and someday, years from now, I'm hoping maybe it'll happen again."

I didn't respond.

I didn't know *how* to respond.

I just stared at her as the guilt flooded over me again, filling up my lungs, making it damn near impossible for me to take a breath. She would have to start all over again one day, and it was my fault.

"So anyway,"—she cleared her throat and lifted her face back to me—"I was just wondering what men considered hot these days. Guess I'll have to up my game, maybe get a tattoo and a boob job."

As she giggled at herself, the corners of her eyes sparkled . . . and my heart broke.

Chapter
21

Michelle

MY HEAD THROBBED LIKE IT was resting on a bass drum instead of a pillow as I laid in bed, silently begging my headache to go away.

Your own fault, Michelle. That's what you get for mixing beer and cocktails.

I hadn't had a hangover in years. Actually, I couldn't even remember the last time, and when I tried hard to think about it, the room spun faster. Thankfully, Maura had decided it was a good day to sleep in, so I was able to snuggle in bed with Matthew a little longer than usual.

"Momma!" Matthew whispered loudly.

My eyes popped open, blinking over and over as my son slowly came into focus. His face was only a couple inches from mine and he was staring right at me with his huge blue eyes. His father's eyes. "Yes, sweetheart?" I asked as I rubbed his soft cheek with my fingers.

"Stop snoring. I can't hear the *Ninja Turtles*."

"Sorry, baby." I rolled over to face the other way, smiling to myself as he snuggled into my back.

A glowing light on my cell phone caught my attention from the nightstand. I grabbed it and slid the lock across the screen blinking against the brightness of it. . My daily text message from Viper.

> V: How are you today? Need anything?

I noticed he'd sent it an hour earlier at quarter to seven, so I decided against my typical *thanks-but-no-thanks* text.

> What the heck were you doing awake at 6:45???
> And other than an awful, head-crushing headache
> for me, we're okay over here. Thanks.

I tucked the phone under my pillow, pretty sure that he'd probably gone back to sleep and wouldn't answer for a while. To my surprise, my phone buzzed just a few seconds later.

> V: I don't know. Couldn't sleep. I'm not surprised
>   about that headache. You were feeling pretty
>   good last night. Hopefully you can just lay
>   around today and chill while it goes away.

I tried to force my brain to think.
What day is it? Shit. Sunday.

> I wish. Matthew has storytime at the library today.

> V: Can I take him?

My eyes glazed over as I stared at my phone, convinced that my brain had somehow mixed up the letters of what he'd really said and I was reading them wrong.

> No, that's okay. You don't have to.

V: I know I don't have to, but I want to. I haven't seen my little buddy in a week anyway. Please?

I rolled back over toward Matthew. His little profile was tinted blue from the light on the TV.

"Matthew?"

His head turned toward me, but his eyes stayed glued to the screen.

"Matthew, listen to mommy for a minute." I waited a second for him to finally look at me. "You have storytime at the library today, and Viper was wondering if he could take you."

His eyes grew as big as I'd ever seen them as his mouth dropped open. "Yes! Yes! Yes!" he cheered, pumping his little arms in the air. Suddenly, his excitement vanished and he looked at me sadly.

Oh no. Here it comes.

"Um . . . Momma?"

"Yes, honey?"

The knot in my stomach was the size of a basketball. Was this the sad face I would have to deal with for the rest of my life? This disappointment, this devastation of not having his father around?

"You're gonna stay home, right? Just me and Viper are going?"

I stifled a laugh. "Yes, baby. Unless you *want* me to go."

He shook his head furiously, clearly wanting me to stay away. "Just Viper. I'm gonna show him the Lego table."

"I bet he'd love that." The excited look on his face warmed me on the inside. I hadn't seen him smile that big since . . . well, last time Viper was over. "Hang on a sec, buddy."

I rolled away from him and grabbed my phone to text Viper back but was surprised to see I had another text waiting.

> V: C'mon, pleeeeease? Our reading level is
> probably the same so we'd be a perfect match.

I shook my head, smiling to myself as I typed out my response.

> Well, when you put it that way, how can I say no?
> Storytime starts at 11.

As I hit the send button on my phone, Maura started to fuss on the monitor.

"Matthew?"

Again, his body turned to face me, but his eyes were left behind on the TV. After a minute of me not saying anything, he looked at me, wondering what the holdup was.

"Maura's finally up and Viper is picking you up in a couple hours. What do you say we go have some breakfast?"

He nodded excitedly as he jumped off the bed, doing a ninja kick in midair, and ran down the hall to Maura's room.

I had just finished cleaning up breakfast and barely had Matthew dressed in his khakis and blue plaid button-down shirt when the doorbell rang.

"It's Viper!" Matthew's legs moved so fast that he ran in place on the hardwood floor for a second before finally gaining traction and bolting toward the front door.

"Calm down." I chuckled as I followed him to the front of the house. "He's not coming for another hour."

"It *is* him!" he squealed as we got closer.

Viper waved through the glass of the front door.

Suddenly I worried that I'd maybe told him the wrong time. I frowned as I opened the front door. He was standing on the porch carrying a cardboard drink holder with different cups in it.

"Viper!" Matthew threw his arms around Viper's leg and

squeezed tight, closing his eyes.

Viper reached down with his free hand and rustled Matthew's hair. "What's up, champ?"

"I feel horrible. Storytime doesn't start until eleven. I must have told you the wrong time," I apologized.

"No, you told me eleven. I just thought I'd come by early and bring these." He held the cups up.

Confused, I looked at the drinks in his hand. "What is that?"

"I don't know what you drink, so I brought a coffee, a hot tea, an orange juice, and a chocolate shake."

I pulled my brows in tight and shifted my glance from the cups back up, eyeing him skeptically. "Chocolate shake?"

He grinned and shrugged his shoulders. "I got that one for me, but if you want it, it's yours."

"That's okay. I'm not really a chocolate-before-noon kind of girl anyway." I laughed and took the cardboard holder from him, carrying it to the kitchen. He scooped Matthew up into his arms and followed along behind me.

"Viper, have you ever been to the library?" Matthew's voice squeaked with excitement.

"I have, but not in a really, really long time. You'll have to show me around, okay?"

Matthew was so close to Viper's face they were practically touching noses. "I will. They have this cool Lego table there and the top is all Lego stuff and you can build right on the table and there's this net right in the middle of the table and they have Legos right in the table for you to use!" Matthew rambled without taking a breath.

"Really? Did you eat yet?" Viper asked.

Matthew nodded.

I took the coffee out of the cardboard holder and poured cream into it as Viper turned toward me, whispering under his breath, "Is it okay if we go early?"

"Sure." I shrugged and licked the cream off of the spoon

before turning around and dropping it in the sink. "The library opens at nine on Sundays."

Viper looked back and Matthew and tossed him up in the air. "Wanna go now?" he asked excitedly.

Matthew could hardly contain himself. He threw his arms around Viper's head and squeezed again. "Yes!" he yelled.

I took a quick sip of the warm, delicious coffee and started toward the garage door. "I'm gonna grab his car seat. Can you keep an eye on Maura for me?"

He looked at me for a quick second and nodded before Matthew continued going on and on about the Lego table again. I hustled out to my minivan and slid the door open, reaching into the backseat to unhook Matthew's booster. The garage door creaked as I shut it and walked back through the mudroom to the kitchen.

"What's the matter, huh?" I heard Viper ask in a soft voice.

I rounded the corner from the mudroom and he was standing next to the highchair Maura was just in, which now sat empty. His back was to me, and I could see that he was holding her. She sat up in his arms, looking him straight in the eye with a frown on her face.

"What's wrong? Why are you fussing?" he asked again.

I stopped and listened with my hand over my mouth, trying not to laugh out loud. Why was it so funny when grown men tried their hardest to do a baby voice?

Maura reached out and grabbed both of his cheeks in her chubby little hands and shrieked while squeezing as hard as she could.

"Ow, ow, ow, ow." He laughed as he tried to pry her hands from his face.

I couldn't contain my laugh anymore and spit all over my hand as I finally let it out. Viper turned to face me, rubbing his cheek with one hand.

"Watch out for that grip," I warned, still chuckling as I walked through the kitchen with Matthew's seat. "She gets a hold and doesn't let go."

"Holy sh—cow," he caught himself. "Who knew those tiny fingers could be so deadly?"

"You're a hockey player," I joked. "Treat her like one too. You gotta try and predict her movements and dodge them. I'm gonna go buckle this into your car, okay?"

He nodded, keeping a watchful eye on Maura's quick hands.

I went out to his car and opened the door, pleasantly surprised by what I saw. I don't know why I was expecting Viper's car to look like a disgusting frat house on wheels, but it was the exact opposite. Actually, it made *my* van look like a disaster.

"Hey, stranger!" I heard someone call from behind me.

I set Matthew's seat down and stood up, closing the car door. My neighbor Jodi was walking over.

"Hey! How *are* you?" I wrapped my arms around her when she got to me.

She squeezed me tight. "Me? How are *you?* I feel like I haven't seen you in forever."

I pulled back and sighed. "I know. I've been a bit of a recluse, just . . . getting used to everything, ya know? Trying to form a new normal."

"Yeah." She reached out and rubbed my arm, tilting her head to the side as she looked at me with sad, sympathetic eyes. "How have things been? Are you doing okay?"

"You know what?" I glanced back toward the house, feeling bad that I'd ditched Viper inside with the kids. "Do you wanna come in for a bit? We can catch up?"

"I would love to!"

"Whose car is that anyway?" she asked as we walked through my front door.

As we walked down the hall to the kitchen, Viper walked

across, bouncing Maura up and down gently as he cupped the back of her head and made silly faces at her.

Jodi grabbed my arm and stopped me. "Who is *that?*"

"His name is Viper. He was Mike's teammate and best friend."

"Holy shit, girl, you better introduce me."

"Jodi, you have a boyfriend." I laughed and shook my head.

"Yeah, but he's not here and that guy is *fine.*" She grabbed my hand and pulled me into the kitchen behind her.

"There's Mom," Viper said to Maura in that goofy baby voice again. "We thought maybe she was gonna run away and leave us fending for ourselves, didn't we? Uncle Viper was wondering how the heck he was gonna feed you since he doesn't have those things she has."

"Tits!" Matthew yelled proudly.

Viper's eyes shot up to Matthew and quickly over to mine as I glared at him. Jodi's hand flew up to her mouth to stifle her giggle.

"Ya know,"—I shook my head and tried not to laugh—"I can't get the kid to remember a nursery rhyme that I taught him last week, but he can't seem to forget the one word that you taught him months ago."

Viper's husky laugh echoed throughout the whole first floor as Jodi nudged me and cleared her throat. "Oh, Viper, this is my neighbor Jodi. Jodi, this is Viper."

"Nice to meet you," Jodi murmured in the phoniest voice I'd ever heard her use.

"Likewise," he said quickly before turning his attention back to Maura, who was completely enthralled with watching him at that point. "I'm gonna give you back to Mommy now because I'm taking your brother to the library, and then to the bar."

I cocked my hip to the side and crossed my arms over my chest, glaring at him again.

He peeked at me out of the corner of his eye and then

continued, "Just kidding. The bars don't open until noon on Sunday." Laughing at himself, he walked over and gently handed Maura to me.

"Try not to get kicked out of the library, okay?" I said, half teasing, half serious.

"Hmmm . . ." The corners of his mouth turned down as he looked up toward the ceiling. "I've been kicked out of a lot of places, but never a library. Matthew, come on! Let's make this day interesting!"

"Yay!" Matthew jumped up and before I could argue, they were out the door.

Maura lay in my arms with her eyes glazed over, sucking her thumb.

"This one is just about to fall asleep," I whispered as Jodi sat at the kitchen table. "I'm gonna lay her down and we can talk for a bit, okay? Make yourself at home."

It didn't take long for Jodi and I to step into stride like friends often do. She was doing a fantastic job of making me laugh with all of her inappropriate stories about her younger, much younger, boyfriend, Vince.

"Wait a second . . . he proposed? Like on his knee? With a ring?" I asked with my mouth agape. Jodi was just a little older than me, in her midthirties, and had already been married and divorced. Twice.

"Yep." She nodded, sounding almost embarrassed about it. "In front of his whole family. What was I supposed to say?"

"So wait, are you going through with it?"

"Why not?" she shrugged. "He's hot. He makes good money. The sex is off-the-charts amazing. Might as well go for it and see what happens. They say third time's a charm."

"You're insane, you know that?" I laughed as I walked over to the counter and grabbed the coffee pot to refill her cup. "Have you guys talked about this wedding at all?"

"Yeah," she sighed, leaning her chin on her hand. "I was hoping to go to the Bahamas or something for one of those destination weddings, but he wants a church, tux, flowers, DJ, the whole nine yards."

I sat back down across from her. "Seriously?"

"Well, he's never been married. I can't take the wedding experience away from him just because I've already done it twice."

Licking my lips as I pinched them together, I stared down at my coffee cup.

"What?" she challenged.

I held my hands up in the air innocently and shook my head. "I didn't say a word."

"No, but you thought something. Spill it."

I looked back down at my coffee cup and ran my finger around the edge. "I was just thinking that maybe you should see if the bridal shop can give you some sort of VIP discount for being such a great return customer." I tried unsuccessfully to stifle my laugh.

"You're such a bitch." She reached over and smacked my leg.

We sat for a minute, laughing and enjoying the moment together without saying a word.

"Think about it," she added. "By the time you're ready to get married again, I'll be such a pro at wedding planning that you can actually pay me to do yours."

I shook my head sternly. "No way."

"Come on, I promise I'd do a good job."

"I wasn't saying no way about paying you, I was saying no way about getting married again."

Her lips parted and she frowned at me as I picked my coffee cup off the table and carried it over to the sink. "Why not?"

I turned to face her and shrugged, leaning back against the counter with my arms crossed. "I don't know. It seems silly. Will I date eventually? Maybe, but I just don't see the point in

marrying again."

"Michelle, you're young, you're hot, and you still have a lot of life left." Jodi stood up from the table and walked over, leaning against the counter next to me. "There's no reason for you to spend it alone."

"I don't know," I answered honestly, staring down at the floor. "Some days I'm great and I feel like, okay, I can do this. I can be a single mom and still give these kids the best life ever. And then the next day, I miss Mike so bad I feel like I can't breathe. There have been days where I've barely gotten out of bed."

Jodi wrapped her arm around my waist and laid her head on my shoulder, but didn't interrupt.

"And don't even get me started on nighttime," I continued. "It used to be my favorite. Mike and I would put the kids to bed and start off watching TV, but by the end of the night we were either having some deep conversation, wrestling, or making love on the floor in the family room. Sometimes all three in the same night." I sniffed and she squeezed me tighter. "I hate nighttime now. Once the kids go to bed, that's when the sadness peaks. I sit down here all alone reliving what we used to have. I hate it."

Jodi lifted her head and looked over at me. "Why don't you come get me? I would love to unwind with you at the end of the day, as long as there's wine."

"Thanks." I smiled. "But you have enough going on over there with Mr. Teenage Sex Maniac."

She rolled her eyes and hip bumped me. "He's not a teenager. Not for a couple years now."

We both laughed at the ridiculousness of what she'd just said.

"And now here I am, thirty years old and hungover so bad that my dead husband's best friend offered to take my son to storytime." I sighed heavily.

"Yeah, what's up with that? Fill me in." Jodi pulled her arm back and turned around to lean again the island, facing me this time.

"There's not really anything to tell. He was Mike's best friend, has been for a while, and I guess when Mike died—" I paused and swallowed hard. "—he promised him he'd look after us."

She pulled her brows in tight and narrowed her bright green eyes at me. "Why would he do that?"

"He, uh . . . was the one that caused the accident . . . kinda."

Jodi's hand flew up to her mouth as her eyes grew huge. "You're kidding me!"

I shook my head. "Nope. So he feels this . . . obligation . . . to make things right. And I appreciate it, but I don't need it. Today was the first time I texted back and took him up on one of his offers."

She dropped her hand from her mouth and frowned at me. "Offers?"

"Not really an offer, I guess, but he's been texting me every single morning to say hi and see if we need anything."

"Wait a minute." She cocked her head to the side and narrowed her eyes again. "That guy, that hot, beefy, tatted-up guy texts you every day to say 'good morning' and see if you need anything?"

My eyes shifted around the room as I nodded.

A tight smile spread across her lips. "That's the cutest thing I've ever heard."

I don't think it would have been physically possible to roll my eyes any more dramatically than I did at that moment. "You're such a romantic. Not everything is a romantic gesture, Jodi. Some things are just that—things. Gestures."

Thankfully, before our conversation could go any further, the front door opened and Matthew came sprinting in.

"Hi, Miss Jodi! Mom, I had the best time!"

"Did you? I'm so glad." I pulled him against my leg for a hug.

"You should've seen it. We all had to sit criss cross applesauce on the friendship rug and Viper could hardly do it!" He threw his head back and laughed wildly. It felt so good to see joy on his face from something other than *Ninja Turtles* for once.

"Hey, in my defense," Viper bellowed playfully as he rounded the corner carrying Matthew's booster seat, "that rug is really small. The worst part was I was the only one in the room who didn't know what criss cross applesauce was. Matthew had to tell me."

Matthew walked over and stood next to Viper. "Can you take me again next time, Viper?"

"If that's okay with your mom, sure."

They both looked over at me with big puppy-dog eyes. "Fine by me." I shrugged.

Matthew threw his arms up and cheered as Viper held his fist out for Matthew to bump it. "It's a date, my man."

Chapter
22

"COME IN, COME IN!" DR. Roberts said excitedly, waving me into her office Monday morning. "I've been dying to hear how your week went."

I walked through the door, sat in my usual spot on the leather couch, and waited for her to take her seat across from me.

"So?" she said impatiently when I didn't start talking right away.

"You're the devil." I glared at her.

"Oh, come on!" She sighed and threw her hands in the air dramatically. "It couldn't have been *that* bad."

"It was fine for the first few days, then it got tough."

"What was the hardest part?"

The thirteen-year-old boy that lived deep inside of me started laughing at her word choice, and before I knew it, that laugh had traveled up my throat and out of my mouth.

Dr. Roberts frowned for a brief second, then shook her head and rolled her eyes. "Fine. What was the most *difficult* part?"

"Saturday night, for sure."

"Tell me more," she ordered as she stood up and walked over to the fridge to retrieve the two water bottles that typically kept us company during our meetings.

"Well, you made me go to the bar, remember?"

"I remember."

"That's like my *place*. That's where I go to meet people."

"People?"

"Women," I corrected myself.

"And . . . did you meet any women on Saturday?"

"Nope. You told me I couldn't."

"That's not true," she defended, shaking her head at me. "I said you couldn't have *sex* with any women, not that you couldn't *talk* to any women. I think talking to them actually would have been good for you, given you a bit more of a test."

"Portland was working. That fact alone was a test."

She leaned forward and grabbed her water bottle. "Who's Portland?"

"She's a waitress at that bar we always go to. I've been trying to get into her pants forever."

"Why?"

"Why what?"

"Why her?"

"Why anyone? She's hot."

"Here's what I'm wondering, though . . ." She paused and chewed on her bottom lip as she twirled a piece of her dark hair in her fingers. "From the things you've told me, I've gathered that you don't have a problem getting women to talk to you, or even go home with you at the end of the night. Is that a fair statement?"

I nodded once. "Sure."

"So, why doesn't it work with this woman? And if it doesn't work, why don't you give up and move on to someone else? Why keep chasing her?"

"Why . . . ask so many questions at once?" I joked.

Dr. Roberts clenched her jaw and inhaled loudly through her nose, clearly annoyed with me.

"I don't know, probably because I hate losing. I'm not used to being turned down, so when she doesn't fall for my lines, it pisses me off."

"Do you hit on her every single time you're there?"

"Pretty much, and when she finally comes to her senses and calls me, it'll be the most glorious day of my life."

"Okay, enough about Portland, for now. How was the rest of your weekend? Any other tests that I should know about?"

"Nope." I shook my head, thinking back. "Other than that it was pretty uneventful. Wait! Something did happen; not a test but still exciting in other areas."

"Fill me in."

"I went to Michelle's."

"Really? Was it a last-minute thing like last time or was this a planned visit?"

"Both, actually. She was out with all of us on Saturday night and then I sent her my daily check-in text on Sunday. Instead of just saying she was fine like she normally does, we chatted a little. She told me she had a headache, so I offered to take Matthew to storytime at the library."

"And?" She leaned forward in her chair, anxious to hear more.

"And . . . I took him to the library."

"How did that go?"

Thinking back to the weekend and my morning with Matthew, I struggled to contain my smile. "It was pretty cool. We sat on this big rug that looked like the Earth and sang songs, and the librarian read a couple of books. It was Space Day. Next week is On The Farm."

She jerked her head back in surprise. "You're going again?"

"Yep," I said confidently. "We got back to the house and he asked if I'd take him again next week. Michelle said yes so I'm all over it."

She stared at me with her mouth hanging open, not saying a

word.

"Stop looking at me like that." I laughed. "I told you, it was fun."

"Okay, okay. Enough about storytime or we aren't going to get anything accomplished today." She cleared her throat. "I'd like to try it one more time. Two weeks this time. Can you do that?"

"What? Why?" I snapped.

"Relax." She held her hands up calmly. "It's just something I want to try."

I bolted up from the couch in frustration and started pacing her office. "I don't get this. I don't get what this is supposed to teach me. Why do you care if I fuck or who I fuck?"

"This is something that might help you, Viper. It's not for my benefit."

"Fine," I groaned as I sat back down on the couch, shaking my head. "I'll try, but I'm not making any promises. I won't go looking for it, but should a situation present itself, I'm taking it."

After a mostly shitty meeting with Dr. Roberts, I needed a break. I needed to go where I could be myself and I wouldn't be judged for it.

I headed straight to Gam's.

She opened her front door, beaming when she saw me. "To what do I owe this surprise?"

"I missed my favorite old lady." I wrapped my arms around her and hugged her tight, lifting her off the floor just a little.

"Well, this old lady missed you too." I could tell she was smiling as she talked. "Come on in. I was just baking."

I set her down and pulled back, eyeing her skeptically. "You? Baking?"

"Okay, I was *thinking* about baking, but I was just about to pour myself a drink. Want one?"

"There she is!" I joked, following her to the kitchen. I noticed she was limping more than normal. I motioned toward her leg. "You okay?"

She waved me off. "I'm fine. Don't worry about me. What can I get you?"

"Do you have any root beer?" I grinned.

"Of course I do!" She winked at me. "I keep it stocked for surprises like this. She took a bottle of IBC root beer out of the fridge and set it on the table in front of me before turning back to the counter to mix her own drink. She was just about to sit down at the table across from me when she stopped and put her hand on her hip. "Actually, it's nice out. Wanna sit on the back deck instead?"

"Absolutely."

Gam's backyard was just as amazing as the front. Flowers of every color sat in planters in the corners of her deck and a dozen more birdhouses hung from the trees. Two turquoise Adirondack chairs I'd bought her a couple years back sat right in the middle of the deck overlooking the lake her house was on. It wasn't a big lake, certainly not as big as the one Kacie and Brody lived on, but it was big enough to have a boat out on, and she loved to sit and watch them and, of course, protect her birdhouses from those bastard squirrels.

"It *is* nice out today." I walked over and set my root beer on the small table that sat in between the chairs.

"You say that like it's the first time you've been outside all day. Don't tell me that you've just rolled out of bed."

"No, I was up early, actually," I said in my best know-it-all tone.

"Oh?" She sat down in one of the chairs and set her whiskey and water down next to my bottle. "What were you up so early for?"

Other than Coach Collins, his assistant Mia, the big wigs in the office, Brody, and Dr. Roberts herself, no one knew I was going there to see her on a semi-regular basis. I hadn't yet told

Gam about my meetings in general, and no way in hell was I *ever* going to tell her about the "restrictions" I'd been put on, but it was time to let her in . . . at least a little.

"I had an appointment with my therapist." I looked at her and waited for her reaction.

She looked over at me quickly with her dark brown eyes narrowed at me, her hand raised up to shield them from the sun so she could see me better. "A therapist? Seriously?"

I took a deep breath. For obvious reasons, Gam's opinions and judgments of me ran much deeper than anyone else's.

"Yes, seriously. The dickwads in the front office thought I was spiraling out of control with what happened with Mike, so they sent me to her. Oddly enough, we're talking about all sorts of things now. She's trying to make me better as a whole."

Her eyebrows lifted. "She?"

"Yeah. Dr. Roberts. You'd like her. She doesn't put up with any of my shit."

"Good, she shouldn't." She nodded. "You think that smile of yours can get you out of just about anything, and you're mostly right. At some point you needed to grow up and deal with life head-on, not hide in the weeds and wait for it to drive by before you showed your face again. You're good at that, Lawrence."

I'd just been schooled by my eighty-nine-year-old grandmother.

"I know. And I'm trying. You have to give me *some* credit."

"Okay, you win . . . for now." She smiled, staring out at the water. "How is this going to affect your season? Don't you start soon?"

"Yeah." I nodded. "We report back in two weeks, actually. I'm just going to have to work around my schedule. It is what it is. If it's important enough, you make time for it, right?"

Her head turned toward me again, eyeing me warily. "You're freaking me out talking like that. Knock it off."

She turned her head back toward the lake and closed her eyes as a small, tight smile appeared on her lips. I didn't say anything.

We just sat in the warm sun, enjoying the quiet together. In that moment, as in many other moments throughout my life, I wished she were my mother instead of my grandmother. She would have protected me.

Chapter
23

THE WEEK WENT BY FASTER than I remembered any other week going by in my whole life. My workouts and practices were priority number one, but I found that not concentrating on where my next woman would come from gave me a lot of extra time on my hands. I did a complete overhaul of my house, going through every cabinet and closet and getting rid of carfuls of shit I didn't need and didn't use anymore. How does one single guy accumulate so much junk anyway?

Before I knew it, it was Sunday. Library day. I'd still been texting Michelle every single morning asking how things were going, and most days it was the same answer, though once in awhile we'd chat for a minute too.

That morning, instead of my typical text, I sent a different one.

> See you at 9?

She answered almost immediately.

> M: Yep. Matthew hardly slept last night. He's so excited.

> Good. Tell him I am too. Any chance I could take him for lunch after?

M: Absolutely. It might change his excitement
into convulsions but I'm sure he'd really like
that. Thank you, Viper. This means more to me
than you know.

That last text made my day. Knowing that Matthew was so excited was one thing, but knowing that Michelle appreciated it brought everything full circle for me.

I told you, Mike. I told you I'd help, buddy. I'm trying.

Nine o'clock rolled around and I was standing on Michelle's porch pushing the doorbell. Like a herd of buffaloes charging through the house, Matthew came flying toward the front door from the kitchen with Michelle following right along behind him, shaking her head.

She laughed as she opened the door. "Seriously. This kid is nuts."

"What's up, buddy?" I cheered as excitedly as I could. Matthew's skinny little body jumped up toward me, completely trusting that I'd reach out and catch him. Of course I did.

"I can't wait. Today is On The Farm day. Remember?" he babbled excitedly, his eyes gleaming.

"How could I forget?" I answered, looking over at Michelle and winking.

She wrapped her arms around herself and smiled at me with closed lips.

"Did you tell him?" I asked her.

"Um . . ." She frowned at me and shook her head slightly, clearly confused about what I had asked.

"About after?"

Her eyes grew big. "Oh. That. No." She laughed. "He was already so excited about the library that if I'd told him about the second part, I would've had to lock him in his room all morning."

I turned my attention back to Matthew, who was staring a hole through me about two inches from my face.

"So, after the library today, how about we stop and get some lunch? I know this cool place that let's you open peanuts and throw the shells on the floor."

"No way!" Matthew whispered loudly, moving closer to my face, if that were even possible.

"You don't think much of personal space, do you, buddy?"

He pulled back and crinkled his little nose up. "What's that?"

"Never mind." I laughed. "You ready to go? Let's leave early so we can get a prime seat on that friendship rug."

"What's a prime seat?" he asked again.

Michelle covered her mouth with her hand and laughed quietly. "You'll learn," she joked as she shook her head and handed me Matthew's backpack.

I threw the backpack over my shoulder and we were out the door.

A couple hours later, we'd read one book about a calf who'd wandered away from his farm and couldn't find his way home, sang the longest version of "Old MacDonald" I'd ever heard, and done a dance where we all had to pretend to be a different animal. I wanted to be an elephant with a huge trunk, for obvious reasons, but Matthew told me I couldn't since they don't live on farms, so he made me be a duck.

Storytime ended and I buckled him into the backseat of my car.

"Where are we going again?" he asked in his squeaky little voice.

"There's this restaurant I like called Cowboy Phil's. When you sit down, they put a bowl of peanuts on the table and you get to eat them and throw the shells right on the floor."

In the rearview mirror, I could see his little mouth drop open and his eyes grow huge. "Whoa!" he whispered.

"Yep, and they have an arcade there and all these cool animals that were alive a long time ago, but now they're stuffed. It's pretty awesome."

Without saying another word, he folded his hands in his lap and looked out the window, smiling. Again with that damn smile.

The hostess led us to a table right in the middle of the restaurant and set our menus down, along with the peanuts. Matthew hadn't even climbed onto his chair yet and he was already grabbing at the bowl.

"Hang on, hang on." I laughed as I helped him into his seat.

The hostess smiled and walked away as I settled into my chair next to him.

Before we even picked up the menus to look at them, my phone beeped with a text alert.

It was from Michelle.

> M: Hi. I know this is totally neurotic, but I'm not used to being away from him for this long. How's it going?

I couldn't help myself.

> He's great. We just picked up two hookers and we're heading back to the hotel to smoke a couple of joints. Why didn't you tell me he hated vodka? Rum it is!

I'm so dead.

I looked up at Matthew, who was furiously pounding peanuts with his fist like a hammer and throwing them on the floor without eating them first.

"You're supposed to eat the peanut first, goofball."

He looked up at me innocently and shrugged. "I don't like peanuts."

As I laughed at him again, my phone beeped.

> M: You are SO not funny.

Instead of texting back, I leaned in close to Matthew. "Hey, take a selfie with me to send to your mom, okay?"

He nodded excitedly. "Should we duck face?"

"Really? You don't know what personal space is, but you can make a duck face?" I rolled my eyes.

"Huh?"

"Never mind." I pulled his little face against mine and we both smiled as I took the picture and sent it off to Michelle.

"So what do you want to eat?" I picked up the menu and scanned it.

"I want pepperoni pizza, chicken nuggets, and noodles," he answered without looking up at me from his busy peanut-crushing session.

"They don't have noodles and I'm not ordering you a whole pizza, so how about chicken nuggets?"

He shrugged. "Sounds good."

My phone beeped again.

M: Look at that happy face!

His or mine?

The waitress finally came over and took our order. Matthew's face lit up when I suggested we check out the arcade while we wait for the food. On the way to the arcade, I stopped at the bar and traded a twenty-dollar bill for two rolls of quarters. One for Matthew. One for me.

It didn't take long for us to become fully engrossed in the games. I was well on my way to setting a new record on the Elvis Presley pinball machine, while Matthew was a few machines down, spinning the steering wheel on a racing game.

I heard a couple kids come into the room but was too engrossed in what I was doing to pay much attention.

Within a minute or so, Matthew yelled out. "Hey!"

My head snapped toward the right to see Matthew standing next to the game he was just on with his hands on his hips, frowning at one of what I thought were boys but were more like teenagers, now sitting in his seat. "That was mine. I was here first."

The little fucker didn't even look up; he just scoffed. "Sorry, kid. This is *my* game. I play it all the time when I'm here and I'm here, so I'm playing it."

I walked up behind the bratty punk and placed my hands on the seat, right behind his shoulders, as his friends took a few steps back. "I'm sorry, did you not hear him? He was here first."

"Did you not hear *me?*" he spit back without looking up. "I said I wanted to play it, so I'm gonna play it."

"Okay." I tapped his shoulder. "Here's the deal—if we're in the business of doing what we want to do when we want to do it, whether it's right or wrong, I'm in the mood to beat the shit out of some snot-nosed, pimple-faced teenage shit-for-brains who likes to pick on little kids. The only one I see in this room is you, so could you stand up, please?"

He let go of the steering wheel and jumped off the seat in one swift motion, turning to face me but not expecting to be looking at my chest. His eyes slowly drifted up to mine as his mouth fell open.

"I'm guessing mine are the only tits you've ever seen, son."

"Listen, I'm sorry." He held his hands up and backed away. "I didn't mean to be mean to your kid."

"So what? You were *accidentally* mean to him? Don't give me that shit. You had no problem being a little prick until you saw that I could crush you with my pinkie. Now get the hell out of here before I actually do it."

He turned and started toward the door when I called out to him.

"Hey! I believe you owe this young man a dollar."

"Yes. Yes, sir." He shoved his hands in his pockets and pulled out a five-dollar bill. "This is all I have."

I crossed my arms over my chest, flexing just a little bit. "And your point is?"

"Here. Sorry, kid." He shoved the money into Matthew's hand and quickly bolted for the door.

Matthew looked up at me and his chin trembled.

"Hey, hey . . . it's okay." I knelt down in front of him and put my hands on his shoulders, looking him straight in the eyes. "You did good, Matthew. Always do that, okay? If anyone picks on you, you defend yourself. Don't let them treat you like that, okay?"

He stared down at the ground and swallowed, and I couldn't help the urge I had to hug that kid. I thought I might explode if I didn't, but I didn't want to freak him out.

"Matthew, is it okay if I hug you?"

The words were barely out of my mouth when he threw himself into my chest and squeezed. I cupped his little head in my hands and pulled him even tighter against me.

It was my job on the ice to protect my teammates, but other than them and Gam, there weren't too many other people I cared about in the world, let alone felt the need to protect—until that moment.

Chapter 24

"**H**EY!" MICHELLE SPUN AROUND IN the kitchen as she heard us come through the door.

"I hope it's okay that I didn't knock. It was open." I pointed back toward the front of the house.

"No problem at all." She waved a dish towel toward me and then flipped it over her shoulder. "How did it go? How was storytime?"

Matthew tucked his hands under his armpits and flapped his wings as he walked around the kitchen. "It was awesome. Viper danced like a duck!"

"Viper danced?" She turned her head toward me slowly, a playful gleam in her eyes.

"Viper did." I nodded proudly. "I figured if he was willing to do it, why the heck shouldn't I?"

She laughed. "I'm impressed. What else happened?"

Matthew stood up from his duck position and put his hands on his hips. "There were big boys in the arcade who were mean."

She pulled her brows in tight, looking from Matthew to me. "What's he talking about?"

"That big boy took the game I was playing," Matthew continued, "but Viper pulled him out of the seat and told him to give me money."

Michelle's eyes were full of panic as they flashed from Matthew's over to mine. "What is he talking about?"

I held my hands out in front of me. "Wait, I promise it's not as bad as it sounds. Let me explain."

She cocked her hip to the side and crossed her arms, staring me square in the face. Quite intimidating, actually.

"So we went to storytime and danced like ducks, then I took him to Cowboy Phil's, that place I told you about?" I paused so she could add something, an mmhmm, a yep, a nod of the head, anything to let me know she didn't want to rip my face off right then.

Crickets.

"Anyway, we ordered our food, and while we were waiting for it to get there, we went to the arcade to donate some quarters to the place. I was playing pinball and he was playing a driving game. Before I knew it, some punk-ass teenagers took his game, so . . . I very politely asked them to get up and give Matthew his game back. At first, the kid wasn't exactly willing, but once he stood up and turned around, he changed his tune very quickly."

Chewing on her bottom lip, she narrowed her eyes and shifted them over to Matthew and back to me again. "What was he talking about when he said they paid him?"

"Oh. That." I shrugged. "Well, as he was rushing out of the room, I reminded them that they owed the young man money."

Matthew reached into his pocket and pulled the money out, proudly showing it off to his mom. "I got five bucks, Mom!"

"The game was five dollars? What kind of an arcade was this?" she asked.

"Well, no. The game was one dollar, but all he had was a five, so we'll just consider the other four punitive damages." I grinned at her.

"And Mom, Viper only said 'tit' one time, so don't be mad," Matthew added.

Michelle glared at me and inhaled deeply as her nostrils flared like an angry bull's.

"I swear it made sense during my bully beatdown," I defended.

She slapped her hand over her eyes and shook her head just as I reached over and high-fived Matthew and Maura started making noise through the monitor.

Michelle looked up at Matthew and winked. "Someone must have sensed her big brother was home and now she wants to get up to play." She kissed the top of Matthew's head and started out of the kitchen. "Be right back."

I wandered into the family room and sat down on the couch. Before I could call him over, Matthew was already sitting next to me, leaning into my side. I draped my arm over him and squeezed harder.

We sat through almost an entire episode of that annoying talking sponge again, and I pulled out my phone to look at the time. I glanced down at Matthew, who was half asleep on my arm, his eyes completely glazed over. I carefully lifted his head and slid out from under him, laying him gently on a pillow. I headed toward the front of the house but felt guilty leaving without saying good-bye, so I took a deep breath and quietly climbed up the stairs.

I'd only been upstairs in Mike's house a handful of times. Whenever I'd been there, we'd mostly hung out in the family room or down in the man cave in the basement, so I had no idea where I was going. Once I got to the top, I heard singing and followed it to the left. The first door I came to was about halfway closed, but the singing was definitely coming from there, so I stopped to listen, leaning in close.

It was Michelle.

She was singing "Hush Little Baby," I assumed to Maura, in the most beautiful voice I'd ever heard in my life. I stood there with my eyes closed, listening to the calming sound that was coming out of her. When she got to the last verse, I decided to sneak back downstairs and just wait to say bye, but when I went to take a step, the wood floor creaked under my feet. I cringed and a second later, the bedroom door opened.

"Hey." She smiled at me as she carried Maura on her hip.

"I'm so sorry. I didn't mean to interrupt you. Matthew fell asleep downstairs, and I didn't want to sneak out without saying good-bye, so I thought I'd come find you, but then I heard you singing, and I didn't want to bug you . . . ." I rambled incoherently.

"Viper!" she interrupted. "It's okay. I was just about done anyway. Lately, it's been hard for me to find time alone with her. Matthew gets my undivided attention when she's napping, and the couple times you've gone to the library, she's been napping, so I just wanted to steal a few minutes with her. Sorry it took so long." She reached out and wiped drool off Maura's chin.

"No way, please don't apologize. It was nice. I didn't know you could sing like that."

"Oh, thanks." Her cheeks flushed and she bit her lip, trying to hide her smile. "I can't cook to save my life, so thank goodness there's one good thing she'll remember from her childhood, right?"

After a brief, awkward shift right there in that hallway, I cleared my throat. "Anyway, he's out and I'm sure you have things to do this evening, so I'm gonna take off."

"Do you have plans tonight?" she asked as she followed me down the stairs.

I shook my head. "No."

"Then you can't go."

Once we got to the bottom of the steps, I turned back to face her. "Huh?"

"You bought my son lunch and saved him from the arcade antagonizers. Throwing a piece of pizza on a paper plate for you is the least I can do."

"You don't have to buy me dinner." I laughed.

"Fine." She turned and started toward the kitchen. "In that

case, stay right there while I get you money for today."

"You're *not* paying me," I called to her sternly.

She stopped in the kitchen doorway and spun back around, balancing Maura on her hip as she raised a defiant eyebrow at me. "Fine again. Sausage or pepperoni?"

Since Matthew and I had just eaten lunch an hour before, once he woke up from his short catnap, we passed the time until dinner building Legos together.

"Sit down with me." He tugged on my shirt as I walked through the family room.

"Hey, look!" I pointed down at him. "You're sitting criss cross applesauce. I will too."

I heard Michelle chuckle from the kitchen as she loaded the dishwasher.

A huge bin of Legos, a million different shapes and sizes, sat next to Matthew. "What are we building?" I asked him.

"A fire station." He was looking down at his project. The harder he concentrated, the bigger his frown grew.

"Do you want me to help?" I wasn't sure what to do. Lego creations were sacred to some kids.

He sat up excitedly. "Can you make a fire truck to go in my fire house?"

I nodded. "Consider it done."

We sat in silence, working diligently on our respective projects for what felt like hours without saying a word, just concentrating. After a while, I heard Michelle chuckling, so I looked up. She was standing behind the couch with her arms folded, smiling at us with her head tilted to the side.

I glanced down at Matthew and back up at her, lost as to what she'd laughed at. "What?"

"Have you ever seen the movie *Forrest Gump?*" she asked.

Random.

"Yeah, a long time ago."

"There's that scene at the very end of the movie where big Forrest goes in to watch TV with little Forrest and Jenny is watching them from behind. She smiles to herself because they look the same and sit the exact same way. You two just reminded me of that."

I hadn't even noticed that Matthew and I were sitting the exact same way with our legs out to the side and our pile of Legos in the middle between us.

"Wasn't Jenny cooking those hard-working men dinner during that scene?" I teased, grinning up at her as I connected two tiny red Legos.

"I told you I don't cook. I can make spaghetti and French toast. That's about it."

I raised an eyebrow at her. "Scrambled eggs?"

She shook her head. "Nope."

"Meatloaf?"

"Nope."

"Chili?"

"Nope."

"Burgers?"

"I don't even know how to use the grill." She laughed. "Why do you think I ordered pizza?"

Matthew, without looking up from his Legos, exclaimed, "I love pizza!"

"Thank God for that, buddy." I reached over and messed up his hair.

"Oh, whatever. You're telling me you can cook?" Michelle walked around to the front of the couch and sat down, pulling her legs up under her.

"Actually, yes," I said matter-of-factly as I set the Legos down and turned toward her. "I really like cooking, but I never do it because it's just me. Not worth the mess."

She pulled her bottom lip in and nodded. "Impressive. What

can you make?"

"Just about anything." I shrugged. "My grandma taught me."

"Really?"

"Yeah. She was a cook for years. She didn't go to school for it or anything, but she was better than most who did." I stared down at the ground, smiling as I talked about Gam. "She worked at a seminary in the kitchen, so she would cook for the aspiring priests. Huge dinner parties every night. And she would bring home any leftovers for us. Pot roast, rosemary chicken, the most amazing mashed potatoes you ever had in your life. Real stick-to-your-ribs comfort food. She's amazing."

My mouth started to water thinking of all the food Gam used to have just sitting in her fridge.

"Anyway." I shrugged. "I used to ask her how she made this dish and that dish and I paid attention. Even now when I try to make something new, I split it in half and take it over to her for her approval, holding my damn breath as she puts that first bite in her mouth."

Realizing I was rambling on for too long about Gam, I looked up at Michelle, who had a tear running down her cheek.

I panicked. "What did I say? I'm sorry."

"No, no." She wiped the tear away. "It's nothing you said . . . I'm just jealous. I never really had a family. I was adopted, the only child my parents ever had, and they divorced when I was young. We visited my grandparents once a year, if that, and eventually they died. My mom passed when I was in high school, and my dad remarried and moved out to the West Coast. We talk, but not often. So really, it's just me."

"I'm so sorry." I felt terrible. Just when I thought that the guilt had run its course and I was better, something happened to bring it right back to the surface. Mike was her only person, and I took him away.

"It's okay." She smiled the most unconvincing smile I'd ever seen. "I'm used to it. It's always kinda just been me and Mike. I don't know if you know, but Taylor moved here shortly after he died to help me and see the kids more often. She does try, but about a week after she got settled in, she discovered that the young musician in the apartment next to hers was the love of her life, so she's been . . . preoccupied."

"You should go with me to meet Gam sometime," I blurted out. The words were *just* out of my mouth and I instantly regretted them.

She flinched slightly and narrowed her eyes at me. "Why would I do that?"

"I don't know. Just someone to go visit. She only really has me, but I'm a horrible grandson and don't get over there as often as I should."

"Oh, have your parents passed too?"

All it took was one sentence for every muscle in my body to tense up.

"No, they're alive," I said sharply.

"You don't see them?"

"No."

"You don't have to, but do you wanna tell me why?"

Fuck no.

I took a deep breath and looked up at her. I'd never noticed how blue her eyes were until that exact moment when they stared back at me, waiting for an answer to her question.

"Um . . ." I hesitated. "My parents aren't great people. They suck, actually. So once I was old enough to decide who I did and didn't want in my life, they didn't make the cut."

"Hmmm." She looked down at her lap and pinched at the fabric of her pants. "So you're kinda like me . . . alone?"

"Yep." I nodded. "I prefer it that way, though. The closer people are to you, the more opportunities they have to hurt you."

Just as she opened her mouth to say something, the doorbell rang.

"Pizza's here!" Matthew sprang to life and jumped to his feet, hopping up and down excitedly.

"To be continued." She winked at me as she got off the couch and headed up front.

Or not.

Chapter 25

OUR HOME OPENER OF THE season also happened to be the five-month anniversary of Mike's death. Since the Wild had never formally paid tribute to him in terms of a public memorial, they decided the home opener would be the perfect time to do that. Every member of the team stood out on the ice in a single line, shoulder to shoulder, as Mike's jersey was raised to the roof of the stadium during a moment of silence. I watched as the spotlight slowly followed it all the way to the top.

ASHER
88

Every eye in the arena was on me; I could feel them on the back of my head. They were all thinking the same thing—Mike would be here if not for Viper. I wanted the game to start. I wanted that moment to be over, desperately. Rage boiled in my blood stream, and I just wanted to get out on the ice and get it out of me before I exploded.

A hand on my shoulder brought me back to reality.

"You ready?" Brody was frowning.

Looking around, I noticed that everyone else was already skating off the ice, but I was so lost in my own head, I hadn't even realized we were done.

"Yeah, I'm fine. Let's go!"

The game against the Oilers was more like a blood bath. One guy needed four stitches to close a cut in his chin, another guy lost two teeth, and medical glue fixed another cut on a hand—and that was just *their* team. In the end, the Wild came up with the win, barely, with a score of 3–2. A power play near the end almost tied it, but thanks to Murphy and his fast glove, he snatched the puck out of the air and saved the day.

After every game, we typically hung out for a little bit while the crowds thinned, but that night I took an extra long shower, hoping the crowds *and* reporters would be gone by the time I was done.

I wrapped a towel around myself, and my lonely friend that hadn't seen action in almost three weeks now, and went to the locker room to get dressed.

"Just about everyone is gone. Except Kacie," Brody said from the other side of the room. I whipped around to face him. I hadn't even seen him sitting on the bench.

"Oh. Whatever." I shrugged like it was no big deal.

"Don't give me that shit. I know you." He laughed.

"It's just hard," I admitted. "Not only was it the first game but also Big Mike's tribute, and you know the reporters are gonna be hungry. I don't want to say or do anything that's gonna get me fined."

"Like breaking a camera?"

I glared at him. "That cost me ten fucking grand."

"You deserved it, but so did he. Hurry up and get dressed. I'll walk out with you."

Throwing my sweats and hoodie on, I decided I didn't give a shit about drying my hair. I just wanted to go home and crawl into bed.

I grabbed my bag and followed Brody out of the locker room with my hood up and my head down, in case anyone was hanging around outside.

The wooden doors of the locker room thudded as they shut behind me, and within seconds, my name was called out.

"Viper!"

I looked up to see Matthew sprinting down the hallway toward me.

Immediately dropping to my knees, I held my arms out to catch him. "What's up, buddy!" I was genuinely shocked to see him there. Michelle hadn't mentioned anything in her text this morning about coming to the game tonight, but I was beyond excited to see her and Matthew.

As soon as he got close enough, I scooped him up in my arms and tossed him into the air. Lucy and Piper ran straight for Brody and wrapped their arms around his legs as Emma walked as fast as her little legs would let her, staring straight at her dad. Michelle and Kacie followed along behind them.

"Nice game, stud," Kacie said in a sexy voice as she leaned in to give Brody a kiss.

"Do you two ever stop?" I rolled my eyes.

Brody looked at me as he reached down and palmed Kacie's belly, which seemed to be getting bigger by the day. "Clearly not."

"Hi, Uncle V!" Piper called with Lucy waving at me from behind her.

"What's up twinkadinks?" I reached over and high-fived both of them, giving Emma a raspberry on her cheek as I went by.

I turned my attention to Michelle, trying hard not to stare too much. She was smoking in her jeans and boots and fitted Wild jersey. "Hey." I reached over and gave her an awkward hug with Matthew still in my arms. "I didn't know you were coming."

"I didn't either." She laughed, glancing over at Kacie and back at me. "I knew what they were doing for Mike, but I wasn't sure

I could sit through it. Kacie talked me into coming at the last minute, and I'm glad I did." She reached out and squeezed Kacie's hand.

"I'm glad you did too. Otherwise, I wouldn't have had a chance to see this guy again!" I threw him up in the air again and he rewarded me with a giggle. "Wait, where's Maura?"

"I left her home with Taylor. I figured it'd be too loud and crazy here."

Kacie looked from Brody to me to Michelle. "Do you guys have to go home right away? I know it's late, but it's not that late. Wanna grab a late dinner at Stumpy's?"

"I'm game." I nodded.

Michelle held her finger up in the air. "Just let me check with Taylor real quick." She pulled her cell phone out of her back pocket and took a couple steps away as Matthew wiggled out of my arms to go stand by his mom.

"Come here, girls. Let's put hoodies on, please. It's getting chilly out there." Kacie waved the girls off to the side and started to dress them. I waited for Brody to follow and help her, but he pulled his brows in tight and narrowed his eyes at me. "You guys have been seeing each other a lot lately."

"Who?"

"You and Michelle."

I nodded toward Matthew. "It's because of him. I like the little guy."

"Is that all?"

"What the fuck are you trying to say?" I growled at him. "You think I'd move in on my best friend's wife?"

He shook his head. "That's not what I'm saying at all. And even if there were something starting between the two of you, I wouldn't judge."

I glared at him as hard as I ever had in my whole life. "Fuck you!" I spat before heading up the ramp toward the parking lot.

I pushed the glass doors open and took a deep breath of the

crisp air as I paced around outside the door. I shouldn't have snapped at Brody like I had, but what kind of an asshole kills his best friend and then goes after his wife? What the fuck kind of person was I that Brody would think for a second I would do something like that?

Before I could turn to go back in, the whole group filed out. Kacie, Michelle, and the kids went on to their cars as Brody came over to me.

"Dude. Listen, that's not at all what I was suggesting," he said as he got closer. "I was just noticing that you'd gotten closer and—"

"I know, I know," I interrupted him. "I shouldn't have snapped like that. It just hit a nerve. I don't know why. I'm sorry."

"Hey, no worries, man. Let's go chill out at Stumpy's and have a beer and relax." His hand clapped my shoulder. "It's been an emotional night for everyone. We all need to wind down a bit."

I nodded and headed toward my car, hoping my shitty mood would be gone by the time we got to the bar.

By the time we pulled into the parking lot, my mood had already lifted.

"Viper! Can I sit by you?" Matthew yelled as he caught up with me and slipped his hand into mine.

I let go of his hand and lifted him up onto my shoulders instead. "You *better* sit by me."

Our small gang barreled through the door of Stumpy's, causing quite the scene. People who'd obviously watched the game on TV clapped and cheered as we made our way over to our corner table. Brody and I turned and pulled a couple extra stools over for the little kids while Kacie sat with Emma on her lap, shifting uncomfortably.

"Here, let me take her." Brody laughed. "You don't have much of a lap left."

Kacie straightened her back and rubbed her side with her hand. "Thank God. I'm ready to be done and meet this little girlie."

"How much longer now?" Michelle looked at Kacie as she pulled Matthew's hoodie off over his head. His blond hair shot out in a hundred different directions, but he grinned up at me without a care in the world. I reached over and smoothed his hair, gently leaning down and touching my forehead to his without saying a word.

"Six weeks," Kacie sighed.

I turned back toward Brody. "Whose idea was it to have this baby during the season anyway?"

"Um . . ." Brody quickly glanced at Kacie and back to me. "My penis's."

"Ear muffs! Ear muffs!" Michelle yelled out as she covered Matthew's ears.

"Yeah, seriously!" Kacie glared at him as Lucy and Piper covered their mouths and giggled behind her.

"Sorry." Brody laughed as Portland walked up to the table.

"Hey, guys! Oooh, you brought the little ones today?" She looked from Lucy to Piper to Matthew to Emma.

"Yep. The boys had their opening game tonight, so we're celebrating." Kacie smiled proudly.

"Oh, that's right. We watched it on TV. Way to go! You guys want a pitcher?" she asked.

"Uh, no beer for me. I'll have—"

"A root beer?" She grinned at me.

"Yep." I bent down toward Matthew. "You want a root beer too?"

"Wait," Michelle spoke up, "he's never had pop before."

"Please, Mom?" he whined as he looked up at her with big blue puppy-dog eyes. "I want a root beer like Viper."

"Fine." She sighed. "Just one, but you're not gonna like it."

Brody ordered a beer and Kacie got lemonade for herself and the girls. "What do you guys wanna do for food? Pizza?" she asked as her eyes scanned the menu.

"Sounds good to me." I folded my hands in front of my face and stared up at the TV above us, hoping to catch the highlights from the game.

"Matthew, do you like pizza?" Kacie asked.

Michelle immediately looked up at me, and the second we made eye contact, I laughed out loud.

"Stop it!" she yelled playfully, wadding up a napkin and throwing it at me. "Don't you dare say a word."

My head fell onto my arm on the table. I was laughing so hard I thought I might puke. As if the whole innocent pizza comment weren't funny enough, the fact that Michelle knew what I was laughing at without me even having to say anything made it one hundred times better.

"What did we miss?" Brody asked, looking back and forth between me and Michelle.

Michelle licked her lips and shook her head, still trying not to laugh as she rolled her eyes. "Nothing. Viper's a brat, but I'm sure you already knew that. He likes to tease me about ordering too much pizza because I don't know how to cook, even though I have yet to see him make something as simple as a sandwich." She looked at me and raised her eyebrows, taunting me.

"Whoa. Whoa. Whoa." I held my hands up. "I can cook, damn it. I can cook good."

She leaned forward and batted her eyelashes at me. "Prove it."

Challenge motherfucking accepted.

Chapter
26

"VIPER!"

I was on the ice during morning drills and heard the sound of my name. I glanced up toward the bench to see Mia, Coach Collins's assistant, standing in the box, waving her arms to get my attention.

"What's up?" I called out as I skated over.

"Coach wants to have a quick word with you before practice starts." She smiled and walked away.

What the fuck is this about?

"All right, I'll be there in a minute," I hollered back.

It would have been nice had he called this little meeting before I put my skates and pads on, but he's the boss, so I couldn't tell him no. I went to the locker room and spent ten minutes taking all my crap off before making my way to his office upstairs.

"Come in!" he yelled after I knocked on the door.

I opened it and walked through, prepared for anything.

"Hey, Viper." He gave me a tight smile as he pointed to the chair by his desk. "Have a seat."

My stomach sank. I was already pissed off and he hadn't even started talking yet. Why the hell would they have let me start the season if they were going to let me go? What city was I going to end up in? I'd have to move and take Gam with me. What about Matthew? My mind raced with questions as Collins stared at me for a long time without saying anything.

He finally relaxed back into his seat. "Well, I'm impressed."

Huh?

"Huh?"

"We had a phone conference with Dr. Roberts this morning. She told us how well you're doing with therapy, and she gave the green light for you to go ahead and continue with the season." His chair squeaked as he rocked back and forth with his fingers locked behind his head.

"Wait. You talked to Dr. Roberts? About me?" Panic welled up in my chest. I didn't want anyone, certainly not my coach, knowing what Dr. Roberts and I had talked about in that office.

"Well, about you in general. No specifics. She just let us know that you hadn't missed one meeting and that she felt you were progressing nicely. The head honchos in the office are happy, which makes me happy. So, well done. You can continue to see her or stop, that part is completely up to you, but in terms of your probationary period . . . that's over."

"Oh." I nodded slowly, staring at the pen on his desk. "That's good to know."

"I'm proud of you. Now, go practice." He stood up and held his hand out for me to shake, which I did. Then I quickly left his office.

When I was a kid, there were a million things in the world that could make me feel sick to my stomach. Breaking a neighbor's window, scratching the side of my dad's new car with my bike, having a sealed envelope in my backpack that I had to give to my parents to sign and bring back to school the next day. None of these things even began to compare to being called down to the principal's office, and that's how I'd felt every time I was called up to Collins's office, but not that time. That time, I left his office with a smile on my face and a *Star Student of the*

Week kick in my step.

In my haste to get to the rink that morning, I'd forgotten to send my typical morning text to Michelle. The minute practice was over, I grabbed my phone.

> I'm a little late today, but how's it going over there?

I gathered up my sweaty clothes and shoved them into my bag as I waited for her response.

> M: Awful. I tried to make chocolate chip pancakes this morning and started a small fire. The kitchen is a total loss. I don't know what I'm going to do.

Holy fuck.

For the second time that day, my heart sank.

> Holy shit. Are you serious? What can I do? You guys can come stay at my place for now.

My hands shook so hard I almost dropped my phone twice. I sat down on the bench and stared down at it, silently begging it to beep. I needed her to respond.

> M: Just kidding. LOL

What? LOL?

> Are you kidding me right now? That was a joke?

> M: Consider it payback for the hookers text. ;)

Holy crap. What a little shit.

> There's a big difference between women you pay for sex and your entire kitchen burning down. Thanks for giving me a damn heart attack.

"Who are you texting?"

I looked up and Louie was staring at me from across the

213

locker room.

Brody walked up and stopped next to him. "Yeah, you're smiling like an idiot."

"No one," I said defensively as I stood up and shoved my phone into my bag. "See you ladies in two days."

I headed outside and tossed my bag down in the passenger seat just as my phone started buzzing like crazy. Before I started my engine, I checked my messages. Three of them, all from Michelle.

> M: Ha! A little scare is good for you from time to time.
>
> M: Viper, answer me. I was just kidding.
>
> M: Hey! You're not really mad, are you? Please answer me.

I couldn't stop the mischievous smile from forming on my lips as I drove out of the parking lot and headed straight for her house, after one quick stop.

Doing my best to look pissed off, I rang her doorbell. I had to concentrate on keeping my eyebrows down low and not smiling when she rounded the corner and walked toward the door. The look on her face made it really hard, though. She was biting her lip and her eyes looked sad as she pulled the door open.

"Listen, I know my joke was stupid. I never should have scared you like that," she rambled as I stepped inside, keeping my hands hidden behind my back. "I feel so bad and I'm really sorry."

I kept my eyes down on the floor, because I knew if I looked up at her, I was going to start laughing. "I don't even know what to say to what you did, Michelle. Except . . ." I pulled the pizza out from behind my back. "A little scare is good for you from time to time."

She looked down at the pizza and back up at me, her mouth

dropping open as her blue eyes grew huge. "You big jerk!"

I flinched as she balled up her fist and punched my arm.

"I thought you were mad at me!" She hit me three more times. "I felt bad."

"You can't fool the master," I said in my cockiest tone with a smirk on my face.

She rolled her eyes and groaned in annoyance as she grabbed the pizza box from me and stomped off toward the kitchen.

I followed along behind her, enjoying the view so much it made me angry with myself.

We walked into the kitchen and Maura was sitting in her highchair, desperately trying to pinch weird little pieces of cereal or something in between her fingers.

"Hey, little one." I bent down and kissed the top of her head, pausing to take a closer look at her tray. "What are these?"

"They're called Puffs. Kinda like cereal for babies, but they pretty much melt in your mouth so even without teeth, they can have them." She flipped the lid off of the pizza and got a stack of paper plates out of the cabinet.

I grabbed one of the pieces of cereal and put it in my mouth as Maura stared right at me.

"They're pretty good, huh?" I said. A huge grin broke out across her face as she picked up another piece and tried to feed it to me. I opened my mouth and she slowly put the cereal in, craning her neck just a little to watch me chew it. "Mmmm, so yummy. Thank you." I rubbed her soft cheek as I stood up. "Hey,"—I looked around the kitchen and into the family room—"where's my little buddy?"

Matthew always came running to greet me at the front door.

"He's in there,"—she nodded toward the couch—"curled up under a blanket, sick."

I walked around the couch and sure enough, Matthew was wrapped in a little ball, staring at the TV.

"What's up, my man?" I said softly as I sat down next to him.

His eyes shifted to me when he heard my voice, but he just groaned.

I set my hand on his head, rubbing his forehead with my thumb. "What's wrong with you?"

"My tummy hurts." His voice cracked as his eyes started to water.

I didn't know what to do. "Can I get you anything? You want some pizza?"

"No!" Michelle shouted from the kitchen. "He's been throwing up on and off all day. Food is out of the question for now, especially pizza."

"Throwing up is bad, right? He can dehydrate?" I called to Michelle as I stared down at Matthew. The poor little guy was as white as I'd ever seen him, with dark circles under his eyes. He looked awful. I had to do *something*.

"Yeah, he can,"—she put her hands on her hips and shrugged—"but I can't get him to drink anything. I filled that cup on the coffee table at nine o'clock this morning. He's barely touched it."

She was right. The Thomas the Train cup was filled almost all the way to the top.

I leaned down close to him. "Hey, buddy . . . did you know sometimes I get the stomach flu too?"

He turned his head just a little toward me. "You do?"

"Yep, sometimes. And you know what makes me feel better?"

"What?" he asked in a gravelly little voice.

"When I drink Gatorade. It has these magic little electrolyte thingies in there that make your stomach feel so much better. Want me to run and get you some?"

He didn't look too enthusiastic, but he did nod, so I kissed his forehead and walked back to the kitchen. "You don't have Gatorade in the house, right?"

Michelle looked around the kitchen, thinking for a quick

second, before shaking her head. "No, we haven't had Gatorade in the house . . . for a long time."

I knew what that pause was. She knew what that pause was. Neither of us wanted to acknowledge the pause.

"Okay, I'm gonna run to the store. Do you need anything else?"

"Nope." She sighed. "We're good on everything else."

"Okay, be back soon."

About half an hour later, I walked back through the front door carrying four plastic bags.

Michelle stared at the bags with wide eyes as I walked through the kitchen and set them on the table. "How much Gatorade did you buy?"

"A lot," I sighed, looking at the bags and then back at her. "It's not just Gatorade, though. The pharmacist said saltines would be good for his tummy if he felt like eating, so I got two boxes. Then I was trying to think of fun ways to try and get him to drink, and I found a package of silly straws, so I got those too. Then I thought maybe we could bribe him to drink, so I got him a color book and crayons."

Michelle sucked in a quick breath and swallowed as she looked back and forth between me and the bags on the table. "You got *all* that stuff for him?"

"Of course," I replied. "He's my buddy. I feel bad that he's so sick."

All of a sudden, Matthew's little head popped up on the other side of the couch. "Did you get blue Gatorade? It's my favorite."

"Ha!" I pumped my fist in the air in celebration. "I sure did. Would you also like a silly straw?"

Matthew cracked a small smile as he nodded.

"Coming right up!" I called to him. I turned to ask Michelle where his cups were, but she was gone. A sniffling sound came from around the corner and I followed it. Michelle was leaning against the dining room wall, wiping her eyes on the sleeve of her shirt.

I leaned my shoulder against the wall so I could face her, not saying anything for a second. After a few more sniffles and another wipe on her sleeve, I finally asked, "Are you okay?"

"Yeah." She shoved her fingers into the corners of her eyes before wiping the tears on her jeans.

"What is this? What's happening?"

She shrugged. "It's just . . . nice. It's been a while now that I've been doing it on my own and to have you here and the way you jumped into action and helped out . . ." Her voice cracked and trailed off. I stepped into the kitchen and grabbed a box of tissues off of the counter.

Matthew poked his head up from the couch again. "What's wrong? Is Momma okay?"

I looked down at the tissues and back up at him. "Oh yeah, she's fine. She just has a really big booger and I'm giving her tissues."

He giggled and lay back down.

I slowly slid back around the corner and pulled a tissue out of the box.

"Thanks." She sniffed again as she took the tissue from me. "I'm sorry. This is so stupid. You probably think I'm a neurotic moron now."

"Not even a little bit," I said in my most serious tone.

Her eyes flipped up to mine as they started to water again. "I don't know why I'm so worked up to begin with. My son gets the stomach flu and it sends me into a fucking tailspin."

I don't think I'd ever heard her swear before. I found it inappropriately hot.

"Hey. You don't have to justify anything to me, okay? And about the Gatorade, I was happy to help out. He's really become my little buddy lately, and I feel bad that he feels so crappy."

"You *have* been around a lot more, and it's been really nice . . . for him and for me." She wiped the mascara from under her eyes. "He's smiling more than he has the last several months, and I didn't realize how lonely I was. The texts you send me in the morning are usually the highlight of my day." She looked up at me quickly and shook her head like she'd said something wrong. "I didn't mean it like that—"

"I know." I reached out and swiped a tear from her cheek. "It's okay."

"Anyway." She wiped her eyes again and looked up at me with a forced grin. "Enough boo-hooing for one night. I'm gonna get my boy some Gatorade while you cut the pizza, okay?"

I narrowed my eyes at her. "I have a better idea. Toss that pizza."

Two hours and a quick trip to the grocery store later, Michelle and I were sitting on the couch in a total food coma, stuffed to the brim with peach BBQ chicken over roasted potato wedges and Parmesan asparagus.

"Oh my God," Michelle moaned. "That was the best thing I've ever eaten in my entire life."

"I'm glad you liked it." I smiled at her. "You can apologize when you're ready."

She lifted her head and frowned at me. "Apologize?"

"You know darn well that when I told you I could cook, you doubted me. What did you say to me? I believe it was 'prove it'?"

"If I could get up, I'd walk over and hit you," she threatened, pulling the corner of her lip up in a smirk.

"And you"—I leaned over and rustled Matthew's hair—"are doing so good with the Gatorade. Keep it up, champ."

Matthew was on his second glass of Gatorade and so far, so good. Nothing had come back up, and he even had a little color back in his face.

"The night finished off a lot better than the morning started out, I'll tell ya that." Michelle yawned. "And you're right. I'm sorry."

I peeked at her out of the corner of my eye. "Huh?"

"You're right," she repeated, sterner this time. "When you said you could cook, I totally thought you were lying, but you definitely proved it, and I'm sorry."

"Wow!" I teased. "Bet that was fun to say."

"Not at all." She rolled her eyes.

I looked at the clock on my phone. "All right, well I better get going. I have some errands to run tomorrow morning before we head out of town for our road trip."

"Wait." She sat up suddenly. "I want to ask you something, but you have to promise not to laugh at me."

"Okay." I laughed. "I promise."

"You're already laughing." She sighed.

"My bad. Here, let me try again . . ." I cleared my throat and put on my best serious face. "Okay, try again. I'm ready now."

"So, I've been thinking about this for several days, but I wasn't really sure I wanted to ask until tonight. I really don't want Matthew and Maura growing up remembering their mom was on a first-name basis with the pizza delivery man. Will you . . . teach me?"

My eyebrows shot up. "Teach you to cook?"

She bit her lip and nodded.

"Hell yeah. I would love to."

"Really?" Hope filled her eyes and made them sparkle like I'd never seen before.

"Yeah, really. I'll be back tomorrow after I run my errands, at like two o'clock, and we'll work on dinner, okay?"

"I'll be ready," she said confidently.

Chapter 27

Up early with a bounce in my step, I ran my errands in record time and grabbed a few things from the grocery store that I was pretty certain Michelle didn't have stocked in her kitchen. I had a little extra time to kill before heading to Michelle's, so I stopped by Gam's and brought her a box of almond crescent cookies, her favorite.

She put the cookies on a plate and set them down in the middle of the table before she grabbed a root beer and handed it to me.

"What?" I laughed, suddenly defensive as I noticed her staring at me with narrow eyes.

She leaned her chin on her hand and kept staring, her eyes moving all over my face as I tossed a cookie in my mouth. "You. Something. What's going on?"

I shrugged. "Nothing's going on. What are you talking about?"

"I don't know. I can't pinpoint it, but you seem . . . giddy."

"I don't do giddy," I argued as I opened my root beer and took a huge gulp.

"I know. That's my point."

"Anyway, what's new on your end?"

"Lawrence, I'm nearly ninety years old. Just waking up is exciting." She sighed and grabbed a cookie off of the plate.

"That's right. Someone has a birthday coming up." I grinned at her as I wiggled my eyebrows up and down.

"Yes, and I want a big damn party. This will probably be my last birthday."

I rolled my eyes at her. "You've been saying that about every birthday for the last ten years."

"Well, I really mean it this time, so you better go all out. I want a huge cake and some of those Chippendales dancers, okay?"

I frowned at her and shook my head. "You're out of your damn mind. I am *not* ordering you a stripper."

"Really?" She let her hand fall hard against the table and glared at me. "You're not gonna grant a dying old lady her last wish?"

"Have you always been this dramatic?" I laughed as I ate another cookie.

"Pretty much, yes."

Wiping the powdered sugar off my hands onto my jeans, I stood up. "All right, sorry to cut the visit short, but I have to be somewhere. I'll stop by when we get back into town, okay?"

I bent down and kissed her wrinkly forehead.

"Where do you have to be? What's better than me?"

"Uh . . ." I stammered. "I'm teaching a friend to cook today. Just something easy for dinner. No big deal."

Her eyes sparkled and she hit the table with her hand again. "I knew it!" she yelled.

"Knew what?"

"Is this little someone a woman?"

I sighed, not wanting to answer her question. She stared at me pointedly, tapping her fingers on the table.

"Yes," I finally admitted. "It's a woman, but it's not what you think. It's Mike's wife."

"Oh." Her head jerked back a little in surprise. "That's not at all what I was expecting."

"Exactly. It's just a cooking lesson. Let's leave it at that,

okay?"

"Okay," she said unconvincingly. I gave her a wave and turned toward the front door. "Most men wouldn't put cologne on for a cooking lesson, though!"

I shook my head and reached for the doorknob as she yelled out one more time. "And don't forget about my party. And the strippers. Maybe they can jump out of the cake!"

"Good-bye!" I waved as I shook my head and closed the door.

The best sound ever greeted me as I walked through the front door of Michelle's house.

"Yay! Viper!" I heard the thud of Matthew's footsteps running toward me.

"My man!" I set the grocery bags down so I could catch him when he jumped into my arms like he always did.

"How are you feeling today?" I scanned his face. Nice pink color. No dark circles. "You look great."

"I feel better." He smiled as he wrapped his arms around my neck and squeezed so hard he made me cough. "You were right, the electricity worked!"

I frowned at him. "Electricity?"

"In the Gatorade."

"Oh! The electrolytes!" I laughed. "Yep, they seemed to work. I'm so glad. Want to help me carry these bags?" I lowered him gently to the ground, and he immediately grabbed two of the bags and dragged them along behind him on the wood floor. He dropped the bags in the doorway, almost making me trip on them, and ran off to the family room to watch TV.

I pushed the bags on the floor into the kitchen with my foot. Michelle was standing by the island with the biggest smile on her face.

"Oops! I'll get those." She ran over and picked up the

abandoned bags. Her blond hair was pulled back in a messy ponytail and a pink apron hung from around her neck. She looked completely adorable standing there, all ready to go. "I'm *so* excited. I hardly slept last night."

I laughed as I set the bags on the kitchen table. "Really? For lasagna?"

"I love lasagna!" She licked her lips and sighed happily.

"Me too. It's one of my favorites." I started pulling things out of the bags. "I also got the stuff for an awesome salad, garlic bread, and a bottle of cabernet sauvignon." Turning back to face her, I pulled my brows in tight. "Do you drink wine?"

"Not often, but yes. Tonight, yes." She nodded excitedly. "What can I help with?" She grabbed one of the other bags and started pulling things out. "Holy cow, this is a lot of stuff."

I sensed the intimidation in her voice. "Don't worry, it's not a tough recipe. I promise."

"Okay," she sighed. "But if it sucks, I'm blaming you." She winked at me and started moving the ingredients to the island.

Once everything was out of the bags and set up, it was time to start.

"Okay." She clapped loudly and put her hands on her hips, swaying back and forth as she eyed the stuff on the island. "What do we do first?"

"First, you relax." I smiled. "You're not gonna wrestle it, you're gonna cook it."

"Sorry." She laughed. "I'm a little pumped."

"I can tell." I motioned toward her apron.

She looked down at herself and back up at me. "What? You don't like my apron?"

"Oh, it's fantastic," I teased sarcastically as she frowned at me. "Let's get moving or we're gonna be ordering pizza again." I piled up the ground beef, Italian sausage, onion, and garlic. "Why don't you start browning those?"

"Okay." She nodded, then shifted her eyes up to mine. She

looked tiny and innocent and adorable. "Um . . . how do I do that?"

"How do you brown something?" I repeated back to her, positive I'd heard her question wrong.

She bit her lip and nodded.

"Whoa. Okay, let's start with the basics. Where are your pots and pans?"

"Ugh. This is so embarrassing." She covered her face with one hand and pointed to the cabinet behind me with the other.

I opened the cabinet and pulled out a frying pan that had clearly never been used.

Trying hard to contain my shock, I held it up and looked at her. "Is this brand new?"

Still hiding her face behind her hands, she nodded.

I reached out and moved her hands from her face. Her cheeks were as pink as her apron and she looked down at the ground, avoiding my eyes.

"How long have you had these?" I asked as I lifted her chin to face me.

"That's not important," she snapped playfully as she grabbed the pan from me and put it on the stove. "Teach me how to brown this stuff."

She turned to face the stove and my eyes moved slowly from the top of her head, down her neck, then down to her collarbone. I swallowed hard and forced myself to look away.

Get your shit together, Viper. You're teaching her to cook dinner and then you're leaving.

"Okay." I cleared my throat. "Open the meat and drop it in the pan, turning the heat between medium and high."

Michelle's movements were very slow and very graceful as she did everything I said, just the way I said to. Every time I gave her instructions on something, her tongue stuck out just a bit as she concentrated.

We worked together in the kitchen like a well-oiled machine,

225

and before long, dinner was ready.

Maura woke up from her nap just in time to eat. While Michelle went up to get her, Matthew and I set the table. I moved the tray of lasagna over to the table and poured two glasses of wine while Michelle buckled Maura into her highchair. Matthew sat in his seat, Michelle sat in her seat, and I pulled the chair out at the end of the table.

"That's daddy's seat," Matthew said innocently, staring up at me.

Michelle gasped quietly and covered her hand with her mouth, turning away from him.

"You know what, buddy? You're right. That's your dad's seat and I don't want to take it. Can I sit in this one next to you instead?" I moved over to the chair next to him as he nodded eagerly.

I looked up at Michelle, who had tears in her eyes, and winked at her. "It's okay," I mouthed.

She nodded, but I knew she was rattled.

I cut the lasagna and scooped squares onto everyone's plates as Michelle cut a section into microscopic pieces for Maura, who was squealing for food.

"At least we have one fan so far." I nodded toward Maura.

Michelle scraped pieces of the lasagna off of her plate and onto Maura's tray as she laughed. "Well, she eats dirt off the floor and chews on shoes, so don't get too excited."

Dinner was fantastic. Matthew had not one but two huge pieces of lasagna and ate the salad like he thought someone was going to take it away from him.

"I've never seen him eat this good—ever," Michelle whispered as he kept shoveling it in.

"Good." I nodded. "What do you think?"

"I think if we continue these lessons, I'm gonna have to start going to the gym." She giggled.

I scooped up another piece of lasagna and without thinking,

said, "Oh, please. You have the most perfect body I've ever seen."

Her eyes flashed up to me for a quick second and I cringed. "I'm sorry. I didn't mean to say that. I mean, it's true, but I shouldn't have said it. I'm gonna stop talking now." I closed my eyes and rubbed my forehead, suddenly wishing I were anywhere else.

"It's okay," she said softly. "I appreciate it. I don't get too many compliments hanging around here all day. It was nice to hear, actually."

Thankfully, we finished dinner without any other fuckups from me. Michelle wiped down Maura's face and put her in the playpen in the family room while Matthew took off down the hall toward his playroom. She took a plastic container out of the cabinet and started scooping the leftover lasagna into it. I was stacking the dirty dishes on the counter when a few dots of something hit the side of my face. I wiped it off with the back of my hand and stared down at it. Sauce.

Michelle's eyes were huge as she covered her mouth with her hands, stifling a laugh. "I'm so sorry," she mumbled from behind them. "I was scooping the lasagna into the container and the spoon caught the edge and when it flicked, sauce went everywhere."

"No problem." I shrugged, grinning innocently at her. As soon as she turned back toward what she was doing, I picked up the wooden spoon, which also had sauce on it, and flung it her way. Drops of tomato sauce peppered her hair and the side of her face as she gasped.

With her mouth hanging open, she spun to face me. "Mine was an accident!" She reached into the salad bowl and grabbed a handful of lettuce, launching it in my direction. Using one of the extra plates on the counter as a shield, I grabbed a handful of the mushrooms we didn't use and threw them at her, laughing hard as they bounced off of her head.

"That's it!" she growled as she took the spoon out of the bowl and snapped it toward me again. Huge globs of sauce splattered all over the cabinets, the counter, and me.

It. Was. On.

I took a huge spoonful of sauce out of the pan and launched it at her. She ducked behind the island for most of it, but one big blob landed on the top of her head.

"Okay, okay!" Both of her hands stuck up from behind the island. "Truce! You win. I concede."

"Deal." I set the bowl down with a smug grin on my face.

She stood up slowly and I couldn't contain my laugh. Her whole front—her face, her shirt, and her pink apron—was dotted with red sauce and the big blob that had landed on her head was now dripping off loose flyaway pieces of her hair from her ponytail.

"We're not gonna do that every time, right?" she pouted playfully as she walked over, grabbing a dish towel off the counter. I had the sudden urge to pull her to me and lick the sauce off that pout, but I blinked hard to force the thought out of my mind.

"Hey, you started it," I teased, bumping her with my elbow as I wiped my hands on another towel.

"Yeah, but I also got the worst of it," she whined, turning to face me.

She wasn't kidding. Little spots of sauce were on her forehead, cheeks, even in her eyebrows.

I reached out and gently swiped at a tiny dot on the end of her nose as she blinked up at me. "That'll teach you not to start something you can't finish."

As her blue eyes bore into mine, something shifted between us. I had no idea what the fuck it was, but I couldn't look away if I wanted to, which I didn't. As we stood there and stared at each other, not talking, that familiar feeling of guilt tugged at my heart again. But it wasn't the guilt from hurting Mike; it was different. I liked this. I liked being in the kitchen with her. I liked being with her, period.

"Momma!" Matthew called out from down the hall. "My movie is over. Can you get the Legos down for me?"

Michelle blinked and looked away, wiping her face with the dish towel before leaving the kitchen.

Fuck. Leave the house now.

I turned toward the sink and gripped the edge of the counter.

"Calm the fuck down," I said to myself quietly. "It was just a food fight."

Yeah? Then why is your heart racing, asshole?

While Michelle was down the hall with Matthew, my phone beeped. I frowned at the screen, not recognizing the number. I hit the button anyway and opened it.

> Hey, Viper! It's Anna . . . Portland. Listen, I can't stop thinking about the other night and how sweet you were when you were in here with the kids. I'm off tonight and was wondering if you were free? Let me know! XOXO

I stared down at that message for about ten seconds and deleted it.

"Ahhh, Legos to the rescue," Michelle joked as she came back into the kitchen. She noticed my phone in my hand and motioned toward it. "Who's that? Do you need to go?"

"Nope. No one important." I set my phone down on the counter and turned back to Michelle. "Let me help you clean up this mess before the sauce dries onto your cabinets."

Chapter
28

Michelle

THE MORNING AFTER LASAGNAGATE 2015, I sat at the kitchen table, zoning out while Maura and Matthew slept in. Technically, they weren't sleeping in, but I was up earlier than normal. I hadn't slept much the night before, not in a while, actually.

I stared out into the backyard, replaying the night before over and over in my head. The way Viper's arms had flexed when he stirred the onions and mushrooms in the pan. The way he'd smelled when he leaned in close and put those same arms around me to show me how to layer the noodles just perfectly. The playful grin on his face as he'd flicked red sauce all over me. The way he'd looked at me when he wiped the sauce off the end of my nose. All those memories made the butterflies in my stomach, which were still there from last night, wake up and start fluttering again.

We'd had a moment. A definite moment where I'd stared up at him, begging for something, but I wasn't sure if it was for him to kiss me or leave and never come back.

My phone beeped, and it scared me so bad I nearly fell out of my chair.

My daily Viper text.

V: Good morning.

I took a deep breath, silently begging the butterflies to not only calm down, but to go away altogether. This couldn't happen. *We* couldn't happen.

Good morning.

V: I would ask if you needed anything, but I'm about to board a plane for a three day road trip, so if you needed anything, I wouldn't be much help anyway. I still wanted to say hi though.

His words made me smile.

I'm good anyway. Don't need anything, but thank you. Good luck on the road.

He didn't text back again, but I was sure he wanted to; and I know he wanted to because I wanted him to. Every time we were together, this pull between us got stronger and stronger, but neither of us was willing to acknowledge it, and that's the way it needed to stay. For Mike.

I took a deep breath and puffed my cheeks out, determined to get out of the house and do something fun with Matthew and Maura. We'd spent enough time cooped up in the house as depressed balls of nothingness. I quickly packed up lunches and a bag for the day and woke my babies, ready to go have some fun. Ready to show them a momma who could handle anything life threw at her.

Hours later, I pulled onto my street and hit the garage button on my visor. I turned into the driveway, startling Jodi, who was stepping off of my porch. She waved at me and crossed her arms,

walking over to my van.

"Hey, you," I said as I opened the van door, gently lifting a sleeping Maura out of her car seat while Matthew hopped out on his own.

"Hi. Where have you guys been all day? I've knocked like three times." She reached over, took my bag from me, and threw it over her shoulder.

"Thanks." I hit the button to close the van and scrambled to find my house key on the ring. "First, we went to the petting zoo, and Matthew fed a goat while Maura ate the goat food off the ground."

"Gross."

"Then we went out to lunch at this place Viper took Matthew, and I spent the whole time pulling whole peanuts out of Maura's mouth." I laughed, finally getting the door open. "Needless to say, I'm ready for a glass of wine. Wanna join me?"

"Yes, please," Jodi answered eagerly.

I put Maura in her bed and put *SpongeBob SquarePants* on for Matthew before pouring two very large glasses of wine for Jodi and me.

"Look at you today." She shook her head. "You're supermom."

"Ah." I waved her off. "I'm just trying to be a regular mom, Jodi. I've spent the last several months since Mike died sitting around here feeling sorry for myself, when I should've been thankful I had nine years with him at all."

"Wow. Just when I think you can't impress me any more, girl, that's exactly what you do." She held her wine glass up for me to clink.

We touched glasses and I took a big long drink.

"Oh! I almost forgot . . ." She set her glass down and jumped off the chair, pulling a small silver envelope out of her back pocket. "This is for you."

I looked down at the shimmery envelope.

Mrs. Michelle Asher and Guest

I dropped the envelope into my lap and rolled my eyes dramatically at her. "Is this what I think it is?"

"If you're thinking it's a wedding invitation, then yes." She gave me a thumbs-up as she took another sip of wine.

"I love you, but you're a bitch. Don't make me do this."

Jodi frowned at me. "What do you mean? Weddings are fun."

"You would know. You've thrown enough of them," I teased, glaring down at the invitation again. "I've barely left my house for six months and before that, I hated social situations as it was. Weddings are so *not* my thing."

"Well, next month, they're going to be your thing at least once."

"What if I RSVP no?" I laughed.

Jodi winked at me. "Then I egg your house."

I looked up at the sky and tilted my head back and forth like I was considering it as she kicked me under the table. "Ow!" I yelled out, rubbing my leg. "Fine, I'll be there."

"What about your plus one?" she asked slowly, avoiding eye contact with me.

"What about it? No. It'll just be me," I said sternly. "And do not even think about trying to set me up with one of Vince's stupid friends, got it?"

"Mmhmm." She nodded, grinning at me unconvincingly.

After Jodi left, I gave both the kids baths at the same time in the same tub because let's face it, the petting zoo wore me out more than them. I sang a little bit to Maura before curling up in my bed with Matthew to read a few books.

We were on our fourth *Clifford the Big Red Dog* book when my phone beeped on my nightstand.

It was a text from Viper.

> V: Hey. I know I don't normally text at night, but
> I'm in the hotel room and bored, so I thought
> I'd say hi again and see how your day went.

"Matthew, lean in close to me. Let's send a picture to Viper, okay?"

"Can we make silly faces?"

"Good idea!"

He lay down next to me and we squished our cheeks together, crossing our eyes and sticking our tongues out as I snapped the picture.

"Too bright," Matthew complained, rubbing his eyes.

"I know, buddy. Sorry." I hit the button on my phone and sent the picture to Viper as my response to his text.

My phone beeped while we were reading the rest of the book, but I left it until we were done. I desperately wanted to know what he said back, but I didn't want to ditch Matthew for my phone. Once we got to the end of the book, Matthew sighed. "Can I sleep in here, Mom?"

Matthew had asked to sleep with me several times since Mike died, but I'd been hesitant about starting that habit simply because we both slept better apart. That night, though, it sounded fantastic.

"Yes, you can. I'd love it, actually. We can be snuggle buddies all night long."

He grinned at me and leaned over, kissing the tip of my nose. "You're the best mom in the whole wide world."

My eyes watered. "Thanks, buddy. It's pretty easy to be a good mom with a good son like you."

He lifted his arm, I thought to give me a hug, but he handed me the remote instead. "Can you put on *Ninja Turtles* for me?"

I laughed out loud as I took the remote from him and put his show on.

Suddenly I remembered my phone under my pillow. I pulled it out as fast as I could.

V: I miss those faces . . . a lot.

Six words. Six words were all it took and those damn butterflies sprang into action again, bumping into each other as they swirled around in my belly. I also didn't know how to respond. Was it appropriate to tell your dead husband's best friend that you missed him too?

Same here.

Nice, Michelle. Way to be lame on that one.

Within a couple seconds, my phone beeped again. This time it was a picture message. My mind raced inappropriately for two seconds before I came to my senses. I opened it. It was obviously a picture he took of himself. He looked like he was lying in a hotel bed. The way his free arm tucked behind his head made his bicep muscle flex, and my mouth water. Tattoos covered his whole body, all the way up most of his neck. I was used to seeing the ones on his neck pop out of his shirts, but I hadn't ever taken a close look at the ones on his chest and arms. A huge grin was plastered on his face, and suddenly he didn't feel like he was a thousand miles away.

"Look, Matthew. Viper sent us a picture too."

Matthew's eyes squinted through my dark room to look at the picture, his face breaking into a huge smile as soon as he saw his friend.

"I like him," he said casually, turning back to the TV.

Don't do it, Michelle. Don't go there. There's nothing but heartache there.

**All right, me and the little man are heading to bed.
Hope you sleep well.**

V: You too. Talk to you in the morning.

I already can't wait.

Chapter
29

BEING AWAY FOR THREE DAYS royally sucked. In the past, road trips meant fucking new girls in different cities, but not anymore. Not since Dr. Roberts made me promise not to. I was pretty sure that even if Dr. Roberts weren't in the picture, I wouldn't be fucking any girls anyway. My thoughts lately had been too consumed with a certain blonde, who I wasn't supposed to be thinking about yet I couldn't wait to get home to.

The minute my plane touched down in Minneapolis, I shot Michelle a text. I was anxious to hear how Matthew's first soccer practice went . . . and talk to her.

> Hey! We just landed. How was your day?

> M: Hope you had a good flight. My day was awful. I'll explain everything tomorrow. I'm too tired now and heading to bed. Text me in the morning?

I didn't like that answer at all. It stressed me the fuck out, and I wouldn't be able to sleep without knowing what had happened. Instead of heading ten minutes south from the airport to my house, I headed north to hers.

I pulled in the driveway and cut the lights.

I'm in your driveway.

M: What? You are?

I looked up to the second floor master bedroom window. The curtains moved back a couple inches, then shut again quickly. I stayed in my car, not knowing if she was going to come let me in or text me and tell me to go home. The front door opened and relief flooded through me. She was wearing a light blue tank top, blue and pink plaid bottoms, and her hair was in a messy bun with all those sexy pieces falling down around her face. For a minute I worried she might have already been sleeping.

"Hey," she said, offering me a tight smile as I walked through the front door.

"What's going on? Are you okay?" I'd barely let the question leave my mouth when her chin started quivering and her eyes welled up. "Whoa, whoa. What happened?"

She shook her head and covered her eyes. I reached out and gently pulled her head against my chest, thankful that she didn't resist. She didn't say anything as she cried silently in my arms, her shoulders shaking. I'd planned on standing there in her foyer, holding her for as long as I needed to, but she pulled back after just a couple of minutes.

"I need a tissue." She sniffed and walked to the kitchen, flipping the light on as she passed it. In the light, I could see her eyes were puffy and her nose was all red. She'd been crying before I got there. She blew her nose and took a deep, shaky breath. "Wanna go sit in there?" She motioned toward the family room.

"Sure." I nodded, following along behind her.

We sat down on the couch and she pulled her legs up to her chest, hugging them tight. I wanted desperately to ask her what was wrong, but I knew that whatever it was, she'd tell me when she was ready.

Finally, she turned to face me. Laying her cheek on her knee, she took another big breath. "My dad died today."

Holy shit. I wasn't expecting that.

"What?"

Her face crinkled up and she started to cry again. "My stepmom called. Apparently he went to sleep last night and never woke up this morning. They think he had a massive heart attack in his sleep."

I scooted closer and put my arm around her shoulders. "I'm so sorry."

She pulled the tissue out of her pocket and wiped her eyes again as she leaned against my chest. "We weren't close. He'd never even met Maura. I feel silly being as upset as I am."

"He was your dad. It doesn't matter if you didn't talk often. It doesn't matter if you hadn't talked in years, it still sucks. Don't feel silly." I kissed the top of her head, leaving my mouth against it as I rubbed her bare shoulder with my thumb.

She sniffed again. "He was the only family member I had left. Now I'm completely alone."

Right there, sitting on the couch in her living room, my cement heart broke into a million tiny pieces.

"You're not alone," I reassured her. "I may not be family technically, but I'm here, and I'm not going anywhere."

She pulled away from my chest and leaned back against the couch, picking at the tissue in her hands. "How long do you really think you're gonna want to keep hanging out with your dead best friend's wife?"

"Listen, at the beginning, yes . . . I came over here because it was something I told Mike I would do, but it quickly evolved into more. *Much* more." I turned to face her on the couch, pulling one leg up in front of me. "I like being here. I like hanging with Maura and Matthew. I like hanging with you. You guys make me less lonely too."

She turned her head toward me, blinking a couple times as she searched my face. The moonlight peeked in through a slit in the curtains, shining right on her face as her blue eyes sparkled.

Her head lay back against my arm and she bit her lip like she was holding something in.

"What?" I asked, tilting my head to mirror hers.

"Why don't you talk to your parents?"

"Oh," I groaned. "That's a long story that you don't want to hear and I don't want to tell."

"What if I do want to hear it?" she asked softly.

I shook my head and stared down at the couch. "It's not pretty."

She pressed her lips together and sighed. "None of those stories ever are."

"You're right." I nodded slowly. "Okay, here goes . . . When I was little, my life was normal. Like you, I was an only child. I don't know exactly why, but in fourth grade, everything changed. It started with getting picked on in school. Ruthlessly. I walked through the halls and the kids bounced me around like a Ping-Pong ball, literally shoving me back and forth. Eventually, that wasn't enough. They would take my lunch and throw it away before I could eat it or trip me in the halls." I finally looked up at Michelle, who was staring back at me so deeply I just wanted to lay my head in her lap and stop talking. Reliving my childhood was so exhausting.

"Anyway,"—I cleared my throat—"finally I'd had enough and decided to defend myself. I started punching anyone from that group of boys who came near me, and of course, *I* was the one who got in trouble because they never got caught. The principal called a meeting with my parents and I was actually relieved. I had told them about the bullying many times, and I remember thinking, this is it. It's finally going to end. My parents will give the principal a piece of their mind and all this will be over. But it wasn't. My mom wanted to take me to a doctor who would pump my body full of pills that would calm me down, but my dad had other ideas. He thought the key to ending the bullying was to teach me to be tougher, so that's what he set out to do."

Michelle reached out and put her hand on mine, squeezing it as her brows pulled in tight.

"He immediately threw me into hockey so I could get my ass kicked and really learn how to fight, but the real fighting started after I got home. If he sensed I was about to cry, over any little thing, he would stand in front of me, inches from my face, and scream at me until I pulled it together. Or he'd make me do three hundred push-ups in one night, until I couldn't even lift my arms to brush my teeth before bed. This one time, I remember getting into a fight at school, and they sent a note home saying that I would have a twenty-minute detention the next day. That night, he made me sit in the bathtub full of ice and freezing water. Every time I complained or cried, he would pour more freezing water over my head and add another minute to the timer. He never actually hit me or anything like that, but I almost wish that he had. The bruises would have gone away, but the shit I had to put up with has lasted so much longer."

I took a deep breath and laced my fingers together in an attempt to stop my hands from trembling. "Anyway, thankfully, it turned out I was good at hockey and had my pick of colleges. I left home the summer after my senior year of high school and never looked back. Instead of going home during summers, I would stay with friends or live on campus. I was drafted straight out of college, and I've been on my own ever since."

"Where was your mom during all this?"

An awkward laugh escaped me. "Sitting in the living room watching *Wheel of Fortune*."

Michelle closed her eyes and shook her head as two tears ran down her cheek. "So instead of protecting you from the bullies—"

"My father became the ultimate bully," I finished her sentence.

"I think about Matthew and someone doing that to him," she stuttered through a sob, "and I think I would kill them with my own bare hands."

"That's how it should be," I said, "but not all parents come with that built-in protective gene, I guess."

"Have they ever tried to contact you?"

"Oh, yeah. When I got drafted, it was all over the news, especially in my hometown. They called, wrote to me, even showed up at my first apartment once. The last thing I remember saying to my father was that I was bigger and could fight a lot better than when I was twelve, so he needed to get the fuck away from me fast. My mom stood next to him, sobbing into a tissue."

"I'm so sorry." Michelle squeezed my hand again.

"Eh, it is what it is, right? Like you said, we all have our fucked-up stories about our childhood. I just know that if I ever become a father, I'm gonna go to the ends of the fucking earth to protect my kids. I'll slay bullies, principals, dragons . . . it doesn't matter. No one will hurt my kids." My eyes started to sting but not because I was thinking about my future unborn children; I was thinking of Matthew and Maura sleeping upstairs.

"Do you ever cry?"

The house was so quiet you could hear the clock ticking in the kitchen, but that question rang out in the darkness loud and clear.

"No," I replied. "Since I moved out of that house, I've only cried once."

She didn't ask when that had been. She knew.

I put my feet up on the coffee table as she curled up on the couch with her head on my lap. Gently, I pulled her bun down and slowly combed her hair with my fingers until she was snoring softly, and for a long time after that until I fell asleep.

"Viper!"

My eyes snapped open at the sound of my name, but my back was locked up. I blinked a couple times, trying to get my bearings and remember what the hell had happened the night before. I lifted my head to look around and realized I was lying on my side on Michelle's couch with my arm wrapped around her waist. She must have been exhausted because she slept right through

Matthew's morning wake-up call. I carefully lifted my arm off of her and brought my hand to my lips, signaling for Matthew to be quiet. I slid out from behind Michelle and scooted down the couch like an inchworm as Matthew covered his mouth and giggled. I finally stood and stretched my arms up as far as they would go.

Matthew wrinkled his nose and jerked his head back as he pointed at my morning friend pitching a tent in my pants. "What's that?"

"Uh . . . we'll talk about that in a few years," I whispered as I adjusted myself and turned him around to walk toward the kitchen. I grabbed a blanket off the nearby chair and carefully draped it over Michelle. We went upstairs to check on Maura, who was standing, bouncing up and down in her crib.

"Good morning," I said as I walked over to pick her up.

She grinned at me and shot her arms out, anxious to be picked up. I gently scooped her up and sat on the floor of her bedroom with her and Matthew.

"Why are we up here?" Matthew asked, completely confused.

"We're just gonna stay up here and let your mommy rest for a little longer, okay?"

He nodded.

I lifted Maura and felt that her bottom was damp. "Uh-oh. Your sister is wet. Wanna teach me how to change a diaper?"

He turned his nose up again and shook his head.

"Thanks for nothing, bud." I rustled his hair, which was already messy from sleeping. "Brody does this all the time. Surely I can figure it out, right?"

I scanned the room for a diaper storage area.

Nothing.

"Do you know where Mom keeps the diapers at least?"

He jumped up and opened a drawer in the white dresser. It was stocked, full of diapers and wipes and weird creams and potions. I grabbed one diaper and turned back to Maura, who was staring as nervously at me as I was at her.

· I laid her on the ground and pulled her pajama bottoms off, tossing them to the side. Paying careful attention to how I took her diaper off, I figured I could just reverse that to put the new one on. Easier said than done.

It took me three attempts to get the new diaper situated under her, but eventually I did. I pulled the little tabs out and secured them, feeling like I'd just walked through some daddy rite of passage.

"Look at that. I did it!" I lifted Maura proudly to show Matthew, who covered his mouth with his hand and giggled as he pointed behind me.

Michelle leaned against the door frame with her arms folded across her chest, smiling at us. Her hair was a little wild, but sexy as hell. She totally rocked that morning-after look like a fucking boss.

"Good morning."

"Morning." She grinned as she came over and sat down with us.

"I tried to let you sleep a little longer. Sorry if we woke you."

"No, that's okay." Matthew plopped down in her lap and she wrapped her arms around him, kissing the side of his head. "I appreciate it, though."

"Look what I did." I pointed to Maura's diaper. "First time ever trying it, and I nailed it."

Leaning down to inspect my dirty work, she pulled her bottom lip up and nodded. "Oh, you nailed it all right . . . assuming the backward diaper thing is in these days."

Matthew giggled so hard that he tipped right off her lap as she took Maura from me and fixed her diaper.

I held my hands up. "I get points for trying, though, right?"

Michelle reattached the tabs on Maura's diaper and sat her up straight. She looked straight into my eyes and smiled sweetly. "You get points for a lot more than that."

Chapter
30

"**Y**OU'RE LATE." DR. ROBERTS WAS standing in her office doorway waiting for me when I walked through her small waiting room door.

"I know," I sighed. "Sorry."

"It's okay. Come on in. Have a seat."

She closed the door, walked over to get our water bottles, and then sat down.

"So, you haven't been here in a couple weeks. What's new?"

Every fucking thing.

"I don't know. Nothing really, I guess. Life has just been busy."

"Tell me about it. Fill me in." She ran her tongue between her top lip and teeth as she relaxed back in her chair and crossed her legs.

"Well, my season started, so that in itself makes my life more interesting."

She nodded. "I bet. More time restraints and things requiring more of your time and focus."

"Yeah." I stared down at the coffee table, deciding whether or not to take a leap of faith right there in her office.

Fuck it. Why not?

"Focus isn't something I've had a lot of lately," I continued.

She pulled her brows in tight, frowning at me. "How come? Is the abstaining thing throwing you off?"

"Surprisingly, no. I'm actually not hating that part."

Her eyebrows shot up. "Really?"

"It's weird. I feel like I've had more clarity since that whole thing started, if that makes any sense." I grabbed the water bottle from the table and opened it, convinced I sounded like a total douche.

"It absolutely makes sense. This thing, the sex thing, is like a weight you've carried around with you for so long, something you feel like you *have* to have, but the minute you shed it, you find that you didn't really need it after all."

I laughed, shaking my head back and forth. "I wouldn't go that far, but it has definitely had an impact."

"So you said you feel like you've had more clarity because of this, yet you're having trouble focusing? I'm confused."

"The trouble focusing isn't because of that. It's because . . . of a person."

Her lips parted as she stiffened in her chair. "I was not expecting to hear that. Is this someone new in your life?"

"Not really." Shifting uncomfortably on the couch, I crossed my ankle over my knee. I knew Dr. Roberts wouldn't judge me, but I was still reluctant to tell her who was stealing all of my brain space. "I've known *of* her for a long time, but just recently I've grown to know her much better."

"Ahhh." She nodded. "Michelle."

"Bingo."

"So, what's going on there? Lust? Feelings? Both?"

"Lust for sure, but I can't go there. And definitely feelings, but I *really* can't go there." Just saying those words frustrated me. For the first time in my life, I'd met a woman who I wanted to hang out with constantly, wanted to know every single thing I could about her, wanted to protect her fiercely, yet she was untouchable.

"Why can't you go there?"

I looked at Dr. Roberts like she was nuts. "She was married to my best friend."

"But she's not anymore."

My blood started to boil. "Yeah, because I killed him."

"Viper, you didn't *kill* anyone. It was an accident. You have to realize that."

I closed my eyes and rubbed my temples with my fingertips, completely ignoring her. While I did feel a certain new level of positivity in my life since I'd been seeing Dr. Roberts, sometimes she still frustrated the fuck out of me.

I sighed and opened my eyes, dropping my hands into my lap.

"I know you just wished me away, but I'm still here," she said, staring right at me. "And still saying the same thing I did two minutes ago. You need to stop beating yourself up over that accident. Let me ask you this—if Mike hadn't died the way he did, say he passed in a car accident instead, would you still feel this guilty about falling in love with Michelle?"

"Whoa, first of all, no one said *love*. I said *feelings*. There are many feelings other than love. Second, probably. She was still the wife of my best friend. Any feelings I have for her above and beyond friendship make me a dick."

"Shit happens, Viper. People die. Life goes on. You are still alive, and you can't keep living worried that you're going to hurt someone who's not here anymore." Her voice was gentle but stern as she leaned forward in her chair, resting her elbows on her knees. "Feelings are weird little things. We have absolutely no control over them. You can try and tell your feelings which way to go, but they're defiant bastards who don't always listen and tend to go wherever they want, paying no attention to time or circumstance."

Interesting way to look at it.

"Do you think she feels the same way about you?"

I locked my fingers on the top of my head, letting it fall back against the couch in frustration as I stared up at the ceiling. "Who knows? Women are so damn confusing."

"Don't give me that. You've been with and around enough women to know when they're into you and when they're not. Be straight with me."

"Fine." I dropped my hands and looked straight at her. "Then yes, I think maybe she is."

"You can't completely shut the door on this, Viper. If you need to close it for a little while and think about it some more, that's fine, but don't shut it completely. Sometimes once you shut a door, you can't open it again."

The lightbulb flipped on and caught my attention.

"Wow." I looked from it to her. "That went fast."

She gave me a tight smile. "That's what happens when you're half an hour late for an appointment."

"My bad." I stood up, grabbed the water bottle off of the table, and headed for the exit door.

"Hey, Viper?" she called after me. "Wanna keep going? Maybe a whole month?"

I got to the exit door and rested my head against it without turning around. "Fine," I agreed. "I'm getting pretty good with my left hand anyway. It's kinda like having a new girlfriend."

Once I got to my car, I checked my messages. To my surprise, I had one from Michelle. She never texted me first.

> M: Hey, I know you said you were busy this morning, but I wanted to shoot a quick text anyway and tell you thanks for last night. It was a super shitty day, but you really turned it around when you showed up. I appreciate it.

I stared down at my phone, thinking about what Dr. Roberts had just said about the door. At that moment, I didn't want to just fling it open, I wanted to pull it off its fucking hinges and throw it away so it could never close again.

> Don't thank me. It was a no-brainer.

> M: By the way, I wanted to ask you . . . I looked at your hockey schedule. You guys are in town on December 12th, and there isn't a game at all that day. Care to accompany me to my neighbor's wedding so I don't have to sit by myself like a loser?

> Sure, but Viper still doesn't dance.

> M: I wasn't even gonna ask. ;)

Sleeping on that couch had done my back no favors, so I decided to head to the stadium and see the trainer. After a little heat and a little ice, I figured I'd get in a quick workout while I was there, even though it was our day off. I needed something to keep my brain occupied anyway.

I was on the treadmill with my earbuds in when Brody walked by the door. He looked in but kept going, backing up when he realized it was me.

He said something but I couldn't hear him and lip-reading was not one of my specialties. I hit the pause button and stood on the sides of the treadmill as it slowed to a stop, then plucked my buds from my ears. "What'd you say?"

"I said, 'What the hell are you doing here?'"

"I had an appointment with the mind reader this morning. My back was all tight, so I came in to see Pete and have him work on it." I leaned against the rail of the treadmill and crossed my arms.

Brody glanced quickly around the room, making sure no one could hear him. "How's that going, by the way? The therapist thing?"

I shrugged. "Good, I guess. I've been given the all clear from her with the office, so at this point it's my choice to keep going."

"Nice!" He reached out and punched my bicep.

"Yeah, I guess."

"What? I thought you liked her?"

"I do, but her . . . *practices* . . . are a little unconventional."

He frowned at me. "Like what?"

It was my turn to look around the room for nosy ears. "A while back, she challenged me to abstain from sex for a week, so to humor her, I did it. Then she upped the challenge to two weeks. Again, I did it. Now, she has me going a month, and I'm sure after that, it'll keep going."

The corners of his mouth pointed down as he nodded his head to the side. "That's definitely interesting, especially for you. Has it fallen off yet?"

"No, asshole," I said sarcastically. "It hasn't been all that bad, actually. Different, yes, but not bad."

"Well, whatever this doctor is doing seems to be working. Tell her I said to keep it up." He winked at me and tossed his hoodie over his shoulder as he turned for the door. "By the way,"—he stopped suddenly and spun back toward me—"at the risk of you going off on me again, what's up with you and Michelle?"

"Nothing. Why?"

"I don't know." He shrugged. "I guess Kacie talked to her the other day, and she said something about you giving her cooking lessons?"

I nodded and put my earbuds back in. "That's exactly what I'm doing. Now, fuck off."

Chapter
31

"**W**HAT ARE YOU GUYS MAKING?**" Matthew climbed onto the stool next to the island and studied the stuff spread out on the counter, wrinkling up his little face as he did so. He leaned in closer to the garlic and plugged his nose. "Ew! It smells gross!"

"You're gonna like it, I promise," Michelle said as she lifted him off the stool, patting his butt as he ran away. She turned to me. "He's gonna like it, right?"

"Hey," I said, holding my hands up, "you made the promise, not me."

"The odds are in our favor, though, right? So far we've made the lasagna, tilapia, and rosemary chicken. He's loved all of those. Oh! And burgers that were so good they've ruined me for all other burgers for the rest of eternity."

"The rest of eternity, huh? That's pretty big."

"Yep." She nodded. "You're going to have to supply me with burgers at least once a month for the rest of my life, okay?"

I'm totally cool with that.

When I didn't answer, she grinned and nudged me with her sharp little elbow right in the ribs. "All right, what next?"

"Now you're gonna take that bowl with all the seasonings in

it and rub your meat." I tried my hardest not to laugh.

Michelle tilted her head to the side and pressed her lips together.

"What?" I defended. "I swear I'm not being dirty. That's what you're supposed to do."

"Fine." She picked up a small handful of the seasoning and dropped it on top of the pork tenderloin, massaging it in with her hands.

I walked up behind her and leaned in close above her shoulder. "Oh yeah, that's it. Rub it real good. Get it all the way in there," I growled as dirty as I could.

She laughed and elbowed me again. "Knock it off."

"I can't help myself. When you rub the pork like that, it really gets *my* spices flowing." I danced in a circle around the island.

She pretended to ignore me as she bit her lip and concentrated on what she was doing, but I could tell by the pink in her cheeks I was getting under her skin.

"Okay. Now you're gonna flip it over and rub it again. Make sure you really get in there and massage that meat. Tell it you love it. Show it."

Her blue eyes flashed up to me before she rolled them toward the ceiling. "There's something seriously wrong with you, you know that?"

I tilted my head left and right. "So I've been told."

She finished with the spice rub and held her messy hands up in the air. "Now what?"

"Now smack it."

She pulled her brows in tight, frowning at me. "Huh?"

"Smack the meat," I repeated.

Her shoulders slumped and she glared at me, narrowing her eyes suspiciously. "I'm not gonna smack this piece of meat."

"You have to. It helps in the cooking process," I said as seriously as I could. "It loosens the juices."

"Oh." She straightened up and paused, thinking about it. "Okay."

Turning back toward the stove, she took a deep breath before slapping the pork with her right hand. "Like that?" She glanced back for my approval.

Holding my laugh in at that point was physically painful, but I was determined. "Yep, just like that. Smack it again. Harder."

She hesitantly raised her right hand and brought it down hard against the tenderloin two more times. By the second time, my gut was ready to explode. I laughed out loud so hard that I startled her.

"You're such a jerk!" she shrieked playfully, charging at me with her wet, spice-rubbed hands. I caught her wrists and held them away from my face.

"I'm sorry, but you were so adorably naive about the whole thing. I couldn't help it."

She wiggled her fingers, trying to get close enough to slather that stuff all over my face, but I wasn't about to let her. I pushed her back, pinning her between me and the counter, gently moving her hands so that I had them securely behind her back.

"The minute you let me loose, you're dead." Her eyes were wild and mischievous.

"What makes you think I'm letting you go anytime soon?"

She pulled and wiggled, desperately trying to break free before she finally gave up and sighed, blowing the pieces of loose hair off her forehead. "How long do you think you can keep this up?"

I leaned in close, breathing onto her cheek. "Oh, I can go all night, baby."

Redness started at the base of her neck, quickly creeping up to her face as she swallowed hard.

"Give up yet?" I asked.

"Fine," she snapped. "I give up."

"Now, when I let go, you promise you're going to go to the

sink and wash your hands?"

She stared me straight in the eye and nodded.

"All right, then." I slowly released her hands and backed away.

She pulled her arms around to the front of her and inspected them. In a flash, she swiped her hand across my face and bolted out of the kitchen.

I covered my eyes with my hands. "Ow! Ow! The spices went in my eyes!" I called out, peeking through my hands to see if she had come back yet.

After a couple more whimpers from me, she peeked her head around the corner cautiously. "Are you serious? Oh shit." She hurried over and pulled a dish towel out of the drawer, running it under cold water for a second.

I continued to writhe in pain, waiting for her to get closer.

She stood in front of me on her tippy toes, carefully lifting the damn cold cloth to my face, when I reached out and grabbed her around the waist. "Gotcha!"

"Crap!" she shouted, kicking and squirming to try and get out of my grasp. As I stood with a tight grip on her, laughing smugly, her heel connected with my balls. Not a full-on kick but a graze, and any guy will tell you, a graze is a hundred times worse than a straight kick to the junk.

The jolt of her heel made me lose my hold on her waist. Just as she wiggled loose and was about to run, I reached out and spun her, grabbing both of her wrists and pinning them against the wall above her head.

"You done yet?" I panted, inches from her face.

Her lips were parted slightly, her chest rising up and down as she stared right into my eyes. I could feel her warm breath on my skin as I searched her face, noticing a tiny scar she had above her lip. I wanted to kiss it. "Not even close," she said barely above a whisper, arching her eyebrow in challenge. "Someone once told me not to start something I couldn't finish, so—"

The doorbell rang, startling both of us. In unison, our heads snapped toward the front of the house. Michelle's neighbor Jodi was standing on the porch, frantically waving at us.

"Damn it," Michelle mumbled under her breath as she pulled her hands out of my grasp. "Can you let her in while I wash up?"

"Got it." I sighed, annoyed that I had to let her go.

I opened the door and waved her in. "Come on in. Jodi, right?"

"Thanks." She sniffed as she walked through the doorway. Her eyes were red and puffy, and a wadded-up tissue was clenched in her hand. Anxiety spread through me. I avoided crying women like the fucking plague. Except for one. When she cried, I ran toward her, not away. "Uh . . . Michelle's in here. Follow me." I turned and started walking, hoping she would just follow so I didn't have to face her again.

As we got to the kitchen, Michelle was wiping her hands on another towel. She took one look at Jodi and rushed toward her. "What's wrong?"

Jodi's lip quivered and she crumpled into Michelle's open arms. "I'm not getting married," she wailed.

"What are you talking about?" Michelle asked. "Come here, sit down. Tell me what happened."

I tried to move out of the way but somehow got caught sitting at the kitchen table with the two of them. Panicking like a trapped animal, my mind raced with possible escape routes. If I went to the living room to watch TV, I would look like a dick, but I didn't really want to sit there and witness whatever was about to take place.

Got it!

I stood up and leaned in just a bit toward them. "I don't mean to interrupt, but Michelle, I'm gonna work on dinner while you guys chat."

She looked up at me with guilt in her eyes. "Are you sure? I'm so sorry."

"No, please. Don't worry about it. I got this." I scooted out from behind the table and moved quickly over to the counter. I could still hear them talking, but at least I wasn't expected to be a willing participant anymore.

"So what's going on? Your wedding is next week," Michelle said.

Jodi sniffed and blew her nose like a bullhorn into her tissue. "I don't even know. We're sitting around having coffee before work and all of a sudden, I'm in the middle of a meltdown, freaking out about whether or not this marriage is gonna work when the others haven't. I can't be divorced three times, Michelle. I just can't."

I watched in the reflection of the microwave as Michelle put her hand on Jodi's shoulder. "Okay, okay. Slow down. One thing at a time. What even brought this on?"

"I have no idea. He said something about wanting to plant lilies in the backyard next summer. I hate lilies."

"Honey, then all you have to do is tell him you hate lilies."

"But it's not that. Shouldn't he know I hate lilies? Why do I have to tell him? And it's just lilies this time, but what if next time it's the kind of car he wants me to buy?" Jodi's voice was rising in a panic, and I couldn't help but roll my eyes as I slid the pork into the oven.

"Okay, let me ask you something. Do you love him?"

"Yes," Jodi answered quickly.

"No," Michelle continued. "Like really, truly, from the bottom of your soul love him? Can't picture spending another day without him kind of love?"

Jodi took a small pause this time. "Yes," she said quietly.

"Then you have nothing to worry about. I was only married once, but here's what it taught me. We grow up, become adults, and get married. From the moment the ring is on our finger, we have these grand ideas in our heads of how our life is supposed to go forever—how things should end up—but it's not really up to us, is it? I don't know who it's up to, but we just have to go with it. We have to keep riding the waves of life, trying not to get sucked too far out and get lost at sea, ya know?"

At that point, I'd stopped cutting the potatoes and was listening closely.

Michelle had waves.

I had doors.

Maybe we could sit on my door and float on top of those waves together.

"You're so right." Jodi sniffed again.

Michelle continued, "If you love him, fight for him, fight for both of you. And plant some damn lilies."

Chapter
32

WEDDING DAY! NOT MY OWN, but Michelle's neighbor Jodi and her soon-to-be husband, Vince, who I had yet to meet. It probably made me a total douche, but when we'd been at Michelle's the week before and Jodi was having her pre-wedding freak-out, I wasn't all that disappointed at the thought of it being canceled. I had to get dressed up enough when the team traveled. Having to do it on my downtime was pure torture. The one positive thing about the wedding was I got to have Michelle to myself for a handful of hours, and that was worth wearing a monkey suit any day.

I pulled into Michelle's driveway and straightened my jacket as I got out of the car. The front door opened as I walked up the steps, and Matthew stood there, shielding his eyes from the sun as he waited for me. The ground was already covered in snow, but the bright sunshine that day made it seem not so bad.

"What's up, buddy?" I held my arms out.

He stared down at the ground, not as excited to see me as he normally was. "My mom said I can't jump on you today or I'll wrinkle your clothes," he pouted.

"Oh." I stepped in and closed the door behind me. "Well, she didn't tell me I couldn't hug *you*." I knelt down to his level, holding my arms out again. His face lit up as he eagerly crashed into me so hard I almost fell over backward.

"I'll be down in a minute!" Michelle called from up the stairs.

Matthew pulled back and rolled his little eyes. "She said that ten times already."

"It's best you learn it now, Matthew." I laughed. "They never mean it when they say that."

He nodded like he knew exactly what I was talking about and we walked hand in hand to the kitchen. A young girl sat at that kitchen table shoveling spoonfuls of yogurt into Maura's mouth. When Maura noticed me walk into the room, she smiled so big yogurt oozed out the sides of her mouth.

"What are you smiling at, silly?" She followed Maura's eyes over to me. "Oh, hi. I didn't hear anyone come in. Sorry. I'm Desi, the babysitter."

"Hi, Desi. I'm Viper."

"Viper's my best friend," Matthew told Desi proudly as he stood next to me.

I looked down at him. "That's absolutely right."

"Ahhh!" Michelle yelled out as she carefully ran into the kitchen in her heels. "I can't find my favorite lipstick." She opened drawer after drawer, slamming them all shut again.

I don't know shit about fashion and even less about women's clothes, but when we'd texted earlier, she asked if I had a silver tie. I lied and said yes, immediately going out to buy one. I had no idea it would be to accompany *that*.

She had on a silver dress that clung to her in places that made me want to weep. Silver heels with straps and more straps wrapped around her beautiful little feet. Her hair was down and wavy, and it looked sexy as fuck. She didn't wear her hair down often, and I had to close my hands into fists to keep from marching over and running them through it.

"Here it is! In the battery drawer. Makes sense." She laughed, finally standing up straight. Our eyes locked and my mouth went dry. "I'm hurrying, I promise. I'm almost ready. Why are you

staring at me like that?" She looked down and inspected herself before flipping her eyes back up to me.

I put my hands in my pockets and shook my head as I slowly moved my eyes from her face all the way down and back up again. "I was just thinking that if *that* is *almost* ready, I'm the luckiest man in the world."

Her lips parted on a soft gasp as she walked over to kiss my cheek. At the last second, I turned and our lips touched. Not a full kiss—just the corners—but that almost-kiss was more intense than *any* other kiss I'd had in my entire life. I waited for her to pull back, but she didn't. She closed her eyes and sighed, holding it right there, just as scared as I was to make it official and turn her head. Eventually, she did move away and smile at me. It was a sad smile. A smile that confirmed to me that she felt the same way I did, but she knew just as much as I did that it could never happen.

She swallowed hard and took a shaky breath. "I'll be back in a couple minutes, okay?"

I nodded and watched her walk out of the room, already excited for when she'd come back.

Thirty minutes later, we finally kissed the kids good-bye and headed out the door. The short drive to the church bummed me out because, selfishly, I wanted to hog Michelle to myself all night long. Once seated in the pew, things got a little awkward. People whispered and stared. I even caught a couple of wedding guests snapping pics. I wasn't the most famous guy on my team, but all it would take was for one person to recognize me and it would spread like wildfire. The last thing I wanted was to take away from Jodi and Vince's day.

Michelle rested her hand on my knee and I practically jumped out of my skin. "Whoa. Are you okay?"

"Yeah." I looked straight into her eyes and focused hard on drowning out the rest of the church. "I'm good. Just ready to get the show on the road."

As if the wedding gods themselves were smiling down on me, the ceremony started right then. And even more awesome was how quick it went. Flower girls, ring bearer, bridesmaids, groomsmen, bride, vows, rings, kiss, done. My kind of ceremony.

Time to party!

The reception room was badass! The tables were decorated with red cloths, and there was a bar in the corner made out of ice. Very quickly after we sat, they introduced the bride and groom, cut the cake, and announced we could start eating, but there wasn't a waiter on the floor.

I leaned in toward Michelle. "Clearly I don't go to enough weddings. Where's the food?"

Michelle giggled and leaned in closer, her hair brushing against my jaw as she did. "Vince had a very specific idea of what he wanted, so there's a mashed potato bar over there." She pointed toward the far corner of the room. "A stir-fry bar over there." She pointed to another corner. "A meat bar over there, and finally, in that corner"—she paused and laughed again—"a pizza bar."

I sat up straight and looked at her. "You've got to be shitting me."

"I wish I were."

After I'd made two trips to each food station, I was pretty sure someone was going to have to roll me to the car and take me to the hospital to have my stomach pumped—but it was worth every delicious bite. Before long, the DJ turned off the dinner music and started playing something more upbeat. Drinks were flowing at the bar and the brightly colored DJ lights were shining on all of our faces.

"Michelle?" We both turned in our seats at the sound of her name being yelled.

I had no idea who they were, but Michelle's eyes bulged and her mouth fell open in shock as she stood and ran straight into

the arms of two women. Then they all began squealing and jumping up and down together.

They hugged and celebrated for at least five minutes before they eventually made their way over to our table.

"Viper?" Michelle shouted my name as loudly as she could over the music. I stood and turned around as she motioned toward the women. "These are my friends from college, Sarah and Nicole. Ladies, this is my . . . friend Viper."

"Hi, nice to meet you." I held my hand out and shook both of their hands. "Did you all know you were gonna see each other here tonight?"

"No." Michelle shook her head. "These two were my sorority sisters back in college, and by some weird twist of fate, they both teach at the same school Jodi does. I had no idea."

"It's the best surprise ever!" Sarah hollered as she clapped her hands together and tucked them under her chin while Nicole stood next to her, nodding like a bobblehead doll.

"It really is. It's been like what . . . nine years since we've seen each other?" Michelle asked.

"Yeah, you had just started dating Mike," Nicole answered, flashing me an awkward glance like she'd said something she shouldn't have.

"We really should get together and catch up sometime, for sure." Michelle leaned in close so they could hear her.

"Absolutely, but we'll let you get back to your date here." Sarah nodded toward me. "It was nice meeting you, Viper." They both offered up a small wave.

"You too," I called back as Michelle and I returned to our seats. I pulled Michelle's chair out for her and bent down into her ear so she could hear me. "That was interesting, huh?"

"It really was." Her eyes dropped sadly to the table as she picked at a spot on the tablecloth.

I rested my hand on her knee and leaned in toward her again. "What's the matter?"

She shrugged. "I don't know. I just forgot how much I missed them until I saw them. I really haven't done a good job of keeping in contact with my old friends."

I lifted my hand to her shoulder, enjoying the feeling of her soft, bare skin under my fingers. "I'm sorry."

"No biggie." She waved her hand. "I'm just in a funk tonight. I don't know why."

The loud music faded out as the DJ grabbed the microphone. "We're gonna slow it down just a bit here, so grab the one you love and take them for a spin around the floor."

I recognized the song as soon as he started playing it. I'd heard it on the radio every five minutes lately, and it made me think of Michelle each and every fucking time. "Thinking Out Loud" by Ed Sheeran.

Completely oblivious to me staring at her, she turned around in her seat. She rested her chin on her arm and her arm on the back of her chair as she gazed out at the couples dancing around the floor. The white lights coming from the electronic disco ball bounced off her face, illuminating her sadness to the point that I couldn't take it anymore.

I stood up and offered my hand to her. She frowned down at it for a second before realizing what I was asking. Her eyes flashed up to mine and she licked her lips as she gently put her hand in mine. "I thought Viper doesn't dance?"

I kissed the top of it. "Viper breaks his own rules sometimes . . . but only for someone very special."

As we walked out to the dance floor hand in hand, I was beyond proud to call her mine, at least for that night.

I stopped and held my hand up, twirling her out away from me before pulling her back against me as tight as I could.

"What was that?" She looked at me incredulously with the biggest grin I'd seen on her face all night.

"Don't get your hopes up. That's the only move I have," I

joked, wrapping my hands around her waist. She rested her forearms on my shoulders and gently rubbed the back of my neck, sending shivers all the way to my fucking toes. As we swayed to the music, she closed her eyes and rested her head on my chest.

After a minute, she straightened and glanced around the room quickly, dipping her face toward the ground just a bit. "People are staring at you."

"I am absolutely one hundred percent certain that I'm not the one they're staring at."

Her eyes glistened and she pressed her lips together. "Viper— "

"Don't," I interrupted, smiling at her as I brushed her cheek with the back of my hand. "I know exactly what you're going to say because you should say it, but don't. For now, for just this song . . . let's pretend, okay? You're not Mike's wife, and I'm not Mike's best friend. Just this one song."

A tear fell from her eye, but she didn't argue as she laid her head back on my chest, right where it belonged.

Chapter
33

O UR SONG ENDED AND WE made our way back to the table, both a little depressed that our time together was over.

"Hey, Michelle!"

I didn't bother turning around. I knew it was Sarah and Nicole again.

"The party is dying down around here, and we were thinking of going to grab some coffee, or a martini." She giggled. "Anyway, would you want to join us?"

"Oh, thanks, you guys. That's so sweet of you, but I can't tonight," Michelle answered.

All I could think about while she turned down their offer was the look on her face when she'd talked about how much she missed hanging with her friends.

"Wait." I turned in my seat to face her. "Why not?"

She shrugged. "I don't know. I have the sitter and kids at home."

"The kids are sleeping, and I can pay the sitter. You should go."

She leaned in close. "You don't have to do that."

"I know I don't have to. I want to. Seriously . . . I'll go relieve Desi, and you go out for a bit with these two." I turned to Sarah and Nicole. "Can one of you give her a ride home?"

Sarah nodded. "Absolutely."

I shook my head slowly. "You have no reason not to go. You said yourself you missed them."

"Oh, please, Michelle?" Nicole begged. "Just for a little while? I swear we won't stay out late."

Michelle's eyes grew hopeful as they bounced back and forth between me and the girls. "Okay. Let's do it."

Sarah and Nicole shrieked in excitement at an ear-piercing level as Michelle bent down close to me. "You sure this is okay with you?"

"Yes." I laughed and nodded. "Go. Have fun. Keep your dress pulled down, please."

I drove myself back to Michelle's house, replaying that dance over and over in my head.

Could we make it work?

Could we both let go just enough to make it possible without letting go completely?

When her head had been on my chest and her arms were around me, I felt like anything was possible. That sounded so stupid and cliché, but it was true. Michelle made me feel invincible.

Once I was back at Michelle's, I gave Desi a hundred-dollar bill and sent her on her way. I took my suit jacket off, hung it on the back of a kitchen chair, and unbuttoned my pants to let my full belly loose. I grabbed the baby monitor from the kitchen and lay down on the couch in the living room, flipping to *SportsCenter* on the TV.

It was weird being in that room without Michelle there. As I sat there, in the quiet house with *SportsCenter* muted, my mind started to wander. It was in that very room less than a year ago that Big Mike had told me he could see me married with kids. He'd told me he thought it would soften my cement heart. How fucking ironic that it was his wife I was falling for and his kids I was helping parent? My eyes shifted around the room. Pictures of Mike and Michelle's wedding still hung on the wall. A bookcase in the corner was filled with framed pictures of their family.

The four of them at the hospital after Maura was born.

Mike and Matthew in the front yard, riding bikes.

Mike, Michelle, and Matthew at Walt Disney World.

Mike grinning with his hand on Michelle's pregnant stomach.

Mike and Michelle kissing.

My chest started to hurt like I'd been punched square in the sternum. For a second, I thought maybe I was having a heart attack. Then I realized I wasn't that lucky.

The living room started closing in around me as I paced the house, on the verge of a panic attack. What the fuck was I thinking hanging out there all the time? Why had I let myself get so close to Matthew and Maura? Why the fuck had I let myself fall for Michelle as hard and fast as I had? Why did I let myself fall for her at all?

Because of Big Mike, you dumb son of a bitch. You promised Big Mike you'd take care of his family, but instead you stole it.

I spent the next two hours sitting at the kitchen table with my head in my hands trying to figure out what I was going to say to Michelle when she got home. I didn't want to walk out of Matthew's life, not at all, but I couldn't keep coming to the house to see him. Maybe she'd let me take him once a week or something. The bigger question swirling around in my head was how long was it going to take for me to recover from this? I'd never felt like this about anyone before, and I'd certainly never lost anyone in this way. Could you ever recover from something like that?

The sound of a key jiggling in the door made my heart sink.

This is gonna suck.

I stood up and walked to the kitchen doorway, and I could tell immediately that Michelle had drank too much.

"Hey," she whispered loudly.

"Hey." My body stiffened as she walked right up to me and wrapped her arms around my waist. "Are you okay?"

"I'm fantastic," she slurred a little. "I had such a fun time with those girls."

"Where'd you guys go?"

"I don't know. Some bar." Letting go of my waist, she wobbled over to the fridge and grabbed a bottle of orange juice. She took a big drink and then stared at the bottle. "We should cook with this."

I tried not to laugh at her, but drunk Michelle was super fucking cute.

"Anyway, are the kids still sleeping?"

"Yep, not a peep out of them." I walked over and sat on the kitchen chair, wondering if it was the best time to talk to her.

"Good." She trailed her finger along the counter as she slowly walked over to me. "I've been thinking about that dance all night. It's driving me crazy, actually."

"Yeah, about that—"

"Shhh." She put a finger over my lips. "Don't say anything now. I don't want to talk. I just want to finish what we started."

Before I could react, she was sitting on my knee and her lips were on mine. She might have been drunk, but she still knew how to kiss. Her lips slowly moved up and down, back and forth against my own. The tip of her tongue darted out of her mouth and into mine as she ran her hands through my hair, roughly pulling me tighter against her. Something inside of me told me to stop, but a bigger something screamed at me to keep going. I hiked her dress up and cupped her ass, lifting her so she was straddling me, all the while praying that the kitchen chair didn't give out. I sat up straight and ran my hands up her back and around the nape of her neck, pulling her hair gently so I could get to her neck. Tugging the strap of her dress off her shoulder, I kissed and sucked along her collarbone.

She moaned, grinding her hips against me. "Let's go in the living room."

I ignored her, kissing my way from one side of her chest to the other.

"Viper, did you hear me?" she repeated through her panting. "Let's go to the living room."

I'd been avoiding that room all night. No way was I going to have sex with Michelle in there. No fucking way was I going to have sex with her at all.

"Wait a minute." I pulled back. "We can't do this."

"Yes, we can." She kissed me again, letting her hand wander over my pants. "Just this one night, remember? You said one song, but why can't we expand it to one night?"

I caught her hand before she shoved it inside my boxers. "We can't." I gently lifted her off of me and stood up, rubbing my temples with my hands as I paced the kitchen, trying to figure out what to do.

"What's going on with you?" she snapped, glaring at me as she pulled her skirt down. "For as long as I've known you, you've fucked anything that walks, and now here I am, throwing myself at you, and you're telling me *no?*"

"I'm sorry. Listen,"—I started panicking again—"I don't think we should be doing this right now. It's not right."

"Why isn't it right?"

"Because of Mike—" I started to explain.

"Oh, I'm *so* sick of you hiding behind Mike." She marched over to me. "I think you aren't attracted to me at all and you just use Mike as your fucking excuse to keep me at arm's length."

I'd never heard anything so insane in my entire life.

"What are you talking about? Not attracted to you?" I grabbed her hand and put it on my hard cock. "Does that feel like I'm not attracted to you?"

"Big deal!" She yanked her hand back. "Guys get hard whenever the wind blows. Matthew gets little boners all the time. Don't be so proud of yourself." She sniffed and turned away from me.

"Listen, Michelle . . ." I gently put my hand on her shoulder. "I just don't want to take that step tonight, because once we do, that's it. There's no going back and pretending it didn't happen."

She took another step away from me, out of my reach. "Get out," she mumbled quietly.

I couldn't believe what I was hearing. "What?"

She spun to face me as tears poured down her cheeks. "You heard me. I said get out. Get the fuck out of my house."

"Okay, please calm down," I begged. "You've had too much to drink and this night just went to shit really quickly. Can we just take a step back and breathe, please?"

"You breathe. You take a fucking step back. In fact, take a lot of steps back—all the way out of my house, and forget you ever came here in the first place."

Arguing with her when she was drunk was just making things worse. The situation needed to be diffused, and the only way I could do that was to leave. I buttoned my pants and grabbed my jacket off of the kitchen chair, trying hard to ignore the sinking feeling that sat heavy in my stomach as I walked out of the kitchen. I couldn't leave without trying to reason with her one more time. "Can we *please* just sit down, have some coffee, and talk about this?"

She was standing by the island with her arms wrapped around herself, staring down at the ground.

"Michelle?"

Her head lifted toward me; her eyes were cold and distant. "Good-bye, Viper."

Chapter
34

How are you? Is there anything I can do?

I HIT THE SEND BUTTON on my phone and slammed it down on my kitchen counter, knowing damn well she wasn't gonna respond. I'd sent the same fucking text every fucking day for the last thirteen days, and Michelle hadn't responded once. Not once. She'd told me to leave the night of the wedding, and I really thought she just needed to cool off, but when I'd texted her the next morning . . . nothing. She'd *always* responded before. I'd been trying to block it out with hockey, throwing myself into my games, staying after practices for extra workouts at the gym. None of it worked. Every blond woman I saw on the street reminded me of her, and every little kid reminded me of Matthew. I felt like I spent every minute of every day wondering what the hell they were doing. She constantly found a way to creep into my brain, and once she did, she would camp out there for the rest of the day.

I'd replayed that night in her kitchen over and over in my head, second guessing myself constantly. What would have happened if I hadn't stopped her? If I'd just let her keep kissing me the way she'd been? If I'd let her hand scoot down into my boxers? When I'd lifted her dress and pulled her toward me, my finger ran along the lace edge of her panties, and it was so sweet, so delicate, just like she was, and honestly . . . it intimidated me.

My phone beeped and my heart took off like a fucking rocket. I'd never grabbed it so fast in my whole life. It was a picture from Brody.

> B: Hey, Uncle V! Look who decided to join the world today! Grace Addison! She got here about 15 minutes ago.

Under the picture was a selfie of him grinning from ear to ear as he held the tiniest baby I'd ever seen in my whole life. She was kinda red and had shiny eyes, but was still oddly adorable.

> Whoa! No shit! Is that hair reddish or is it the picture?

> B: Nope, she definitely has some red in her hair like Kacie. Assuming it doesn't change, my mom might get her wish of a redheaded granddaughter after all.

> Congrats, brother. I'm happy for you. Give Kacie a kiss for me, and tell her I said good job.

I was annoyed. Happy for Brody but annoyed with myself that I couldn't even truly enjoy that moment with my friend because of the shitstorm I was feeling on the inside. How could *one* woman cause so many fucking emotions?

I stood up and shook my head. I'd had enough. I was done—with women and with abstinence.

I picked up my phone again, making an entirely different call before heading to my car.

"Hey, come in. I don't have a lot of time, but you sounded frantic." Dr. Roberts gestured me into her office. I walked past her to the coffee table and slammed my kitchen drawer full of numbers down, startling her. "Um . . . okay. What's that?"

"Those are phone numbers," I answered sharply with attitude as I stood between the couch and the coffee table with my hands

on my hips.

"Okay," she said slowly as she walked over to her seat, still staring at the drawer. "And you brought them here because?"

"I have no use for them anymore. Women are nothing but fucking trouble, and I'm done." I sighed and rubbed the back of my neck with my hand. The tension in my shoulders was making everything else hurt too.

She crossed her arms and leaned back in her chair as she pursed her lips. "Care to elaborate?"

"Since college, I've thought I had women figured out. You smile at them, pay them a few compliments, and before you know it, they're eating out of the palm of your hand. So why is it the first woman I actually *want* to listen to and spend time with has to be the most complicated woman on the planet?"

"Michelle?"

"Yes, Michelle," I snapped.

"What happened?"

"She asked me to go with her to a wedding a couple weeks ago and I went. We had a great time." I finally sat down as I let my thoughts drift for a second back to the way my arms had felt around her out on the dance floor. "A really great time. Anyway, she has too much to drink and throws herself at me. I do the right thing and stop it and somehow I'm the asshole. Now she won't talk to me."

"Wow." Dr. Roberts nodded slowly. "That's a lot of stuff to happen in one night. Why did you turn her down?"

"What?" I snapped, narrowing my eyes at her.

"Why did you turn her down?"

"No, no. I heard you, I just can't believe those words came out of your mouth." I stood up and paced the room, surprised that there wasn't a worn spot from my usual route, week after week. "*You* are the one who told me I couldn't have sex, remember?"

"So you turned her down because I told you not to have sex?"

"Well, no. Yes. I don't know." Frustration had consumed me, and I just wanted to be fixed. My head hurt. My chest hurt. My heart hurt. "I'm so damn confused. All I know is I had the most amazing night with her. I'd even started to think that maybe we could do this, that maybe we could find a way to make it work. And then, being in her house—Mike's house—I panicked."

"Why did you panic?"

"Because I still feel guilty."

"You have to move past that, Viper." She sighed. "It's already eating you alive, and it's going to continue to get worse. What happened was an *accident*."

"I know, but—"

"But what?" she interrupted.

"But it should have been me!" I yelled in frustration as I sat back on the couch.

"Okay, fine. It should have been you," she agreed sarcastically. "Then what?"

"Then what *what*?"

"If it would have been you, what would life be like now?"

Looking at her like she had two heads, I said slowly, "I don't know. I would be dead."

"And?"

"And . . . they would all still be here."

"Because . . ."

"Because life goes on."

"Exactly!" she exclaimed, throwing her skinny, tan arms in the air. "Because life goes on. So you can't keep worrying about what Mike *might* have thought or what *might* have happened if he were alive, because he's not. Before you respond, let me ask you another question." She held her hand up. "If you were dead, would you care what was happening down here on earth?"

"Would I care? I don't know—I'm dead." I shrugged nonchalantly. "But there are several people I'd haunt the shit out of, and you're making your way up that list very quickly."

"Get in line," she joked, rolling her eyes. "I'm serious, though. If you were deeply, madly in love with someone and you passed, especially as young as you are now, would you want that person to stay single and cry over you every day for the rest of their life?"

"Would that be so bad?" I answered playfully.

"Come on, be serious."

I sighed. "No, of course not. I'd want them to be happy."

"Exactly." She sat back and smiled. "Let me ask you one more thing . . ."

This lady makes my brain hurt.

"Do you think you make Michelle happy?"

"I have no idea."

"Don't give me that bullshit, blow-off answer." She glared at me and shook her head. "Think about it. Honestly, do you make her happy?"

Leaning forward on the couch, I rested my elbows on my knees and let my head drop toward the floor as I thought back to the last couple of months with Michelle. "All I know is when I'm with her, we're both happy, and when I'm not with her, I wish I were."

"Then why do you keep fighting this? Mike was your best friend in the whole world, right?"

I swallowed the sudden lump in my throat and nodded.

"Did you ever think for maybe a second that it's him up there pushing the two of you together?"

"What?" My eyes flew to hers.

"Maybe he wants the two of you together. He knows you; he knows your heart; he knows you would protect her and the kids fiercely and never hurt them. He doesn't want to worry about some loser coming in and using Michelle for her money or the house or anything like that."

Her words bounced around in my head. While part of me thought they were an absolutely ridiculous stretch, the other part of me wanted to believe she knew exactly what she was talking about so I could somehow justify what I was doing as a favor to Mike.

"Lawrence?" Dr. Roberts frowned as I stood up suddenly.

"I gotta go."

She blinked quickly, pulling her brows down low. "What? Why?"

"There's just something I have to go do."

"Okay, when do you want to come back?" She followed me to the exit door.

I sighed and turned back, shoving my hands into my pockets as I stared at the ground. "I don't know that I am."

"Oh." She sounded a little sad. "Okay. Well, I'm here if you ever change your mind."

"Got it." I looked up at her. "Thanks, doc."

"You're welcome."

"Thanks, you know, for everything," I said as genuinely as I could. She pressed her lips together and nodded.

I turned and reached for the doorknob when she called my name again. "Hey, Viper?"

"Yeah?" I spun back to face her.

"Don't give up on this. Don't give up on *her*. Any woman that can drive you *this* crazy obviously feels the same way about you. I know that without having ever met her." Her eyes begged me not to throw it all away. "She might have closed the door a little, but she certainly didn't lock it. Maybe she's standing just on the other side, waiting for you to knock."

I stared straight at Dr. Roberts and arched an eyebrow at her. "Well, hopefully she's not too close to it cause I'm about to bust through that motherfucker like the Kool-Aid man."

A grin broke out across her face as she scrunched up her nose. "That's my boy. One more thing . . . ." She giggled and nodded her head back toward the coffee table. "You want your drawer back?"

Chapter
35

Michelle

"**M**OMMA. MOMMA!"

I cracked one eye open just enough to see Matthew's smiling face lying on the pillow next to me.

"Good morning, baby." I rubbed his cheek with my thumb and closed my eyes again.

"Momma! The sun is awake. Time to get up."

Groaning, I rolled over and grabbed my phone to check the time. "Sweetheart, it's not even seven yet. The sun gets up earlier than people. Can't we sleep for a little bit longer?"

"Okay." He sighed and squeezed his little eyes tight, nuzzling in close to me.

I wrapped my arms around him just as I heard a loud growl. My eyes snapped open. "Was that your stomach?"

With his eyes still pinched together, he nodded.

Wow, there goes your bid for mother of the year.

"I'm sorry, honey. I didn't know you were so hungry. Let's go have some breakfast together while we wait for Maura to wake up."

He didn't need me to say it a second time, springing from the bed in his little Ninja Turtle teddy bear suit. How could kids wake up and hit the ground running like that? I practically needed two cups of coffee just to get my eyes open and then I still needed a nap by lunchtime.

This adult stuff sucks. I want to be four again.

I tiptoed past Maura's bedroom door and down the stairs, hoping to steal some valuable alone time with Matthew before Princess Bossy Pants woke up.

"What do you want for breakfast?" I yawned.

"Um . . ."

I looked over and Matthew was sitting at the coffee table in the living room, already engrossed in his latest Lego collection.

"Matthew!" I laughed as his head snapped toward me. "Stay with me, buddy. What do you want to eat?"

"Um . . . scrambled eggs and jelly toast." He turned back to his Legos.

I stood there with my arms crossed and cleared my throat dramatically so that he'd look over at me again. My eyebrows raised but I didn't say anything.

"Please," he added with a grin.

"Thank you." I returned his smile before heading to the fridge and filling my arms with eggs, milk, and cheese. I carried it all over, dropping it carefully onto the island.

"Momma." Matthew climbed up onto the stool, resting his chin on his hands. I loved when he sat like that. It made his cheeks squish out like they had when he was a baby. "Can Viper give me cooking lessons too so I can cook breakfast for you next time?"

His innocent question was like a shot to the gut.

"Well . . ." I sighed, not sure how to answer him. "I'm not

sure about that, sweetie. Viper's really busy with hockey right now so he can't come over."

"What about when he's done? He makes good food."

"He does make good food." I nodded as I reached up into the cabinet to grab a mixing bowl, desperately praying he'd get bored with my answers and return to his Legos, or at least pick a different topic.

Viper and I hadn't talked in two weeks, and honestly, I wasn't sure we ever would again. I was so embarrassed about the way I threw myself at him after the wedding that the thought of facing him again made me cringe. And . . . he'd made his choice. If he'd wanted me even a little bit, he had clear access that night, but he chose not to. It was probably for the best anyway. Nothing good could have come from us having sex.

Stop lying to yourself.

The truth was, I was devastated. Embarrassed. Kissing him had felt amazing. It had felt like the biggest release after months of arms brushing together and little glances that left us both blushing. The electricity between us was so strong there were times I was surprised I couldn't actually hear it popping in the air. Somehow, the man I used to tolerate for my husband had become someone I couldn't go five minutes without thinking about. But he didn't want me. To him, I was nothing but an obligation.

"Momma!"

Matthew calling my name pulled me back from wherever I had been. "Yes, baby?"

"Your phone." His little arm was extended, his finger pointing toward my phone on the corner of the island.

"Thanks." I smiled as big as I could, even though I was dreading deleting that text, just as I'd been doing every morning for the past two weeks. It was almost easier to assume he'd stopped thinking about me, but his morning texts were proof that wasn't true.

I grabbed my phone and was both happy and sad when I saw

the text was from Taylor, not Viper.

> T:　Yo! It's gonna be above freezing today and I
> was thinking of going to Mike's grave to clear
> the snow and ice off. Wanna go with me?

I answered as fast as my fingers would type.

> Yes! Maura is fighting a cold, so I'm gonna text the
> sitter and see if she can stay here while we go.
> What time were you thinking?

> T:　Pick you up at noon?

> Perfect! If you don't hear back from me, all is good.
> See you then.

I sent a quick text to Desi and within seconds my phone beeped again. Hopefully she didn't have plans and wouldn't mind sitting here for a couple hours. I looked at the screen and took a sharp breath.

> V:　How are you? Is there anything I can do?

I'd known that text would be coming eventually, but I was still caught off guard. Every day when he'd texted, I had deleted it immediately so that I wouldn't be tempted to answer. My phone beeped again.

> D:　No problem. I'll be there at 11:45.

I worked my butt off all morning to get the kids dressed for Desi, have lunch ready to go, and pick up the downstairs. Before I knew it, Taylor was at the front door. Of course Matthew and Maura were hanging all over their auntie, begging her to come play with them.

"Mommy and I are going to run some errands, but how about after I drop her off, I come in and hang out for a bit?"

Matthew agreed and reluctantly let her go, and we were off.

The cemetery where Mike was buried was only about ten

minutes from the house. Taylor and I had gone often last summer to plant flowers and keep his gravesite as clean as possible. It was our thing to do together. We both agreed it made us feel good to still have something we felt like Mike needed us for.

"So . . . I've been meaning to talk to you," Taylor said seriously as soon as we pulled out of the driveway.

I turned to her, frowning slightly. "What's wrong? Are you okay?"

"I'm fine,"—she shook her head—"but I feel terrible and I owe you an apology."

"An apology? For what?"

"For being the worst sister-in-law in the world." Her voice cracked.

I tilted my head to the side and pursed my lips. "No you're not. What are you talking about?"

"The whole reason I moved here in the first place was to help you with the kids and be around more, and then I met Isaac . . ." She chewed on the corner of her lip to try and keep from smiling, but when Taylor talked about her new boyfriend, it was impossible for her not to.

"Taylor, I get it. You don't have to apologize," I assured her. "You're young and gorgeous. I figured it wasn't gonna take long for some man to scoop you up."

"We're moving in together," she said hesitantly, grinning at me.

My mouth fell open. "You are?"

She nodded as we turned into the cemetery parking lot. "His lease is up next month, and since we spend all our time together anyway, we figured why pay two rents."

"Well." I giggled. "At least he doesn't have far to move."

She put her truck in park and we grabbed two shovels out of the bed, linking arms as we made our way to Mike's plot. Thankfully, there wasn't too much snow on the ground yet, which meant the cleanup wouldn't be too difficult.

I was staring at the ground, concentrating on not slipping on random pieces of ice, when Taylor stopped suddenly, almost knocking me to the ground in the process.

"What are you doing?" I looked up at her.

Her head was tilted to the side and she was staring straight ahead. "Look." She pointed. I turned my head, following her finger toward Mike's grave.

My head jerked back a little. "Whoa."

Mike's entire area had been shoveled clean already.

"Looks like someone beat us to it. A fan maybe?" she asked as we finished walking the rest of the way there.

As soon as we got close enough, we could see that not only had someone cleaned the snow off his plot, but the ice and snow had also been removed from his headstone, and sitting on top of it, right in the center . . . Lemonheads.

Taylor picked them up and frowned at me. "Who would've left these here? That's weird."

My eyes stung and I pinched my top lip in between my teeth, trying my hardest not to lose it right there.

"Don't you think this is strange?" Her eyes swept up from the box to mine and then bulged. "Michelle, what's wrong? Are you okay?"

"I'm fine." I sniffed and shook my head.

"What's going on? What's wrong?" Taylor's eyes darted around the cemetery like she was missing something.

"Nothing. I'm good." I cleared my throat, looking down at the box of candy. "Those are from Viper. That was their thing."

She looked down at the Lemonheads and back up to me. "Wait, are you crying because of these? Because of *him?*"

"No, I'm not." My chin quivered. "Can we just not talk about this right now, please?"

Her eyes softened and she took a step toward me, placing her hand on my arm. "Are you in love with him?"

"I can't do this. Not here!" I swallowed a sob as I walked over and bent down, placing my lips on the cold granite of Mike's headstone. "I love you," I whispered before I stood up and hurried back to Taylor's truck.

Taylor followed several steps behind me, not saying a word as she unlocked the truck and we both hopped in.

The drive home was horrible and awkward, and I just wanted to be out of the car. Panic flared up in my belly when instead of turning left into my subdivision, she turned right, headed toward the Starbucks.

"What are you doing?" I asked, looking out my window to avoid her eyes.

I felt her hand on top of mine and turned my head toward her. "This is long overdue," she said with a tight smile.

We ordered our drinks—black tea lemonade for me and a chai tea latte for her—and found a small table in the back corner.

Neither of us wanted to start the conversation. That was obvious by the way we both stared out the window not speaking, but I also needed to get home eventually.

"Listen, I'm all for hanging out with you anytime, but this isn't necessary right now. It's really nothing, I swear." I tried to smile convincingly as I shrugged.

"Michelle,"—she cocked her head to the side—"I'm not an idiot. Lemonheads don't make most people cry for no reason."

Just the mention of the candy made my face pinch together as I looked down at the table and tried to hood my eyes with my hand.

"Honey, what's going on?" she said in a soft tone as she reached across the table and rubbed my forearm gently. "Are you in love with Viper?"

I couldn't lift my head to look her in the eye, and if I opened my mouth to respond, I was going to sob, so I just nodded.

She got off of her chair and moved it around to my side of

the table, where she sat back down and put her arm around my shoulder. "Why didn't you tell me?" Before I could say anything, she lifted her hand and slammed it back down onto the table. "Because you haven't been around in months, Taylor, you idiot," she said to herself.

"You're not an idiot." I took a shaky breath as I wiped my eyes on a crumpled-up Starbucks napkin.

"How long has this been going on?"

I shrugged. "I don't even know. One day he was just . . . Viper. Then eventually, the more we hung out and I saw him interact with Matthew, I don't know, suddenly it was just different. I didn't tell you because I'm ashamed. I don't want you to hate me."

"Why do you think I would hate you?"

I dropped my hands to the table. "Why *wouldn't* you hate me? I was married to your brother."

"Right, and you were an amazing wife to him for many years, Michelle. It's not like you cheated on him and broke his heart. Then I would probably hate you, but this is different. So different."

"I know, but Mike hasn't even been gone a full year yet." I stared down at the table, embarrassed at the words coming out of my mouth.

"Oh." She nodded. "I didn't know that was the magic number."

My head lifted. "Huh?"

"One year. Three hundred sixty-five days. I didn't know that was the official 'you can't fall in love with anyone else' waiting period after your spouse dies," she said sarcastically, making air quotes with her fingers. "Give me a break. There is no time frame. There are no rules. And people who tell you otherwise can go fuck themselves. You've known Viper for years. Had you met some random dude in a bar the week after the funeral, I might have thought you were a little nutty, but that's not what this is at all."

Taylor's words made me want to break down all over again. Knowing that she didn't judge me or think less of me meant more to me than anything else.

"I love your brother." I sniffled and corrected myself. "I *loved* your brother."

"I know you do. I know you *did*." Her eyebrows lifted as she smiled and nodded. She laid her head on my shoulder. "And he loved you."

"None of this matters anyway." I threw my napkin down on the table and sighed. "Nothing is going to happen with me and Viper anyway. This whole conversation is pointless."

"Wait,"—she straightened up and looked at me—"why isn't it gonna happen?"

"We got into a fight a couple weeks ago and I told him to leave."

"Awww." She stuck out her bottom lip. "And he hasn't called since?"

"Called? No. But he's never called. That wasn't our thing. He texts me every morning to see how I am and if I need anything. He's been doing that for months and months now."

"And he's still done this since your fight?" Her voice raised in surprise.

I nodded.

"Can I ask what you fought about?"

I felt the back of my neck tingle as my face grew hot. "My neighbor got married and he went with me to the wedding. I stayed out late with a couple girlfriends I hadn't seen in years while he went home to relieve the sitter. Anyway, I had a couple drinks with the girls, just enough for a little liquid courage. I went home and made a move, the move I knew he was too scared to make and would never have made on his own. He thought I was drunk and turned me down."

"But you weren't drunk?" she asked.

"Nope." I shook my head. "I remember every horrible

second of that fight."

"Why did he turn you down, though? What was his reasoning?"

"Mike. He felt like we were betraying him."

"You're right. I'm not the idiot, you are." She shook her head. "I've known Viper for years too, and he doesn't see the same girl twice in a lifetime, let alone hang out with one night after night after night with no sex. He's clearly crazy about you, and you are obviously just as crazy about him, but you two won't be together because you're both scared of the exact same thing—that my brother, who has passed, would be mad at you? Am I getting all that right?"

My eyes darted around the coffee shop. Coming out of Taylor's mouth, it did sound silly. "Pretty much."

"You're both morons," she said sternly. "You guys have to get over this guilt thing that's standing between you. Life is short, Michelle. You more than anyone should know that at this point. Don't let any more time slip away. He's a little wild, but from what Mike's said, he's a good man. You and the kids deserve a good man."

My heart soared at her words.

"Plus, he's willing to put up with your shitty cooking, and any man that would do that gets the seal of approval in my book." She winked at me.

Chapter
36

M Y HANDS DIDN'T SHAKE.

My heart didn't race.

I pushed that doorbell with all the confidence in the world.

Within seconds, Michelle walked around the corner from the kitchen, freezing in her tracks when she saw me looking through the glass. She stood and stared for just a second before she pinched her lips together and came to the door.

"Hi!" I said cheerfully as she opened it, walking right past her and into the kitchen.

I heard the door close, and she didn't start yelling at me right away.

Already a good sign.

"How are you?" I asked nonchalantly as I started taking groceries out of the brown paper bag I'd brought and setting them on the island.

"Viper," she sighed. "What is all this? What are you doing?"

"You haven't had a cooking lesson in almost a month. I'm sure the kids are sick of pizza by now, so it's time." I glanced into the living room and down the hall toward Matthew's playroom, frowning when I didn't see anyone. "Speaking of the kids, where are they?"

"Matthew finagled Taylor into letting him sleep at her house tonight, and she thought she'd give me a break and take Maura too."

"Even better." I grinned at her, wiggling my eyebrows up and down.

"I'm so confused," she mumbled, closing her eyes and rubbing her temples with her fingers.

While her eyes were shut, I stole a quick peek over at her. Her hair was damp from a recent shower, and she had on Wild sweatpants and a baggy T-shirt with no makeup. Frankly, she was one shopping cart full of crap away from passing for a homeless person, but I could not have found her more attractive than I did at that moment. It wasn't about looks with her; it never had been. It was her heart I was in love with.

"What's there to be confused about? We're making chicken marsala."

Her hands dropped to her sides in frustration. "You. Me. Us. This. I told you to leave and I meant it."

"I did leave." I shrugged. "And now I'm back."

"Why?"

"Because."

"Because *why?*" Her voice cracked, and that was all I needed to hear.

In one swift motion, I slid to my left and locked my hands on the counter on either side of her hips, closing her in with my arms. My face was inches from hers, our noses practically touching.

I stared her right in the eyes. I didn't want her to just hear what I was about to say, I wanted her to see it too. To fucking feel it.

"Because I belong here. Because I belong with *you.* Because as much as you try to fight it, you know you belong with me too. Because somewhere in between hearing you sing to Maura, teaching you to make scrambled eggs, and dancing with you at that wedding, I fell in love with you."

She took a shaky breath as a tear slowly rolled down her cheek.

I gently wiped it with my finger, holding it up in the air. "Because I want to make sure you never cry again."

"But that night, after the wedding . . . you didn't want me." She swallowed and looked down at the ground.

"That's not true. It's not that I didn't want you. Jesus, Michelle, all I've wanted for months is you. I didn't want the guilt that came along with you, but fuck it. I'm ready. I'll deal with the guilt every day for the rest of my life if it means I get to wake up and you're still mine."

"Really?" Her voice cracked again as tears flooded her eyes. Tears of guilt. Tears of relief. Tears of hope.

"Yes. Really. I've never been more sure of *anything* in my whole life." I wrapped my arms around her and pulled her so tight against me I could feel her heart beating on my chest. "I have no idea what the future holds. But I do know that I've never wanted to try with another person before. Just try. Put all the other bullshit to the side and really, really *try*."

She was quiet for a minute, and I started to worry that maybe I'd misread her tears.

"I wasn't drunk," she finally mumbled into my shoulder.

"Huh?"

"The night of the wedding, I wasn't drunk." She pulled back and stared up at me. "I had two drinks, but by the time I got home, I was barely even buzzed anymore."

"So you kissed me because—"

"Because I wanted to finish what I'd started. I still do." She raised up on her tippy toes and ran her nose along my jawline. "I'll deal with the guilt too. I'm sure it'll be hard, but nowhere near as hard as trying to convince myself that I don't love you too."

Something in me broke, and I just didn't care anymore. I couldn't fight the urge to kiss her one more fucking second.

I cupped her cheek in my hand and angled it up toward me, pressing my lips hard against hers. She sighed and leaned into me. We didn't move our lips. We didn't move our tongues. We didn't move at all. We just stood there, connected . . . finally.

That didn't last too long. Not only had neither of us had sex in a very long time, but the buildup between the two of us was at a complete boiling point. The minute she shoved her hands up the back of my T-shirt and I felt her nails on my back, every nerve in my body sprang to life. I'd seen scenes in movies where a couple kisses for the first time and they show a series of shorts clips—fireworks going off, a band marching, a tea kettle whistling—I was all of those things combined, and multiplied by a thousand.

For the first time in my life I had no clue what to do with my hands. I didn't want to just fuck Michelle; I wanted to show her how much I loved her. I wanted to touch her everywhere, all at the same time.

We moved slow, our lips flowing in sync like we'd been kissing each other our whole lives. With my one hand still on the side of her face, I moved the other one to her hip, gripping it softly. She sucked on my bottom lip, pulling it in and gently pinching it between her teeth.

"If you don't touch me soon, I'm gonna explode," she said with my lip still between her teeth.

I tugged my lip back and grinned at her. "I'm gonna do more than touch you, but you're right—you *are* gonna explode."

I dropped to my knees and quickly pulled her sweats down to the floor. She stepped out of them and flung them off to the side. I started kissing the top of her feet, slowly making my way up her lower legs to her inner thighs. Even from my knees, I could hear her breathing hard. I grabbed the edges of her panties and pulled them down. Light pink and lacy as hell. I expected nothing less from her.

She stepped out of those too and moved them off to the side with her sweats, but before she could put her second leg back down on the floor, I decided to throw rule number two out the window. I lifted her leg, hooked it over my shoulder, and sank my tongue right into her. Out of the corner of my eye, I saw her hands as they gripped the edge of the counter. Her head fell back and she moaned out loud. Really, really loud. The leg that was still on the ground started to shake, and I knew she was right there, but I was nowhere near done with her. My tongue licked and rubbed against her clit until she shoved her hands into my hair and started to convulse, calling out my name over and over.

Once her leg stopped quivering, I pulled back and stood up, softly setting her other leg on the ground.

"That was . . ." She peered at me with a glazed look in her eyes and shook her head. "I can't . . ."

"We're not done." I bent down and possessed her mouth again as I cupped both sides of her face. There was no music playing, but we started swaying back and forth as if there were. This girl kissed me in a way that made me forget kissing even existed before her.

"Come here." She took my hand and started pulling me toward the living room.

"Wait." I squeezed her hand and tugged back. "Not in there. Please."

"Upstairs?" She grinned at me as she chewed on the inside of her lip.

I nodded, desperate to get that lip back in my mouth. "Here, hop on." I turned around and squatted.

"A piggyback ride? Are you serious?" She laughed.

Turning my head to the side just a tad, I ordered, "I'm all kinds of worked up, so unless you wanna do it right here on the wood floor, hop on."

She giggled as she sprang onto my back, and I took the stairs two at a time.

"Take a left," she mumbled as she kissed my neck with the lightest flicks of her tongue, sending shivers all the way down my back.

Once I got into her bedroom, I walked straight to the bed and turned around, dumping her off backward as she let out a playful squeal. She crawled backward up the bed, staring me straight in the eye as she moved. I yanked my T-shirt over my head and pushed my pants and boxers off even faster, grabbing the condom out of my pocket.

Rule number one. Always. Until it's on purpose.

"You brought that with you tonight?" she asked with a raised eyebrow, watching as I rolled the condom down my shaft. "Someone was very confident, huh?"

"It has nothing to do with confidence." I kissed her collarbone. What was it about her damn collarbone that drove me insane? "But I did know I was coming here to tell you I loved you, and I was pretty sure if you felt even *half* as strong about me as I feel about you, we'd end up here."

Michelle lay back on the bed and lifted my face up to kiss her again.

"Hang on a sec." I pulled her up to a sitting position, dragged her T-shirt over her head, and tossed it off to the side. "Much better." My mouth connected with her nipple as soon as she lay back on the bed.

I was ready. I was more than ready. So far past foreplay it wasn't even funny at that point.

As soon as she was on her back, I nudged her legs apart with my knee and positioned myself on top of her. I leaned on my elbow for a second and brushed the hair off of her forehead, looking into her eyes.

"What?" she asked in a worried tone as she ran her nails up and down my side.

"I don't know. Just . . . this. You. It's incredible." I kissed the tip of her nose. She smiled and pulled me down for a kiss, softly gasping into my mouth as I slid inside of her. We continued kissing while I moved in and out, picking up speed. Her nails dug into my back and she started moaning again, turning her face to the side as she closed her eyes. I knew she was close.

"Open your eyes. Look at me," I said in between pants. "I wanna watch you. I want you to look right at me when you come."

Her eyes opened and her brows pulled in tight, making the most erotic face.

"I love you, Michelle."

"I love you too," she whispered, breathing heavier. "Oh God!" She curled into me a little as her body went still, and I pumped harder and harder, determined to push her over the edge again. "Viper! Oh shit!" She pinched her eyes shut.

"Look at me. Please. I need to see you." I'd never felt what I felt in that moment during sex. Before Michelle, sex was just something I did to feel good and fill up time, but with her and with feelings involved, it brought it to a whole new level. Beyond intense.

She opened her eyes again and clamped down on her bottom lip as she came around me, each pulse of her pussy bringing me closer and closer. Finally, I felt my balls tighten, and that was it. I stared back into her eyes and lowered my forehead to hers as I came harder than I'd ever come in my whole life. I grunted, groaned, and told her I loved her two more times before I was done. As soon as I was finished, my body went limp. I was exhausted. I took the condom off and cleaned up before hurrying back to bed with her.

"Should we get up and get dressed?" she asked after we'd lain in bed, hugging each other for about ten minutes.

"No," I said sternly. "Now that I've seen you naked, I'd like you to be that way as often as possible, please." I kissed her temple, leaving my mouth there.

She laughed and I rolled over, propping myself up on my elbow. "I wasn't kidding." I shook my head.

"Well,"—she rolled over and faced me—"I'm thinking that

might make Matthew ask a few questions I'm not ready to answer yet, so I suppose you'll just have to wait until he goes to bed every night."

I tucked a stubborn piece of hair behind her ear. "You bet your ass we're gonna do that every night . . . and every nap time . . . and when he's watching TV . . . and when he's outside playing . . ."

"Easy." She laughed. "I'd like to be able to walk regularly."

"Are you hungry?" I asked.

"Starving!" she said dramatically.

"Well, seeing as how I'm too fucking exhausted to cook any of the stuff I brought with me, wanna order a pizza?"

"Very fitting. I would love to." She chuckled to herself. "And . . . I can think of something to keep us busy for the half hour until the delivery man gets here."

Chapter
37

"**A**RE YOU EXCITED?" I LOOKED in my rearview mirror at Matthew, who was grinning in the backseat, as usual. He nodded.

I turned toward Michelle. "How about you?"

"I'm nervous," she admitted. "I mean . . . this is the equivalent of meeting your mom. She's the most important person in your life."

"Correction." I lifted her hand, kissing the top of it. "One of the most important people in my life."

She smiled at me with her whole face, from her mouth to her beautiful eyes.

"You have nothing to worry about. She's gonna love you." I hopped out of the car and unbuckled Matthew from the backseat while Michelle reached in and got Maura.

We were halfway up the sidewalk to Gam's when she came out on her front porch and waved at us. "Hi, everyone!"

"Whoa," I muttered under my breath before leaning over to Michelle. "Clearly you're not the only nervous one. She's never this chipper."

"Hi!" Matthew waved back, running up ahead of us. "I'm Matthew."

Gam rested her hands on her knees, bending over just a little bit to be closer to him. "Hi, Matthew. I'm Gam. Nice to meet you. You're a cutie pie."

"Thanks." Matthew nodded. "So are you." He climbed the rest of the way up the porch and walked into her house like he owned the place.

Gam stood and looked back at him with her mouth hanging open before turning to us. "I love that kid already." She laughed.

"Hi, Gam. I'm Michelle." She reached her hand out for Gam to shake, but Gam playfully pushed it away.

"I know who you are. You're the woman that made my grandson's brain turn to mush. I shake hands with strangers; I hug family." She pulled Michelle into a big hug, wrapping her arms around Maura at the same time. "And you, you pretty little thing, you must be Maura." Gam tickled under her chin with one finger as Maura smiled shyly and tried to hide behind her mom.

"How are you, you old bat?" I said when it was my turn.

"Wow. For once you don't look like shit. Way to go, kid," she said warmly as she hugged me back. "Come inside. I made lunch . . . unless Matthew already ate it all."

We spent the next hour chitchatting as we sat around her dining room table eating BLT sandwiches and her famous pineapple coleslaw. That was my absolute favorite of hers. I swear I could eat it by the pound.

"That was delicious. I'm stuffed." Michelle wiped her mouth with her napkin.

"I loved the bacon!" Matthew cheered, throwing his little hands up in the air.

"Me too, buddy." I reached my fist out for him to bump it.

Michelle stood up and handed Maura to me as she started stacking the plates on her arm. "I'm gonna start cleaning this table off. Would you mind keeping an eye on Maura for me?" she asked.

"No problem." I nodded, setting Maura down on my knee. Immediately, she squirmed to get down. "Hang on, baby. We'll go play in a minute."

"Oh, let her down." Gam waved. "There's not much here she can get into. Besides, I like watching her play."

I set her down on the floor and turned in my chair so I could keep an eye on her.

"Wow, look at you," Gam said as she pressed her lips together, shaking her head slowly at me.

"What?" I asked defensively.

"The way you are with the kids. It's natural. I never thought I'd see you with kids."

"Eh, Michelle is the real superhero, Gam. I just try to help out where I can and make her life a little easier."

"Well . . ." Her eyes welled up with tears. "It's nice to see."

"You know, for such a tough old lady, you sure cry easily," I teased.

"Oh, shut up, you brat." She took her glasses off and set them on the table as she pulled a tissue out of the sleeve of her shirt to wipe her eyes. "Let's move into the living room where the kids can play while we talk."

Matthew spread out all the Legos he'd crammed into his backpack on the coffee table, and Maura immediately stood up at the edge of the table, smashing all of his little buildings like Godzilla.

"Hey!" Matthew squealed as she slammed her fist down over and over, giggling.

"Uh-oh. No way, missy." Michelle scooped Maura up to keep her away from Matthew. So of course Maura arched her back and threw a fit.

"Hang on. I have an idea." Gam stood up and walked into the kitchen, returning a couple minutes later with a stack of measuring cups and spoons. She set them on the floor next to

Maura and her tiny little eyes lit up. "There. Babies love those things."

"Thank you." Michelle smiled sweetly as Gam reached over and squeezed her hand.

"So, how have things been with you guys?" she asked as she relaxed back into her couch.

"Um . . ." Michelle sighed and shifted her eyes over to mine. In that one look from her, I saw all the stress and chaos the last couple of weeks had included.

"It's been . . . okay." I took over for Michelle. "We didn't make any big official announcements to the world that we were together or anything, but of course as soon as we went out once or twice, there were some pics posted in magazines and the mean tweets began."

"Oh no." Gam shook her head. "All those electronic devices are the devil, I'm telling you. I hate them."

"I know. I have to come over twice a year to change all your clocks to the right time, remember?" I teased her.

She shot me a playful glare. "But wait, what did these tweety people say?"

I leaned forward and lowered my voice so Matthew didn't hear me. "They just said some shitty things about Mike dying and how wrong it is that we're together now. It wasn't that they were lies, but the way they said it just hurt."

Gam ran her tongue over her top teeth as she nodded slowly, looking back and forth between Michelle and me. "You know what? Fuck them."

"Gam!" I blurted as Michelle and I looked over at Matthew, who was so enthralled with his Lego garbage truck that he didn't seem to notice.

"Oh, please." She waved toward him. "Swearing never hurt anyone. I swore around you as a kid, and you turned out just fine."

"I don't know that I'd say *that*," Michelle mumbled under her breath playfully.

"I'm serious, though. Fuck them." She crossed her arms over her chest. "Did you know I was engaged when I met your papa?"

"Wait. What?" I was confused. That crazy woman could switch topics faster than a preschooler.

"When I met your papa . . . I was already engaged. Did you know that?" she repeated.

"No, I had no clue."

"Yep." She nodded. "To Johnny from Mississippi. He was a sailor. Boy did I have a thing for a man in a uniform. Still do." She wiggled her eyebrows up and down.

"Gross." I closed my eyes and shook the thought from my head.

"Anyway, back in my day, people didn't do that. Once you were engaged, you were engaged, but I couldn't help it. I'd fallen in love with your papa. So I broke off my engagement with Johnny and married your papa immediately," she said with a confident nod. "And if I hadn't, you wouldn't be here. But that's not my point. My point is that sometimes just because something isn't necessarily the right thing to do or the socially acceptable thing to do, that shouldn't stop you."

Damn, I love this woman.

"You come from a long line of rebels, rule breakers, and envelope pushers, Lawrence. You've never been one to color inside the lines, and I would expect nothing less of you as a grown man. If those people out there in computer land don't like what you two are doing, who gives a shit? You love her and she loves you. That's the only thing that matters when you put your head on your pillow every night."

Michelle turned her head toward me, pinching her lips together as her eyes turned watery.

"You're such a softie." I grinned, shoulder bumping her.

"Okay, enough of that nice shit." Gam stretched her neck to look through the sliding doors that led to her back deck and stood up. "Come on, Matthew. I want to show you my birdhouses out back."

Matthew jumped up excitedly and took her hand as they walked toward the kitchen.

"I thought they were going out back," Michelle whispered as she leaned in close.

Just then I heard pieces of ice drop from the freezer into a cup, and I couldn't stop myself from lowering my head and laughing.

"All right, now we can go. Do you like squirrels?" she asked Matthew as they went out on the deck, carrying the cup of ice.

Epilogue

OUR SEASON WAS OVER. WE didn't make the playoffs—again. Losing was frustrating, but at least I had a great little crew to hang out with every night to soften the blow. Before summer officially started and everyone went their separate ways for a few months, Michelle and I decided to have a cookout at her house. Sort of as a thank you to everyone for their support throughout the last year.

We'd been in full-on house prep mode all week: deep cleaning, dusting, raking the yard—all the not fun stuff.

"How's it going down there?" I looked over at Matthew, who was supposed to be helping me pull weeds but ditched me to collect earthworms in his bucket instead.

"Fine," he answered flatly as he concentrated on what he was doing.

"What are you doing?"

"I cut a worm in half. Both of his pieces are still moving." He turned toward me with a devilish grin on his face. "It's so cool. His guts are out!"

I was both worried and proud at the same time.

"Hey, you hungry?"

Still staring down at his mutilated new friend, he nodded.

"Let's take a break and see if Mom has any ideas for lunch." I stood and walked up behind him. "Then you should probably have a bath, huh? You have dirt in places I didn't know existed."

Matthew rose to his feet and walked with me to the house,

hand in hand, of course. I'd become used to the fact that if I was walking *anywhere* with Matthew, even someplace close like from the backyard to the house, he would be by my side and holding my hand. I wasn't just used to it, I looked forward to it.

I opened the sliding door and he ran in, heading straight for his playroom.

"Freeze!" I called as he was halfway down the hall. He spun around to face me and I pointed toward the other side of the hallway. "You. Bathroom. Hands. Worm guts."

Michelle was standing in the living room with her hands on her hips and her face crinkled up. "Do I even want to know?"

"Probably not." I shook my head as I washed my hands in the sink. "But if he ever asks for a dog, say no."

I heard her scoff behind me.

Drying my hands on a dish towel, I walked up next to her and looked down at the cardboard box she'd taped together. I motioned toward it. "What's that for?"

She turned and faced the wedding pictures of her and Mike that hung on the wall. "For these. It's time."

I put my hand on her shoulder, turning her toward me slightly. "You know I'm not asking you to take those down. You don't have to do that for me."

"I know you aren't." She nodded as she stared at the wall, deep in thought. "But it's been a year. I think I'm ready."

"Okay." This was the part I hated as a guy. Was I supposed to take them down for her? Hold the box? Hug her? Walk away? "Is there anything I can do for you?"

"No, but thank you." She gave me a tight smile and then turned back toward the wall, taking a deep breath. "Okay. Here goes nothing." Her hands shook as she wrapped them around the black frame and gently lifted it off of the wall, setting it in the box.

I eyed her cautiously. "You okay?"

She swallowed. "Yeah. Yeah, I think I am." She took the

other three wedding pictures down and put those in the box too.

"What are you guys doing?" Matthew asked from behind us.

We both spun around. He was scratching the side of his face as he frowned at us.

"Hey, honey." Michelle squatted down in front of him. "I'm just taking some pictures down so we can put some new ones up."

"Oh." His voice trailed off like he was confused. "So is my dad not my dad anymore? Is Viper my new dad?"

A soft gasp escaped Michelle's lips as she shook her head. "No, baby. He's still your dad."

"Come over here, my man." I held my hand out to Matthew and we walked over to the couch together, where I scooped him up and plopped him on my knee. He chewed on his lip and wrung his hands together as he stared up at me with his big eyes. "I need you to listen to me, okay?"

His eyes grew wide and he nodded.

I bent down so that my eyes were level with his. "Your dad will *always* be your dad, no matter what, okay? I will never, ever, ever try to take his place. I loved him, and I know he loved you more than anything in the world, so I promised to help take care of you and protect you, but I will never try to be him."

Matthew nodded again. I wasn't sure how much of what I'd just said sank into his four-year-old brain, but I'd repeat that speech over and over for years to come if need be.

Michelle stepped out of the room, returning a few seconds later with a tissue for her eyes. She sniffed and walked over, rustling Matthew's hair. "Aren't you lucky? You have a daddy up in heaven *and* a best friend down here to help take care of you."

She wadded up the napkin and dropped it on the coffee table as she passed by it on her way to the cardboard box. Grabbing the edge, she grunted as she pulled it across the room toward the bookcase in the corner.

"What are you doing now?" I asked.

She turned and looked the bookshelf of pictures up and down. "Working over here now."

I glanced down at Matthew just in time to see a small twitch of his eyebrow.

"Don't do that. Leave those," I insisted.

"Why?" She turned to face me with a small frame in her hand.

I nodded down toward Matthew. "He's confused enough about all this. Don't put all his memories in a box. Seriously, leave them."

"Okay," she hesitated, "but I wanted to put up some pictures of us too . . ."

"Then I'll buy you another bookshelf, and we can put our memories on that one, but leave that shelf just the way it is for Matthew." I smiled down at the son of my best friend, the little boy whom I loved just as much as if he were half genetically mine.

Michelle looked down at the picture of her, Big Mike, and Matthew at Walt Disney World and kissed it. She walked over and held it out for Matthew, who kissed it too. She turned to walk away and I grabbed her wrist, pulling the picture toward me so I could kiss it too. Matthew smiled and I realized the best thing I could ever do for him in his whole life would be to show him I loved his dad just as much as he did.

Four hours later, the backyard was hectic, to say the least. Brody, Kacie, and Louie were sitting around the table talking to Jodi and Vince, who had just stopped over for a couple minutes after a long day of planting lilies in their backyard. Baby Grace was sound asleep on Brody's chest while Emma sat on Kacie's lap, shoving pieces of watermelon into her mouth as juice dripped all the way down her arm. I was standing behind Brody's chair keeping a close eye on Maura, who was in the sandbox.

"When did you get a trampoline?" Jodi frowned out into the yard as she watched Lucy, Piper, and Matthew jump around on the trampoline with Becca and Logan, Andy's kids. "I don't remember you having that last summer."

"That's because we didn't." Michelle grabbed a beer from the big metal cooler and twisted the top off with her bare hand. "Viper actually brought it over from his house a couple weeks ago."

Louie's eyes widened and flashed over to mine. I winked at him as he coughed on the gulp of beer he'd just drank.

Andy came through the sliding door, carrying the drink he'd just mixed inside. "Look who I found when I was in there," he bellowed.

Darla and Neil waved at us as they followed him outside.

"Yay! You made it!" Kacie cheered. "I wasn't sure you'd be back from your trip in time."

"We haven't even been home yet. I'm exhausted, but I couldn't miss this. How is everyone?" They made the rounds, giving hugs as they walked by everyone. When Darla got to me, she tilted her head to the side and smiled. "Glad to see you so damn happy. You deserve it." She wrapped her arms around me, and I squeezed her back as hard as I could.

"Thanks. You too," I mumbled into her shoulder. "Look at us, two formerly single whores, each partnered up happily. Who would've thought, huh?"

"Not me." She giggled and pulled back, kissing my cheek on the way by.

"Taylor and Isaac should be here in a bit too," Michelle announced. "And I hope everyone's hungry. I made a ton of food."

"Wait, you cooked?" Jodi's eyebrows raised. "Uh-oh, hope the pizza place is on standby."

"Stop it!" Michelle threw her beer cap at her as she walked over and hugged me around the waist. "I'm actually pretty good now. I've had an incredible teacher."

"Yep, that's me," I bragged proudly, puffing my chest out. "Lawrence Finkle, teaching women across the country new tricks for over ten years now."

The women booed me while Michelle punched me right in the gut and glared.

"It was a joke, it was a joke!" I grunted and protected myself from her onslaught.

"So let's see . . ." Louie looked from person to person around the yard. "Baby Grace is what, five, six months old now? Are we taking bets on who gets pregnant next? Michelle or Kacie?"

"Oh no!" Kacie shook her head adamantly. "This momma needs a break."

"We'll see." Brody reached out and squeezed her leg. "I told you I wanted a dozen little Brodys, remember?"

Kacie rolled her eyes and pushed his hand away playfully.

"I think we're waiting a while too, homie." I laughed, putting my arm around Michelle's shoulders. "We aren't ready to share a house yet, let alone a fetus. And wait a minute, if we're taking bets, I'm thinking the newlyweds over there should be in the running." I nodded toward Jodi and Vince.

"Oh, hell no," Jodi said. "We're sharing lilies, not babies."

"Well if you're throwing baby bets around, can we get in on the running after the wedding?" Darla grinned.

"What wedd—" Kacie's mouth dropped open. "Oh my God, are you engaged?"

Darla proudly held her left hand up, revealing a brand new diamond on her ring finger. Everyone got up and started hugging them in congratulations. Right away, the girls started babbling about bridesmaid dress colors, and I walked over to shake Neil's hand, staring him straight in the eye. "She's a sweet girl," I said sternly. "Be good to her."

"I will." He nodded, shaking my hand back.

"So wait a minute . . ." I turned back toward the group. "Michelle and I are together, Jodi and Vince are married, Darla and Neil are *getting* married . . . that just leaves you, Andy. We gotta find you somebody now."

Andy shook his head and was about to argue with me when Brody blurted out, "Louie's available!"

Four more hours later and everyone was gone. Michelle and I had collapsed on the couch, completely exhausted and trying our hardest to ignore the mess in the kitchen.

"That was fun," she sighed. "We should do it again soon."

"We should," I agreed. "At Brody and Kacie's house, though. Have you seen that kitchen?"

"Don't remind me," she groaned. "Can't we leave it till tomorrow?"

"I say we don't even clean it tomorrow. Let's just throw everything out and buy new dishes," I joked.

"Deal!" She laughed as she looked off to the side, deep in thought about something. "It's been a weird year, huh? Kinda makes you wonder where we'll be a year from now."

"Do you ever wonder what if?" I asked cautiously.

Her eyes turned sad as she shook her head. "Don't." I stared back at her, not saying word. Selfishly, I wanted to know the answer; I *needed* to know the answer. Finally, she took a shaky breath and let it out slowly. "I have thought about it, and it kills me every single time, because while I can't imagine my past without him, I don't want to imagine my future without you."

"Babe, you won't have to. You want my prediction for the next year?"

"Of course." Her voice rose in anticipation as she wrapped her arms around my waist and laid her head on my chest.

"I think we'll be sitting right here with the same two great kids and the same amazing friends, except I'll be begging you to finally let me move in with you."

She scoffed, "You won't have to beg hard."

I closed my eyes as I kissed the top of her head and took a deep, contented breath, filling my lungs. Within a few minutes, her breathing became rhythmic and I knew she was sound asleep. Carefully lifting my feet onto the coffee table, I laid my head back against the couch and looked around the room. The room that Mike had told me I had a cement heart in. The room that my cement heart had finally broken in when Michelle told me about her dad. The room that I'd promised to always be there for Matthew in. The room I'd promised never to take his father's place in.

The room that held a bookshelf full of memories that this family needed to leave up forever. The bookshelf that now held a new framed picture of me and Mike in our Wild uniforms after a game. The frame that now had a box of Lemonheads sitting next to it.

Acknowledgements

As always, this book would never have come to fruition without the help of some truly amazing people.

A HUGE thank you to Letitia, at Romantic Book Affairs for this AMAZING cover! You were an absolute dream to work with and you absolutely nailed everything I wanted in a cover! Follow Romantic Book Affairs here: www.rbadesigns.com

Another huge thank you to Tami at Integrity Formatting! I contacted you last minute and asked you to do not one, but two books for me very quickly and you didn't even think twice about it. Thank you so so much for all of your help! Follow Integrity Formatting here: www.integrityformatting.wix.com/integrity-formatting

To my editor, Megan Ward...There are some people that walk this planet who are a gift to everyone they meet. You are one of those people. You've taken on the daunting task of climbing inside my brain and bringing my mediocre words up ten notches. I'm honored to call you not just my editor, but one of my truly best friends. Thank you, thank you, thank you for all you have done for me.

To Pam Carrion from The Book Avenue Review ... Sometimes you want to wring my neck. Correction: *most* of the time you want to wring my neck but for some reason, you stick by me through thick and thin and I'm beyond thankful for it. Thank you so much for all that you do for me every single day. And lastly, don't talk shit about Total. ;)

To Melissa Brown... What is there to say that hasn't already been said? Not a lot honestly. There aren't many people in the world I can say that I've been friends with for almost 30 years but I'm so glad I can say that about you. Our conversations are anything but normal, but I wouldn't have it any other way. Thank you for sifting through all this muck and drivel with me and battling the JR's of the world.

To my beta readers... Polly, Kristy, Michelle, Melissa, Laura, Mrs. B (Fine, Deb)... thank you SO much for all the work you put into reading this and giving me your feedback. It was extremely valuable in shaping the story the way it sits today. From the bottom of my heart, thank you.

To my family, specifically my husband and my mom... thank you a million times over for all the pitching in you did while I was lost in Viper's world. I know what you did doesn't seem like much, but it was monumental to me. The support from you guys makes my job 1000 times easier. I love you all so much!

About the
Author

Beth Ehemann lives in the northern suburbs of Chicago with her husband and four children. When she's not sitting in front of her computer writing, or on Pinterest, she loves reading, photography, martinis and all things Chicago Cubs and Blackhawks.

Connect with her at-

www.bethehemann.com

authorbethehemann@yahoo.com

www.facebook.com/bethehemann

@bethehemann (Twitter and Instagram)

18626469R00176

Printed in Great Britain
by Amazon